After 49 years' experience in cooking and all facets of gastro-media, (TV, radio, magazines, newspapers, personal appearances), Peter Valentine Howard retired. However, he had to write fictional novels on plots simmering in his brain. With his partner's support, writing and singing his struggles with PTSD are mostly kept at bay, allowing him to live happily.

D1513554

Dedication

For every cook and for all media specialists

Peter Valentine Howard

The Cooking Game....
r u Game?

LET THE SHOOT
BEGIN!

AUSTIN MACAULEY
PUBLISHERS LTD.

A CIP catalogue record for this title is available from the British Library.

ISBN 9781786935212 (Paperback)
ISBN 9781786935229 (Hardback)
ISBN 9781786935236 (E-Book)
www.austinmacauley.com

First Published (2017)
Austin Macauley Publishers Ltd.
25 Canada Square
Canary Wharf
London
E14 5LQ

Acknowledgments

A positive relationship with your editor is crucial for a first time fiction writer like me and I have the best editor – Lyn Rimmer. She immediately got my line of thought and writing style - thanks Lyn for the constant consultation, advice, patience and caring.

So many people read my work and gave me such invaluable feedback including Brian Cartledge, Mary Atkins, Paula Lake, Martin Field and Maggie Christiansen. Thanks so much for your criticism, both positive and negative. Special thanks to Mary-Lou Stephens who has been so diligent with her comments and so free with her advice.

To my partner Gregor, thanks for your patience and support.

The brilliant team at Austin Macauley have been just so amazing. Thanks for your patience and advice in this my first effort as a fiction writer. Thanks you so much Austin Macauley.

INTRODUCTION

Sweet Serendipity

Evan delighted in recounting how his stellar rise to fame had begun. He truly loved telling the story of his gorgeous wife, Lex, encouraging him to believe in himself as a 'natural' and promising that the people of her home town would love him. After all, this is a small town like many small, rural towns and once embraced as part of Lex's well-respected local family, Evan was supported wholeheartedly.

The annual agricultural show represents the highlight of a social calendar that is remarkably bare, so the entirety of the local population is in attendance; ranks swelled with visitors and tourists alike.

There he stands, Evan Pettersen, on the minute stage with clumsily assembled cooking gear and his major assets – his natural charm and winning smile. He recognises, a little self-consciously, that his repertoire is somewhat restricted for this event given lack of equipment and time constraints. However, his hugely successful city restaurant reassures him and countless others that he is a chef on the simmer. His celebrity bubble is about to float to the top of the bountiful celebrity chefs' froth.

Halfway through his second dish, a simple vegetarian pasta, he knew he'd hit the mark. Not a soul stirred from their allocated seat. They sat, captivated by his every move, glued to every word and when he smiles, the sighs are audible. From the female portion of the audience, that is. The few males, invariably farmers, that were interspersed throughout appeared to manage a greater degree of self-control.

Naturally, over the years he had attended cooking demonstrations by superior chefs at numerous trade shows, but had never been tempted to undertake this sort of thing himself, especially before eighty or so people. He would not have done this one except for the persistent encouragement of his lovin' wife, Lex.

He was loving it. The energy flowing back to him from the audience elevated his own spirits to the point that he appeared to almost glow on stage.

He was pleased he'd taken the advice on making the pasta dish, as this was a district big in wheat farming, specialising in Durum wheat. Evan was sure to make particular reference to the value of this flour product with its strong protein that allowed the pasta dough to stretch – essential to create excellent pasta. With his intimate and locally applicable wheat knowledge, and that beaming smile, he was definitely a contender for the best in show stakes.

His mother always said that Evan was born with a grin and that it came naturally to him. Sure, smiling comes easily to many; it takes fewer muscles than frowning, apparently. Evan's God Given Gift was that his smile was evident even while he talked!

A winning combo – smiling the smile and talking the talk! Truly a gift.

By the end of the pasta dish, Evan had really found his form and had relaxed into the easy banter that flows when you are totally in control and yes, enjoying yourself. His next and final dish for the presentation was a lamb dish with locally produced mustard seeds and mustard oil. Although mustard seed production was small in this region, it was gaining acceptance by farmers as an "in between" crop, used to regenerate the soil with nitrogen after the wheat crops were harvested. Oh, how those snippets of local knowledge created an ever growing bond with his people, his audience.

As is the way of serendipity, those meaningful coincidences that can change the course of life, Nigel Herbert-Flyson was also visiting his in-laws and happened to be a member of the audience enjoying this half hour in the glow of Evan's presence. As CEO of the Channel 3 network he observed with avaricious and calculating awe, the power of this charming man on stage.

Nige allowed himself a moment of self-congratulation as he knew that he personally was about to create yet another TV sensation. The package was good, nice looking, maybe mid to late thirties and that fucking smile. This guy was exactly what he was looking for to star in the food/cooking show he was bullying the Programming and Sales Departments to move on. He had convinced both departments of the enormous benefits possible, spelt P R O F I T.

How Nige loved the magic "P" word that got them all going, or leaving. It was Nigel's way or the highway. He shook his head in mild perplexity. Who would believe that here in this tiny, hick town he had found the next star for his network, he was a fucking genius, no doubt about it. He allowed himself what passed as a chuckle as he thought about the smiling, seductive guy up there on stage who was completely unaware of what was about to happen to him and his life. Nigel was about to create a TV star and media sensation, and a shitload of money.

As the demonstration ended Evan found himself surrounded by an audience full of congratulations and questions. Nigel shoved through the annoying throng with his best imitation of hail fellow, well met – after all, these were the same fucking schmucks who kept his station at the top of the ratings game. He grabbed the sweating chef's hand and pumped it as he exploded with, "That was very good, son – no, not just good, but fucking great!" A quick glance around assured him that the F word was not used here as it was in TV land and he wondered momentarily if an apology might be considered necessary. Fuck that! He never did, no matter where. He pressed his business card into Evan's palm with an unambiguous, "Monday morning. My office."

Evan apologetically but firmly explained to the speechless TV magnate that this was simply not possible as he had been absent from his restaurant all weekend, and needed to make sure all was on track.

Nigel was truly at a loss, in his sycophantic world this simply did not happen, he ruled by divine leadership, he spoke and it happened. In other circumstances, he would have marched away with a series of colourful expletives, but he knew in his gut that he was on to something with this guy and managed to swallow his bile, asking when might be suitable with a hint of sarcasm. Tuesday. Network office. Okay.

As they headed back to the city, Evan and Lex chatted on in their usual easy way about how enjoyable the family get together had been on Saturday night, especially as Evan had not been slotted into his usual role as head chef. Lex had a warm and welcoming family and having a rare break from the three kids had allowed them to enjoy this warmth without the usual responsibility. There had been initial disappointment from the grandparents at not seeing the children, but this was soon overcome as all relaxed on a strictly adult level for once.

The kilometres whisked past in Evan's very smart car but conversation about the appointment on Tuesday was avoided – what would be, would be – and they considered their world was already one they were grateful for.

The Fates were smiling on Evan and the Tuesday meeting landed him with his own show. There had been a moment of consternation and confusion amongst some of the Network staffers at the meeting when Nigel explained that he would need to discuss the offer with his wife before accepting; meaningful discourse between loving partners was not a huge part of their facile understanding of relationships.

Evan wanted to become a TV star with his own show on daily morning TV, but he had an inkling of the potential havoc it could wreak with his life and that of his family, and his successful restaurant business.

Could this really be happening to him, it sure as hell seemed to be the case! Just six short years ago, he was a thirty-eight year old successful restaurant chef with an adorable wife and three kids, living in the burbs. Now, he was on the way to stardom – he and that sublime smile!

CHAPTER 1

Let The Shoot Begin!

Evan Pettersen had attended one opera in his life, Donizetti's Lucia di Lammermoor. At forty-four, he still remembered the grey, misty set of the death scene with the deranged and bloodied Lucia terrorizing the wedding party with the knife she had recently used to kill her new husband.

The cavernous studio he walked into each Tuesday and Wednesday during the shooting season for the Game brought that grey, misty scene to mind as the halcyon lights strung high in the ceiling cast that same cool, grey light. Just enough light to see what you were doing, but not enough to intrude on your concentration.

Evan, the star who had made a meteoric rise to fame with "The Cooking Game....r u Game?" loved coming into the studio at this time, around 7am, when the place was just waking up and the early crew members were doing the same, shaking away the cobwebs of the previous night's excess. Another day was beginning and he had no idea what time it would end. Recording a TV show was like that; forget the dinner arrangements.

Evan enjoyed the relative peace, knowing that within an hour or so the industrious calm of studio 3 would be shattered by the arrival of Philomena Watts, executive producer of the Game. Customarily Phil, as she was known around the traps, would arrive at around 8am with a verbal blast. There was never anything like a simple good morning from this female dynamo.

A typical tirade would begin along the lines of "What the fuck is going on here you lazy bunch of shitheads?" and progress along to "I don't get you dickheads ... every week it's the same place for that lounge for the interview segment ... and you've moved the fucking thing ... what the fuck gives?" Then invariably, "when will the main set be done ... where is Max, where the fuck is he?" Naturally Max, the sound technician with uncanny instinct had disappeared, to return later when the coast was clear and with a little luck he would not run into Boadicea, his personal nickname for Phil.

Her outrageous outbursts would never have been tolerated in any other industry, however in the TV business, it was almost the norm. As the progeny of TV royalty and the powerful Executive Producer of a very successful and profitable daily show, Phil was allowed to do and act pretty much as she wished, within reason.

The physical attributes of Phil's "tanties" included the erratic waving of her arms, white knuckled fist clenching and the occasional foaming flecks of spittle at the corners of her mouth. This display was invariably accompanied by threats as to what may or may not happen to various parts of the particular victim's anatomy. Phil's performance was an anticipated weekly event, always on Tuesday and always accompanied by much waving of arms, where one hand held the shoot schedule for the day. The demanding shoot schedule of 20 to 24 segments for the week long daily show meant that each minute was precious and according to Phil, the set was never anywhere near ready.

Phil's tantrums were legendary in the business – famous even. Around Channel 3 headquarters, these temperamental displays were known quite affectionately as "Phil's farts". Her expletives were so explicit and colourful, it was said that she would leave Gordon Ramsey or Joan Rivers speechless and blushing.

The long-suffering crew had learnt that it was prudent to handle Phil's "Tuesday Tornado" with calm humility. A few hushed utterings along the lines of "what is she on about again?" and "why can't she give her arse a go instead of all this verbal shit!" from the stagehands and a silently mouthed, "fuck her!" from the kitchen hand slicing onions in a kitchen at the rear of the set was as close to mutiny as they ever came.

As he sauntered along with recipes clanging around in his brain, Evan slipped into one of his habitual reveries. He remembered such strident scenes from his early days apprenticed to various talented chefs from around the world. He'd learnt to move quickly to avoid a dinted head from yet another flying sauté pan thrown with remarkable accuracy by the French Head Chef. The Greek Chef was more attuned to a friendly but boisterous thump to help remind exactly how to dice meat evenly for the stew. All head chefs had different ideas and their own uniquely cruel methods of endorsing them; and then, there was the text book stuff! Confusing as it had been, Evan had picked up points and techniques that still served him well, long after the thump or unintentional connection with the sauté pan.

He reflected on how abhorrent that type of behaviour had initially seemed to him in his youth and from such a protected background. His parents were strict Presbyterians and, as 'quiet' people, hardly ever raised their voices but rather exacted a reprimand with logical reasoning and perseverance – and sometimes prayer. Family life with his elder brother Greg and his younger sister Eva was humdrum, consistent and peaceful. His father was a successful engineer and, as he liked to say to his children, "There may not be millions … but there's enough." The children grew without concern about their next meal or new set of clothing. School fees were not a subject of household worry even though they attended private Presbyterian Colleges.

Frequently Dad would take the family to a good restaurant, never extravagant but appropriate to the celebration or simply to relieve his wife of the daily drudge of feeding the ravening mob. She, like all good wives of her ilk, never complained and to go out to eat was to give her ideas for family meals. She amused herself by trying to replicate the fish dish or the beef dish that the family had enjoyed the previous evening. While she was critical of her efforts, the family woofed it all down and provided there was dessert, all was idyllic in their gentle world. On reflection, Evan was incredibly grateful for this time in his life as the gestation period for his appreciation of the beauty of cooked foods and he developed a fine palate for food; never alcohol as the folks simply did not imbibe – well rarely, and if so, always extremely expensive and acclaimed wines.

Evan delighted in the fact that he'd had a dream upbringing. When he'd listened to some of the horror stories of his contemporaries as he trained, he knew he'd been blessed with the best of parents and his only real complaint had been the obligatory weekly attendance at church service and the subsequent bible lessons. He'd considered it a real drag, but another of Dad's favourite lines had been, "You're under my roof and while you're here, you go to church!"

End of story as far as Dad was concerned. And his mother for that matter – church on Sundays was de rigueur.

While his dad had been athletic in his distant youth, those days had been left well behind him at university when any illusions he'd had to further himself on the track were quashed by the immense study workload of an engineering degree. Consequently, he applauded his middle child, his 'big son' (Evan was taller than Greg) when he took to the water as an amphibious wonder kid. "That's the Viking coming out in you, Son," was his father's claim; even though it was bullshit, as Evan was to discover later in his life.

The Scandinavian heritage was frequently embellished by his Dad and credited as the reason Evan grew to have the discipline and body of an Adonis. His swimming style of preference and body design was backstroke – he was brilliant and rose to school champion, with aspirations of competing at the national titles. His body developed into something resembling any of Michelangelo's male masterpieces. His shoulders were broad, deep and muscular allowing his squared chest to suspend engagingly and his rippled ribs snapped around the six pack to taper to a waist he would retain for ages. Oh God, he was beautiful and with his burnished hair (which Dad also attributed to his heroic Viking genetic heritage!) haloed his tanned face to create a physical image irresistible to men and women alike.

A single point of difference existed between the master sculptor's marble efforts and Evan in that he was hung; none of that undersized embarrassment those pathetic white Adonis's had to endure in public spaces around the world. No, Evan was very handsomely equipped where it mattered – not that he had any real idea of the delights said equipment could deliver.

Sex was not a topic open for discussion at home and his parents believed he'd gain what knowledge he needed by the process of osmosis (or perhaps the divine intervention of the sex education Angel). Both scientific principle and the Angelic hosts bypassed Evan and it was not until he arrived in France at the ripe age of nineteen that he enjoyed his first sexual encounter with the lusty, lovely Renata. How long has this been going on and does everyone do IT – Holy Shit!

It slowly dawned on Evan where all those friendly conversations at school with the opposite sex and then in various work places, were meant to lead. The guys told him frequently that such and such a girl 'fancied' him – none had bothered to let him into the secret of what 'fancied' meant. Now, with Renata in tow as a most willing and regular partner he intended to make up for lost time regarding sins of the flesh! She introduced him to a couple of her gay buddies but Evan simply could not understand how guys could do that with each other – Renata adamantly assured him that they most certainly could, and did. Bullshit!

So, he revelled living a young man's burn-the-candle-at-both-ends life for three months in the tiny, one room flat he rented not far from the Madelaine in Paris. His miniature den of iniquity served its purpose as he worked, and screwed, and ate out on rare days off but eventually, from sheer exhaustion, he took Renata and they fled to Nice to sleep and fuck. Funnily enough, Sunday mornings never saw them at church.

Evan knew the time was drawing nigh to leave his lusty lover and return home, duty and expectation called. However, before adorning the mantle of adulthood, Spain beckoned and he answered the call. He was mesmerised by the tiny seaside town of Cadaqués, the home of Salvador Dali for many years. He then ventured on to Sitges, Barcelona and Madrid experiencing all he could of their culinary delights in the little time he had left. He would often reminisce on this bustling country, wishing he'd had more time there and promising he would return one day.

He was joyously welcomed home by family and friends and a new work life. Initially, it had been difficult to put his time in France behind him; after all what could any young man crave more than learning, eating and sex – not necessarily always in that order! It was then that the multiple hours of swim training, long days on your feet in hot kitchens and a natural instinct inspired his desire to be the best chef – ever. His cooking skills were as innate as the swimming had been during his school days and his ambitions exploded like the multitudinous sukura – the cherry blossoms of the Japanese spring.

He'd worked passionately and tirelessly and a few years after he married the love of his life, Lex, he schemed to open his own restaurant. Armed with a business plan he'd prepared with his father's accountant, he hit up his old man for the base capital to set up his venture. Sure, they had three young children but Evan was fired by the passionate desire for his own eatery and so, Mangereire exploded volcanically onto the restaurant scene and never looked back.

It was now that Evan gave credit to the hard work, discipline and the lessons learned at school and in his early work life because they were responsible for him achieving his cherished dream. He knew how much also he owed to his parents and not just the money borrowed for the start up. It had been something of a shock to Evan when they had suddenly up and moved to the country after being such an influential part of his life and these days, although they spoke, it was hard to find time to visit within his hectic schedule.

His daydream came to an abrupt end, as it so often did, with picturing himself on the set for the first time six years ago, and being scared shitless. That was when his God given talent as master smoocher of people became apparent down the tube of the TV camera. He became a star immediately.

However, back here in reality, it was nearing time for his staunch support, Phil Watts to arrive and that was enough to curtail any daydreaming.

And so, another Tuesday began – it is 8.07am with the first segment to be shot at 9.30am; but Phil was always on about starting early ... just in case there were hold ups, or fuck ups as she was more inclined to regard anything that did not run to her schedule. She had learnt to be ready for any eventuality during the 13 years she had been an executive producer at Channel 3; the last six of these as executive producer of the Game.

Philomena Watts' father had been the General Manager of the Channel 3 network and Phil was brought up on a diet of TV with its inherent dramas and the high life generally associated with this intriguing business. Phil was no chip off the old block as Terry, her dad, had been a much respected quiet achiever, who had no patience with the type of boisterous behaviour exhibited by his daughter.

Abusive, loud, forceful, achieving and successful, Phil was a truly complex package. Her aggressive tone and butchish clothing often led initiates to presume that she was gay, a suggestion she vehemently denied. The long, golden plait that hung over her right shoulder proclaimed her femininity for all to see; or so she fervently believed. More to the point, this plait provided a precious security blanket. When feeling under pressure, or in a confronting situation, Phil would grasp her plait with her left hand to ease the anxiety. In times of extreme anxiety, Phil had even been known to suck the loose hair that formed the tassel of her security blanket.

Phil believed her divine right was inviable around the sets and hallways of the 3 network, given her father's previous importance and status. But, where staff and business associates would stand by her Dad, knowing they were in the company of a great man, they would stand aghast as Phil took on one of her hissy fits. She firmly believed that it was her right as a woman to have these rambunctious outbursts to get her way in what she deemed "a man's world".

She had been heard to say on many an occasion that women and fags always got the rough end of the pineapple in this crazy business. Though she was possibly right, she had never given any other method of communication a chance, it was always shoot first and ask questions later for Phil.

Then, of course, there was that infamous chair throwing incident during a production meeting. Unfortunately, said airborne missile collected a junior mid-flight who, on completion of his hospital stay, consequently sued the network. The cool $480,000 payout awarded the victim was never, (as threatened at the time), deducted from Phil's expense account. It was true, Phil was definitely known around the network for all the wrong reasons. However, she was still there and still in control of her patch of turf.

This 48-year-old woman from a privileged background never had her ability to produce this show questioned, the powers that be simply whitewashed the issues yet again when another stagehand complained and the union stepped in. Somehow the show went on and not just on, but very successfully; both ratings and profits being pronounced extremely good – inspiring actually. This being the case, top management was loath to touch the "magic" Phil wove every day she was in charge of The Game.

At just 8.12am Phil's Tuesday morning mayhem had ceased and it was business as usual with Max back in action, having managed to avoid Phil in the intervening fracas.

Mel, floor manager extraordinaire, settled down to mapping out the schedule and working with the director, Bill Wiseman, looking at specific shots and other needs for the day's shoot.

The gentle hum of a well-oiled team had returned to studio 3 as Phil marched off in search of the star of the show, the effervescent Evan.

Bill and Mel had become mired in the third cooking segment – twice cooked mushroom and Gruyère soufflés. Bill grimaced as he saw complications with this fancy muck; his own idea of top cuisine was baked beans on toast. He complained, "Why the fuck do you have to cook 'em twice … surely once is enough for this shit!"

Mel didn't answer as she had her concerns also because there were eight steps to this dish and the accepted format was no more than five steps per recipe. How the hell did this one get through, she wondered, just one more win for the star and somehow she and Simon Hacknell, the on-set chef and Evan's right-hand man would just have to sort it. She knew the segment would be a winner though – the Tweets would go off the planet and Facebook would run hot with recipe requests. It was their job to make the recipe work and there were no illusions – both Simon and Mel knew this. The twice cooked soufflés would come out making Evan look like the brilliant chef he was and it was not part of his job description to worry about the intricacies of getting a dish like this to air.

"Come on Bill, let's go talk to Simon and see if we can't work this one out … fuck what a mess!" She sighed as they crossed the busy studio to reach the on-set prep kitchen at the rear.

Here, amongst the recipes, slicing and dicing, the whirring of food processors and the calm hum of spoons stirring was the boss of the back kitchen and the heart of the Game, Simon Hacknell. His organisational skills and knowledge were extremely comprehensive for a young man of twenty-eight. As Evan's right-hand man, not only here at the studio but also in the affiliated businesses that Evan controlled, it was his job to "make it happen" and Simon relished this role with all its attendant responsibilities.

"So, how the hell we gunna do these soufflé sequences, Simon?" Bill asked. "The first segment with the banana and chilli chocolate sundae is straightforward enough – but what about this twice cooked stuff?"

Simon inhaled deeply and released the breath in his controlled Zen-like way, controlling his rising stress level. He looked carefully at Bill and replied patiently, "This may be 'stuff' to you, Bill, but to people like me and our audience out there, these soufflés will be brilliant." After a thoughtful pause he also added, "If you're worried about 'stuff', you just focus on the crappy chilli chocolate and banana dish." End of story – for now.

Simon allowed himself another deep breath wishing he could be included in the planning meetings in the first instance and put a stop to this non-adherence to format. But, quite frankly what could he, or anyone, do to interfere with the whims of an important client like Hothams Chocolates? The 'suits' wanted to show off this part of their new range of chocolates for the young and young at heart, as their TV advertisements banged on about with monotonous repetition. Naturally, the ads in question were exclusive to the 3 network and needless to say, worth a bundle of bucks which made the ad-executives in 'suits' very happy to say nothing of what it did for their commissions! The young chef reflected on this latest example of money overriding good sense, taste and inclination – profit was it at 3!

Back to the soufflé solution and Simon was on top of it – as usual. With the three of them hovering over the ingredients, Simon began, "So sequence one is where we find Evan at the oven with the soufflés beginning to rise. Mel, can you make sure the internal light is on in the oven so we capture the lightly golden tops rising? Evan explains to the audience, showing this is the soufflés cooking. Bill, you then pick him up on camera 2 and he moves to the kitchen bench to show how they come this far. Alright so far, Bill? Mel … okay?" Both nodded in understanding, so Simon went on to explain that Evan would then tell the viewers that the soufflés currently cooking would be the ones that are turned out when cooled. A tray of pre-cooked, cooled soufflés would be introduced to take the whole process further. The many steps of TV cooking were complicated but it was their duty to make it look easy.

"And so, at this stage, Evan will stir the egg yolks into the cooling mushroom and cheese mixture – cool?" explained Simon.

"Hold on … hold on," jumped in Mel, "how will the dumbos at home know how the base got this far?"

Simon exhaled yet another deep Zen breath – may the Gods give me patience – "Well, Evan will have shown the ingredients that have been used and will demonstrate how to get the roux mixture to the correct consistency," he said, pointing to the first saucepan.

He continued with, "In this next saucepan the basic sauce has been made by adding the hot milk to the roux and cooking it out over a low heat, Evan will show this and talk it through." He searched both their faces for comprehension and continued, "Then he'll stir the sweated mushrooms, cheese and egg yolks. The whipped egg whites are then folded in and the mixture is spooned and poured into the breaded soufflé moulds – Evan puts these onto the tray and heads to the oven with them." At this point Simon felt completely validated; he was the maestro and in charge … well, for a moment or so anyway.

"Guys, Evan will emphasise the adding of the whites in two lots and tell 'em why – so a close up on camera 1 would work well, and then get Jonesy to pull out to the boss." Okay so far. This was going almost too well thought Simon and on cue, the indigenous South American flutes of his mobile beckoned for immediate attention.

"Jesus!" cried out Bill. "That fucking phone; always those fucking flutes and always right in the middle of everything." Bill had been listening attentively and planning his shots. He'd already planned Jonesy's close up on the egg whites being folded in and silently offered a sarcastic thanks to Simon for the confirmation. He was, at least, starting to feel more confident as to how this messy segment could be tackled. Bill knew the phone call signalled the end of this so-called briefing, because Simon's calls were always marathon events. So, with a demurring glance at Mel, he offered a hopeful, "Guess it'll all be okay on the day."

Mel nodded agreement and that was that – the other three live segments seemed reasonably straight-forward. Four "live ones" all up and then the recorded wine segment would fill the show. Why they were called "live segments" was something of an unquestioned anomaly as the entire show was pre-recorded. This was the first of the three shows that they would shoot today, so it would be Monday's show for next week; Tuesday and Wednesday's shows would be shot later today. Thursday's and Friday's shows would be shot tomorrow, Wednesday.

It was unsurprising really, that nerves were frayed at this time on a Tuesday morning as so much could potentially go awry and there was precious little allocated time for malfunctions. Funnily enough, once the first segment was actually underway, those same jagged nerves settled. Or perhaps, they were simply beaten into submission with coffee and cigarettes. Somehow, some way, someone had to control getting these shows to air. It was always okay on the day!

With her attendant air of pomposity, Phil had left the industrious studio knowing that within an hour or so, all would be underway. The rush of equipment being moved with its inherent noise was accompanied by the shouts of various crew members; each making sure all was in place as should be. Soon, this noisy, organised chaos would be replaced by the quiet that made good television possible; the masked hush of success.

Phil had every right to feel confident that everything would be okay on the day – after all the Game was now in its sixth, incredibly successful, season; why shouldn't she be experiencing that warm little glow of confidence. She smiled secretly to herself and wondered if the crew had any idea at all that she created the bluff and her Tuesday "farts" were part of it, they were competent professionals and she trusted them. But this was a business that depended on bluff as part of the whole façade and she had learnt how to play the game early. She continued her musing as she approached the green room in search of her Star – Evan. It was a graciously designed room, with that superficial TV ambience of "cool" and was shared by a number of the network's stars. The current incumbent was the star of "The Cooking Game....r u Game?" – Evan Pettersen.

As Executive Producer Phil had plenty to discuss with Evan, but experience had taught her that anything remotely contentious would have to be delayed until the day's filming was completed. Evan could not handle being flustered before a long day of shooting three shows; seventeen segments today including the pre-recorded and outside location ones.

So she kept her demeanour nice and light – carefree but confident. No need to mention the Big Boss's thoughts for the Christmas special; the one he pictured on location. Shit, location shoot at that time of year! No need to stress Evan with Nigel's plans. Mr Nigel Herbert-Flyson, Channel and Network boss would inevitably get his way which would include, as ever, the predictable, profitable suck up to important sponsors, advertisers and the 'suits'.

The Sales Department would undoubtedly have been in his ear and they usually had their way with him. Nigel, or Nige to his mates and those wielding a worthwhile chunk of the mighty dollar, was a network institution and his control over lives and destinies was never in doubt. Phil was more aware of this than most and was somewhat ambivalent about her boss – Nige to her, of course. They went back a long way. Way too long.

She gave her customary three light taps on the green room door and barged in irrespective of waiting for invitation, also customary. "Hi-Evan-you-good-hon?" spoken as a single word and she was seated. Her green tea was delivered by PT. No word of thanks was offered; it never was.

Evan lifted his dreamy, steel blue/grey eyes from his iPad towards Phil's face. It seemed to take him a few seconds to focus and gather his thoughts. That fabulous smile flashed at Phil in sincere friendliness. They had been through a great deal over six years as Executive Producer and Star and had forged a genuine trust and friendship through the trials and tribulations of bringing the adventurous cooking show together. It was an interesting and much discussed relationship that did not involve any sexual dalliance, no matter what the viperous gossips might like to rumour when there was no grander scandal to perpetuate.

They were professionals and friends. This was business – big business. A fact they both appreciated and enjoyed the benefits of.

"Hiya Phil," Evan replied as he lightly rubbed his eyes, not wanting to rub too hard in case his roughness may cause them to appear bloodshot. He wondered if he needed reading glasses and made a mental note to get PT to make an appointment with the optometrist. "Yeah, all cool and ready for a big day ... will be good except for that damn wine segment. Do we really have to use that wanker, Phil? Can't we find someone or something else?"

Evan should know better, she often thought to herself. The power of this place was the Sales Department. Profit equalled power and that was the way it worked for the Boss and the board. The shareholders liked the segment immensely. As a chef, and with his somewhat abstemious Presbyterian childhood, Evan did not have a background in "plonk" as he called wine. Consequently, his ignorance was apparent when it came to this touchy segment.

Phil had known this would come up – Evan loathed the wine segment, mostly because he thought the presenter was a wanker; but there was no doubt that the "wanker" had a huge following amongst would be connoisseurs. There was no way that John Smithton, the wine presenter, was going anywhere as far as Phil knew and certainly as far as the Sales Department was concerned. Smithton was THE man for Alpha Wines and he was good, very good. Evan did not agree, but it was a moot point around the studio. As a result of Evan's rare but heartfelt ennui with regard to the connoisseur, the wine segment was filmed mostly on location. Be that as it may, the P word was the first commandment at the Network and Alpha Wines advertising meant Profit.

Phil said emphatically, "Well, you know as well as I do, bud – Smithton stays as long as THEY say and there is nothing either of us can do about that!" She rarely found it necessary to strong arm Evan, which was fortunate because she really was not into mollycoddling stars. Phil condemned star outbursts as no more than spoilt and childish behaviour and they were only replaceable talent, for fuck's sake. This attitude had, in fact, lost her a couple of jobs, but what was talent without the 'A team' crew to make them look the part, right?

Phil moved round to make herself more comfortable in the comfy chair near the desk of the Star and across from PT. Evan's PA, also known as PT, was the very energetic and capable personal assistant to Evan. Her real name was Joanna Friberg but she had been christened PT (Part Time Wife) by Evan many years ago. She was adorable and invaluable and after eight years had come to know her boss very well. She could second guess him much like his real wife, Alexandra (AKA Lex), who should well be able to do so after 19 years of marriage to THE man.

"Got anything else, Phil?" asked Evan with a slight hesitation, "Are we all set … any surprises?"

"Not that I know of, but as you well know, anything can happen. But then I know you can handle it, you always do. Oh, by the way, there's a little concern about the twice cooked soufflés – are you on it? Can they be that tricky? Bill's cracking a shitty about the segment, saying it's pretentious but then, you know Bill," she concluded with hopeful optimism.

"Yeah … well, we're not here for Bill … it's about our viewers who know a shitload more about food than Bill does. There's more to it than the crap Bill eats. Ever seen what he eats in the canteen? His world would be decimated if toasties were dropped from the menu. Give me strength!"

Evan knew that Bill, as director, would get the shots that were needed and part of his acting out was the same nervousness that skewed everyone's behaviour waiting for the shoot to start, together with the various interpersonal power plays that had to be taken into consideration.

Evan watched as Phil exited the door and with an undefined movement, she suddenly reminded him of his mother. What was it that Phil did? Was it the little swing of her behind as his mum used to do, or maybe the artless wave she gave with her left hand? That tender farewell wave that was a shared ritual as she wished him good night. Whatever it was that Phil did, he was reminiscing about her – his mum. Well, for about three seconds, anyway. He recognised that here in la-la land, this crazy world that was TV, an awful lot of the people he worked with had not had the blessing of a mum like his, or a father either, for that matter.

Evan always considered himself incredibly fortunate in the parental hand he had been dealt. He'd often contemplated the weird dichotomy that his parents presented as sincere and practicing Presbyterians who also embraced the good life and fashioned their children's outlook to enjoy all they were blessed with and respect God, their parents and their elders. This attitude of appreciation for the simple joy of good food had initiated numerous pleasure filled evenings spent in good restaurants for the whole family, which undoubtedly inspired his mother's culinary skills and hence his own passion. These same attitudes were the grounding that Lex and he also worked to instil in their own three offspring.

Today, it seemed somewhat antiquated thinking and behaviour but Evan, his older brother and younger sister, all recognised that their wonderful parents had given them an exceptional start in life.

Lucky? Maybe, more than luck was involved here, and what was luck anyway?

Perhaps this is why Evan enjoyed the success he did. He was lost in this self-examining daydream when PT jostled him to get a move on to make-up. He liked to think of himself as a simple man who had found his passion in life – cooking. Lucky again.

In fact, Evan was not a simple man at all, he just thought in simple terms for the most part. He had a genuine love for the art of cooking, was respected by his peers and adored by his audiences in TV, magazine columns and cookbooks. He was a success and he loved it!

Life is good, he assured himself as he sauntered to make-up.

Make-up was the domain of Marj – Marjorie please; Marj makes me sound like some old cleaning lady! Once that perfect onscreen visage was complete, Evan made his way to the studio engaged in his usual hype ritual and reminding himself that all would be brilliant. Waiting there was the "A team" who would make sure it would be just that – brilliant!

Slipping through the studio doors into the grey pall that was the Lucia haze of the studio, he found his shirts hanging and ready for him beside the studio kitchen. Eleven, as always, in various shades to facilitate his choice – the azure blue caught his eye, it always complimented his eyes. He eased the smooth shirt over his expansive shoulders, buttoned up, and tucked it into his rather tight jeans. His eating regime and the near frantic pace of his life didn't allow any extra grams to creep onto that almost perfect frame.

He was a particularly fine looking figure of a man and he was aware of it. Was it the auburnish hair with the blond tips that sparkled around his forehead, halo like? Was it the steel blue eyes that, contrasted by the hair, lent him that perpetual air of outdoorsy, boy next door charm and ease? Being tall and having been a backstroke swimmer, he had Superman shoulders and a tapered waist

– and he was dressed by the wardrobe department to accentuate each and every attribute.

He was impressive in stature and wore that impressiveness well. He appeared at ease or maybe it was the happy-go-lucky attitude that came from being the possessor of these mere physical attributes. Perhaps success created that sense of ease.

Nothing else, like success, can create its own enticing aura of beauty! He had it all.

As he approached the Game's studio kitchen and Simon he perused the set to see how all the prep was shaping up; the lights flooded the area and the Lucia haze was dispelled by the blaze of the day-making lights. No matter how many times Evan had seen this happen, it still took his breath away and jarred his psyche into realisation of "show time!" As the star, he would be under those brilliant lights creating the magic that was "The Cooking Game….r u Game?"

He was ready.

Chasing him was Max, the sound tech whose responsibility it was to get Evan "wired for sound". This entailed clipping a tiny microphone to Evan's shirt at the neckline and popping the wire to his transmitter down his shirt front, making it invisible. This done, the wire connected to the transmitter which was tidily tucked away into one of the back pockets of the star's jeans. While this was taking place, Evan glanced through the running sheet for the day's shoot – for the umpteenth time. Now, through his earpiece, he could hear his director's instructions. Evan could remember the first time he had used this essential piece of equipment – these days he had his own personal earpiece specifically moulded to his right ear. The hallmark of a Star – your own earpiece.

He was all set.

A simple Hi to Simon, accompanied by the slightest arch of an eyebrow, queried if all was good? This invariably received a swift thumbs up from his right-hand man, and Evan was ready for THE light – his key light.

His skin felt caressed by the iridescent brightness of the lights and his whole being tingled as he changed persona; he was about to claim his kingdom. He was psyched for the first of the fourteen segments that he would mould and manipulate into award winning TV entertainment. This was Evan Pettersen, the wonder kid of the TV cooking world.

The magic was about to begin.

The floor manager, Mel, did a quick whizz around the studio making certain the "A team" were all ready for cueing. It was 9.22am and within a few minutes the first shot and the day would begin. Simon went through the ingredients for the first dish with Evan. Adrenaline was pumping across the studio floor. The clapper board clapped as it recorded the segment for camera 2 and the ethereal Simone readied with her stopwatch.

Chilli Chocolate Ice Cream Sundae. Simon and Evan's collective palates did an instant revolt, but both had an implicit understanding of the value of Hotham Chocolates, a major advertiser. As one, they swallowed their revulsion and as Simon pointed out, it was a mercifully short segment. Four allotted minutes and it would be over – Evan was aiming for three and a half.

Evan allowed himself a quick eyeball around the camera operators – Spikey on camera 3, Jonesy on 1 and Johnno on camera 2 and a reassuring glance upwards to find the locked in overhead camera operated from the director's booth; Marco ready on the boom mic. Everything in its familiar place – nice.

"Quiet!" boomed the voice of the diminutive floor manager, Mel. This was the final signal for mobile phones to be switched off; this excluded Simon's which was switched to vibrate and silent.

Suddenly, the studio was saturated with the instantly recognisable theme music, bright and bubbly. It sounded like an electronic, silvery fountain trickling away and was entirely appropriate for the Game's audience at this time of day – the "mid-morning and coffee set" that relaxed and tuned into Evan once the kids were at school, or having an obligatory nap.

As the music trickled on, the screen was filled with a flashing montage of past segments, mostly Evan and his stunning dishes or Evan at some personal appearance somewhere. Contented cows looked surprised as Evan wandered through some random farmer's paddock, rounds of white mould cheeses cascaded across the screen with luscious appeal and somehow even the carrots of various hues looked entirely appetising.

With that, the screen was flooded with the name of the show – "The Cooking Game….r u Game?"

"Here we go," Mel commanded again and the countdown began. "From 5 … 4 … 3"; 2 and 1 were never counted out loud – silence was crucial.

In the director's booth, Bill was intently selecting his opening shot from the many screened panel that confronted him. Okay, got his opening shot and there he was, Evan Pettersen looking stunning and beaming that impossibly seductive smile. Yep, he was gorgeous.

With the music now fading, that smiling face took Mel's pointed finger to indicate that he was away.

"Hey, so good to see you and welcome to the show. On the Game today … what have I got in store for you? Are you game for a Chilli Chocolate Ice Cream Sundae … chilli, chocolate and ice cream … let's see how that comes together for you … who are the chilli lovers? How about some game? Let's cook quails!"

He looked at the quails as did camera 1. He then came back to the screen on camera 2 and continued his intro. "John Smithton's here from Alpha Wines with his take on Pinot Noir," (only someone who knew him as well as his wife or PT could detect the faintest hint of sarcasm), "there's a funny little carrot salad I've been working on with Simon. You'll love it and we know you'll let us know how much … thanks, you Tweeters'!" The Tweeter account detail is superimposed under the close-up of his face, "… and to finish up; twice cooked mushroom and Gruyère cheese soufflés. Who said soufflés were impossible? Not the way I do them – I'll show you." With that reassurance, his beaming smile once again filled face and screen. The Evan Pettersen trademark was applied with a sincere wink from the right eye this time, and to camera 1.

"Fuck, I wish he'd tell me when he's going to wink," screamed Bill, "then I could get the shot lined up … dickhead!" but of course, Bill got the shot with Jonesy who was always on the ball for that illustrious trademark wink.

And so, the show was under way.

Evan's intro was fantastic; as Bill declared through his earpiece. The Chilli Chocolate segment was introduced as a new product for Hotham Chocolates and the Sundae materialised in a swift 3:51 minute creation. Some of the crew winced as quails were introduced, most notably the vego time keeper/meet and greeter, the ephemeral Simone.

All smiles and no worries so far with Evan being his inimitable self, and the show flowed. Simon had done his usual superb preparation and even Bill had no complaints. Phil's hand was nowhere near the plait, another indication of smooth sailing, as she smiled at her monitor. Even the Sundae was given unanimous approval by the spoilt and somewhat cynical crew. The quails, a different kettle of quails!

John Smithton was given his typical introduction and asked if Pinot Noir was the next "real" wine for apprentice connoisseurs? Whatever that may mean, it was of no interest to Evan who viewed this segment with his usual suspicion. He had no real interest in wine and only drank it when it was a social necessity. This was a definite throw-back to his Presbyterian childhood where alcohol was not consumed either at home or in restaurants.

On to the carrot salad segment and a good introduction! The general opinion of the "A team" however, varied between boring and space filler. "Like there's nothing better to turn into a salad?" said Spikey through his headpiece for all to hear, except the Star who was having a marvellous time extolling the virtues of the humble carrot. How inexpensive they are and how healthy for the kids! Spikey's rhetorical comments prompted silent laughter and approval from the crew.

More commercials … and Bill was a happy traveller, so far. With a song and a prayer, the twice cooked soufflés segment was underway. Four minutes into the six minute segment and all was going really well. The ever beaming Evan was smiling as he said, "… and now that you've got 'em this far and they're cooked for the first time … the rest is a piece of cheese!"

With that appalling pun, Bill knew instinctively that Evan would cover himself with a self-deprecating smile, enough to make a clown blush, and the inevitable WINK. This time Bill was ready for the shot, even though Evan did the eyeball eclipse to camera 2, not camera 3. "Beat you, you bastard," Bill acknowledged to himself with great satisfaction as Johnno nailed the shot of Evan's wink.

Using an overhead shot, Evan got on with it easing the "ones I did before", cooled soufflés from their containers.

"Now you can see why it is so important to grease and line the soufflé containers or moulds with fine, dry breadcrumbs. Don't they slip out easily?" he cooed to camera 2, "and it's best now to invert them into individual ramekins or an ovenproof container to finish them off."

The soufflés looked anything but enticing as they were, given they'd risen and then deflated as they cooled down. They bore a remarkable resemblance to tiny flat tyres!

Evan remained unfazed. "And now spoon over some cream and top with the grated Gruyère. We've used Gruyère in the original soufflé mix but, you know what …you can never have enough cheese … especially Gruyère!" said with another cheesy grin, minus the wink.

"What the hell is Gruyère?" asked Jonesy down the microphone of his headset.

"It's fucking cheese, you dumb shit!" replied the all-knowing Spikey.

"Quiet!" boomed Bill down both their headsets.

Evan slid the tray of soufflés smoothly into the oven, saying, "Put these in at 200 degrees for 15 minutes, and hey, what a surprise … here are four we prepared earlier all ready to eat. How good is that?" An all knowing smile this time and the first show nearly done.

"I serve these little golden beauties with a green salad. Individually they're super, or in a larger presentation mould they make a fab communal dish for all to share!"

With a smile and fork poised to plunge into a soufflé, Evan highlighted the scrumptious surprises in store for the next day's program. The theme music slowly increased in volume as the lights dimmed and the audience viewed the star devouring a mouthful of soufflé with satisfaction and, of course, a huge smile.

Monday's show completed with the usual aplomb. And so, to Tuesday!

CHAPTER 2

A Right Royal Visit

It was Wednesday and the three shows filmed the previous day were in the "can" meaning the three thirty minute programs for the following Monday, Tuesday and Wednesday were ready for air. The shows for Thursday and Friday had been filmed and were virtually ready aside from some minor editing still to be done on the ostrich meat story.

The weekly production meeting, held late on Wednesday afternoon, had more than the usual amount of heated discussion, centred on the special guest star. The special guest star was scheduled to be filmed the following Wednesday for inclusion in the Friday show. There were some hold-ups with his people, who were speaking with the Games' people regarding concerns about his rather unusual needs. The Games' producer, Zoe Hendricks, was well versed in dealing with 'star' talent as they were referred to in these meetings.

The 'star' talent in question was one Rory Overham, superstar of the US food world. His demands were extraordinary and hovered between ludicrous and ridiculous, but he was accustomed as a superstar to having his whims adhered to. The Overham audience was expanding globally and he had agreed to use some of the footage from his Games appearance on his syndicated US program.

The carrot dangling was the opportunity of exposure for Evan's profile in that lucrative US market and Zoe was fully aware what a huge deal it was for the Network. She had already perused the list of demands starting with a particular non-fragrant soap for his dressing room and moved on to "Heavenly Scented Magnolia Tips Tea". Zoe had voiced her doubts to his people regarding the difficulty of finding anyone who even knew of this tea, let alone buying it!

The answer was simple enough … no tea; no appearance!

And these two stipulations were just the beginning – cotton towels with thread count of 800 was another. Zoe had shook her head wondering if this could really be happening – were they for real?

They were.

"So, the question is … do we really need this fuckin' faggot?" the ever eloquent Phil asked, as she tried to get a grip on this fractious meeting. She wondered at the fucking ego required to have to make the sort of sensation someone like Rory caused wherever he went. Phil didn't quite get it no matter how many examples she had seen of 'Star' behaviour, she just loathed being in a position of no choice but acquiescing to the demands. Oh, and the Fairy Queen wanted two segments worth of time not one, so it was a fucking twelve minute segment, or nothing.

Ultimately, Phil's rhetorical question went unanswered.

These production meetings, at the end of two days' shooting tended to go one of two ways. Easy, where all the proposed segments for the following week fell neatly into place, or it could be a train wreck. Today, disaster was in full flight. It had been a particularly gruelling shoot over the last two days and the last thing anyone needed was this confusing and convoluted production meeting. What's more, the sandwiches provided for the meeting were disgusting.

"Before anything else, these freaking sandwiches are a disgrace. Christ Almighty, we produce a show about gourmet and we can't even get a decent sandwich. What gives?" exclaimed Zoe, the exasperated producer. "And to answer your question, Phil – yes, we do need this fucking faggot!"

Someone had to say it and as Phil's potential nemesis, Zoe felt it was part of her job description; there were no punches pulled between the two long-standing protagonists.

"If that's the case, Zoe, and I agree with you about the sad fucking sandwiches, what's so special about Rory fuckin' Overham?" the executive producer drilled on Zoe, who was not intimidated by Phil because they went back too far. "Why should we have him considering the trouble he's been already? We haven't even got him here yet, he's not been confirmed. What the hell will happen once he's on set?"

Zoe explained her reasoning condescendingly: he was so famous that the Game could leverage considerable publicity from his appearance leading up to the show and again after it had been put to air. Rory's appearance was huge promotional material for the Game, including any incidental media coverage of his visit, especially as his intention was to reveal a never-before-seen new product as part of his Tiara food range.

What Zoe really wanted was Channel 3's publicity department to get on board with a competition to send a winner from their audience to the US for a holiday and a meet and dine with Rory in New York City, where he lived. When she'd vaunted the scenario to Phillip Williamson, public relations specialist for the Game, she'd focussed on the massive revenue generated by the competition using a competition call line but no response had been forthcoming, as yet. All because viewers thought they would be the lucky winner. Suckers! Someone always did win, after an inordinate amount of revenue fell into the coffers of the network.

Feeling that the meeting had to be brought to a close before further argument ensued, Phil said, "Zoe, you and I will work this one through and the rest of you … any more questions? Is everyone set for next week?"

There were several comments and more discussion about the quality of the sandwiches and the meeting dispersed. Phil and Zoe remained behind to get down to how they would get the famous, sometimes infamous, American chef onto the show.

The day came for THE appearance by Rory Overham on "The Cooking Game….r u Game?" show. It was a Wednesday and time had been allocated for a 12 minute segment with a commercial break in the middle. Phil had decided to make it the last segment and consequently the last filming segment of the week – for Friday's show. This way, if there were any challenges or problems they could be ironed out quickly (hopefully) and they'd get on with it. This tactic had worked in the past and TV Gods willing, would so now.

Phil's constant grabbing of her plait indicated to the crew that she was more than a little anxious.

Evan was oblivious to all the problems associated with getting Rory onto the show. From watching his appearances on other shows and Rory's own show on a specialty food Channel in the US, Evan's opinion was that the flamboyant Rory was a talent – a huge talent. His show was called "Overham – OTT". He certainly was gay, but somehow it was all a part of the package, when you considered his talent and huge audience. Most importantly, he always seemed to have a lot of fun on his show.

Simon, who rarely attended the weekly production meetings, had done so when the Overham appearance was debated. He'd let Evan know that the dish would be a bitch to do but he could make it work. He always did. Evan was relieved that he did not have to go to those production meetings on a regular basis – what a shit fight!

Rory's dish was the historically famous Gâteau St Honoré – a decadently rich French dessert. The construction, and it truly was a structure, had a circular puff pastry base with a ring of choux pastry around the edge of the circle. Once cooked and cooled, the base is filled with Crème Chiboust, a yellowish, gooey concoction not unlike its cousin Crème Pâtissière; a thickened, yellowish custard. Choux pastry balls aka cream puffs sit on the top of the choux pastry ring, secured using caramelised sugar. These are then drizzled with caramelised sugar syrup. The filling is decorated with swirls of whipped cream dispensed via a special St Honoré piping tip.

Evan had investigated this devastatingly delicious dessert on the internet. WOW! How the hell will Simon bring this one home thought Evan – so time consuming! This will be very interesting. I'll need to be on it for this one. And damn, it's the last segment when so much of his energy and concentration juices had been used up. After 11 segments over the last two days plus the restaurant business, he knew he was going to have to dig deep for the energy needed. He knew he could do it, as he'd done it many times before, but he was wary of the purported brilliance of his Star guest. Would he be out-dazzled on his own show?

The day's shoot had been going very well and the "A team" was humming. Phil was happy and her plait remained untouched – so far. Bill, in the director's booth was as happy as a pig in the proverbial and Mel was silently whistling. The vibe was good and only two more segments to come, including the one with Rory Overham, US food guru extraordinaire. The dishes from the previous segments were being washed down with coffee during a small break, a perk the "A team" relished.

The driveway at the entrance leading to the reception area at Channel 3 was filled with an enormous white limo which slid to a gentle stop. Had the driver been trained at Buckingham Palace? He sprang from his driver's seat and marched gracefully to the rear passenger door to open it. The Star alighted in a most regal manner, his feet barely seeming to hit the ground.

Rory Overham, the famous, super-celebrated chef from New York City was in the building. A sycophantic litter of advisors, assistants and various hangers-on spilled out of the limo after him. One made it to the reception door and opened it for Rory to glide through gracefully, and the others scrambled behind in a gaggle.

Meanwhile, the limo was removed with some difficulty. The exasperated driver muttered a sarcastic, "Thanks for the tip!" as he gave a finger to the departing minions, who had overlooked this odious task.

The two receptionists noted the arrival sharing a quizzical glance between them as Rory's main man, Ziggy, approached, heralding the presence of Mr Rory Overham.

"Just have a seat and Simone will be here presently to escort you to the studio," one of the receptionists said with a welcoming smile.

"Which way is the studio?" replied Ziggy, knowing that his boss, the Star, would not be waiting in any common reception area!

"Oh, it's through that door, but someone will be here in a minute."

"Rory Overham waits for no one!" declared the Star, somewhat pompously, as he pushed Ziggy to one side. The two openly amused receptionists looked on as he twirled away with his cape billowing like a train on some fabulous gown and disappeared through the door, headed for the studio.

As the Overham entourage neared the studio, they were met by the tie-dye clad Simone who, complete with messy dreadlocks, was on her way to collect the American star. She recognised him immediately as he led the theatrical charge to the studio. Quite startled, she gripped her clipboard with whitened knuckles and said, "Mr Overham … it is so goo…" Rory, with minions still in tow swept past her with the demand, "Take me to Evan Pettersen."

Simone, the sometimes dizzy studio receptionist and time keeper of segments, ran past the fast moving group to intercept Rory, "Evan's just finished a segment. He'll be with you ASAP." Leaving his highness standing in his tracks, Simone bolted to Phil who stopped what she was doing and approached the grand visiting chef.

"Well, Rory, I can't tell you how good it is to have you here," said Phil with hand extended in warm welcome.

Rory looked down at her and then further down to her hand as if it belonged to a leper, as he condescendingly explained, "Whoever you are, I am Mr Overham and this is my team – AND I don't shake hands with just anyone; these hands are precious, you have no idea how much they are insured for!"

With hand still extended she replied with sugary sweetness, "I agree entirely Mr Overham, one never knows what one might contract shaking hands with strangers." Nasty, smart little bitch, thought Rory waspishly as she continued, "I am Philomena Watts, the Executive Producer of the Cooking Game….r u Game? and I'm not just anyone." With that the extended hand was raised and pushed into the limp hand of Rory, who shook it, bereft of enthusiasm or good humour.

At this point Phil fully embraced the fact that this was going to be a challenge, not a pleasure. Oh God, where do these fuckwits crawl out from, she mused to herself as she guided his royal imperiousness to Simon's kitchen.

Having seen where Phil was leading him, he stopped. "I want my dressing room. Where is that?" Rory was impatient, to say the least.

Ziggy, sensing the brewing storm, stepped before Rory saying, "Chef, you might want to go through the dessert with the studio chef … Simon, isn't it?" he added, in a brief aside to Phil.

"Yes, this is Simon," indicated Phil as she steered them to a serene Simon, who was up to his Zen elbows creating caramelised sugar.

Mr Rory Overham gave Simon a proficient once over and a beaming ray of sunshine broke through the gathering storm clouds. "Oh, I see," said the lecherous Star chef, "I'll have no problems here," he oozed further to Ziggy.

Phil interrupted the flow making an official introduction with, "Simon, this is Chef Overham."

"Oh, do call me Rory, please," he gushed extending his hand, only to find that Simon was incapable of shaking, covered as he was with sticky caramelised sugar.

"I am so sorry, Mr … I mean … sorry, Rory," stumbled Simon, with a smile, "I'm all sticky … but welcome!" as he flashed his very best smile.

Uummm, I'd like to be all sticky with you honey, thought Rory. He flashed his perfectly even rows of dazzlingly white teeth in a smile, by way of reply.

Phil calculated there was around $45,000 of dental enhancement in that insincere smile.

The Star was left with the innocent and unwary Simon whilst Ziggy was taken to oversee the Star's dressing room.

Evan strolled over to the studio kitchen once he had been alerted to Rory's arrival. Phil cautioned him in passing to be on guard with his royal grumpiness, at which he raised a quizzical brow and grinned.

Simon had Rory's full attention, completely unaware of the thoughts racing through Rory's fertile imagination, as he ladled the dark golden sugary sauce to test its consistency. The doyen of US kitchens gave full marks with a smile that would brown butter.

"Excuse me, Mr Overham and Simon. I am Evan Pettersen, your host today – welcome to the Game." Evan was at his most welcoming with that famous visage that had been known to make women weaken at the knees focussed entirely on his guest.

Rory turned to face that rich, warm voice and was sure he must have died and gone to heaven! Oh, my God, he thought as he returned that glowing smile, is this country filled with stunningly gorgeous men? He extended a hand in his most lingering, alluring, trembling handshake – "Please call me Rory and thank you for having me on your fabulous show." He feared his lust was palpable.

What a strange accent, Evan considered as he shook Rory's wet-palmed hand, and nervous too – you had to respect a guy who never got too big for a bit of stage fright – eh? "It's a great pleasure. Can I show you to your dressing room? I think you'll find everything you need there ... all good Simon?" asked Evan.

Simon signalled confidently that everything was totally under control as the two Stars moved out of the kitchen heading towards the dressing room in question.

Evan ushered Rory into the rather crowded dressing room which had a few vases of flowers distributed about, in addition to all the other expensive accoutrements demanded by the Overham delegation. "You'll be very comfortable here, Rory. We'd like to shoot in fifteen minutes, if that is okay with you?" Evan asked.

"Make it twenty and I'll be there!"

"Where's my goddam tea, Ziggy? I need my tea!" was the petulant demand Evan heard as he departed.

Evan headed back to the studio to check his shirt was still okay remaining blissfully unaware of all the background drama surrounding Rory and his imminent appearance on the show. He was basking in the joy of knowing His show had managed to claim Rory over all the other cooking and talk shows that had competed for the honour. A coup. However, the segment was still to be shot and far from being a "bagged bird" just yet.

He popped his head into the director's booth asking hesitantly, "So, you okay, Bill. All cool for you so far?"

"I'll be fine when this next segment with the queer is over and done. Talk about a convoluted recipe. I think we have the shots set …," he said reassuringly, and then continued, "You know there is an entrance for Rory, not your usual intro?"

The Games' Star took a quick look, yet again, at his running sheet and noted, "no intro for RO required by Evan" and wondered, yet again, how this would pan out. He should have realised right then and there, that this was not going to be a usual Game's segment. As Bette Davis had said famously in Now Voyager, "Hang on, this is going to be a bumpy ride." And it would be!

"Okay Bill, thanks for the reminder. All's good here. It'll be a breeze," Pettersen, ever the optimist, replied.

Meanwhile, the main kitchen studio was being stocked with the ingredients needed by the superstar. Bench space was filling up, but Simon, with that cool Zen aura almost visible, was in charge. Simon had been impressed with the thoroughness of the recipe instructions. He'd taken a couple of lessons out of the prep requirements and layout. Although he was not particularly impressed with the American Star and his imperious manner, the way Rory behaved was really of no concern to Simon, he focused simply on what he was responsible for as far as his appearance on the Game went.

Max was about to experience a little more difficulty with the temperamental Star. He approached the dressing room to apply the mic to Rory's collar or shirt and find a place to locate the transmitter. He knocked and got no reply, so he gently knocked again. A terse, "Who is that? Go away, whoever it is!" was spat from behind the closed door.

"Yep – I'm the sound tech and you need your mic on. It's only 10 minutes before we shoot," Max responded evenly.

The door swung open and he was admitted to a melange of people squeezed into what was a rather small room. He was ordered to be quick about it and leave just as quickly. Fuck, what a rude bunch of queers he thought – what about a bit of respect for a guy just doing his job. He ran back to the studio and reported to Bill that the arsehole was indeed, just that!

Phil was feeling somewhat perturbed and wondered how best to handle this arrogant fucking little prick, while her left hand searched desperately for her plait. Should she discuss the situation with Evan or let it run its course? She decided on the latter, consoling herself that Evan knew how to handle someone the likes of Rory. Little did she realise just how wrong she was.

Phil buzzed PT, Evan's PA to remind her to be ready for the stream of Tweets that was assured to follow Rory's appearance – even though it was a week away. PT was a whizz with the social media aspect of Evan's businesses and in charge of his Facebook, Instagram and Twitter accounts. In fact, she did all the replying, only pestering Evan with the important ones. Well, the ones she considered important, as there was a whole heap of sycophantic nonsense and crap that streamed through cyberspace to their sites, including marriage proposals, even though Evan constantly spoke of Lex, his loving wife – to no avail.

There was an atmosphere of apprehension in the studio as light and sound were checked. All ingredients and equipment were nervously re-checked and the hero Gâteau St Honoré sat to one side ready for the reveal at the end of the segment – the hero shot. All was ready as Mel meandered to the star's dressing room to give him the 5 minute ready call.

"Coming!" was the impatient reply from the royal chamber.

Rory was slightly nervous, as he was before every appearance and he maintained this slight nervousness made him a better performer. At 47 and so well preserved, with a little help from the plastic surgeon's scalpel, he was ready and waiting in full make-up, compliments of his personal make-up artist, of course. A quick re-check of his costume and he was set to go.

How long had he been doing this stuff? Around two and a half decades now and he was always amazed at his nervousness. He put it down to his upbringing, as his parents had been nomadic, with no real concern about putting down roots to provide their children with a sense of security.

It's where the buck is – was his Dad's quotable quote and consequently Dad took the family from city to city, state to state, looking for itinerant work. Rory, having been born in Tampa, Florida then lived in places like Paris, Texas; Phoenix, Arizona and a good stint in Montreal, Canada. This was followed by a swift move to just outside Boston, Massachusetts back in the US. All that taken into account, Rory Overham was a consummate professional and this he professed to himself as he glided toward the studio. He had no doubts about himself as a STAR and that is what saw him through this trying period prior to entering centre stage – his star quality and his belief in the self-generated media hype – that is what and who he was.

In the brighter-than-sunshine studio kitchen, Evan was diligently doing his final, final run through, of the script. Suddenly, the studio filled with the strains of "Morning" from Grieg's Peer Gynt Suite. Surprised, Pettersen turned to his right – stage left. Instantly, he noted his camera was not on him (no red light glowing on top of his camera), for which he was immensely grateful because his jaw had dropped and his disarmingly famous smile had disappeared.

He was flabbergasted at the vision of Rory making an entrance to HIS kitchen.

Sashaying into the lights, with a dazzling smile that exposed THE teeth, every perfect luminous one of them, was the star of the US food world – Queen Rory Overham. Around his shoulders was some sort of bright green cape that dropped just below his waistline. Its draped lines were superb and the embroidery depicted various kitchen utensils, coloured bowls and assorted herbs. Intricate!

Embarrassing – thought Evan.

The camera and floor crews were aghast. Except for Mel who was totally enjoying this farcical production and went with it, a huge grin spreading across her face, having long been a devoted admirer of outrageous fag fashion.

"Holy fuck!" Spikey spluttered, as he slowly exhaled.

"Shut up!" screamed Bill down the irreverent cameraman's headpiece.

From the kitchen bench, at the front of the set, Evan was spellbound in his apparel appraisal. In Rory's right hand was a rampant balloon whisk, held as regally as any King, or in this case Queen, would hold a sceptre. On his left hand sat a round orange ball which was not unlike an orb. Evan surrendered to incredulous disbelief as a supremely sweet, deep male voice cut through the music booming, "And now folks, all the way from New York City and brought to you by Tiara Productions, here's Super Chef Rory Overham … the man to make your culinary dreams come true."

End of announcement and as the music died Rory was full centre stage … beaming. His cape was whipped from his shoulders by a fawning Ziggy to reveal the trim Star in some kind of jump suit in off-beige.

Not quite a Onesie, but oh so close. Max must have had fun getting the mic onto the Star, thought Evan with a mockery that was not his accustomed habit.

Oh my God thought Evan, this'll send Facebook and Twitter nuts, not to mention Instagram and emails.

Evan fought for composure and found his smile saying, "Well, welcome Chef Rory." For some reason beyond his comprehension he began to applaud the man.

He'd never done that before. The crew, taking cue, reluctantly joined in a hesitant, almost slow, clap.

"Oh, I am so happy to be here and thanks for having me on the Game ... The Cooking Game....r u Game? Am I right darlings? Perfectly charming," gushed the visitor.

"It's a pleasure to have you here ... and what brings you all this way to visit us?" said Evan, feeling somewhat back in charge of proceedings, albeit briefly. Rory took over.

"You know, Evan ... what a darling name that is ... family name?" Rory continued without waiting for Evan to answer. "I have been trying to get here for years but somehow ... New York, London, Paris and Rome got in the way ... but I'm here now and that's all that matters." He said this ever so smugly smiling to camera 1.

"Oh, and I have my latest new product which you're gunna love ... a dream come true for us in the cooking world... I'll show you soon." He almost giggled as he said this and at that moment, Evan felt a little pinch on his right leg. What the hell was that?

In a head and shoulders two shot for camera 2, Evan asked with remarkable equanimity considering the disturbing leg pinch, "What's happening today, Rory? And by the way, we hope you enjoy your time while you're here ..."

Before Evan could say anything further and with both of them still on camera 2, there was another little pinch that left Evan with no residual doubt as to who was the culprit. The grand star was hitting on him live, on national

TV and Evan was more than slightly flustered by this covert intrusion on his leg as he tried to hold it all together. Nothing like this had ever happened before in his six and a half years of television. This segment was turning into one big set of new experiences for the local Star who thought he knew it all.

No need for him to worry too much about keeping it together because Rory was now in full flight about his Gâteau St Honoré, explaining to camera 1 that this was a very famous dessert from France and that he loved to take a classic like this and do a modern take in his own inimitable style.

Evan almost made a comeback as Rory looked briefly his way and said, "This dessert is named after the patron saint of baking, St Honoré and also Chef Chiboust made it famous in his pastry shop on the Rue St Honoré in Paris … Isn't that divine? Sorta like a double whammy, isn't it darlings?" Again he giggled and commandeered the cameras – the studio was in Overham hands. It was going to be fabulous.

Phil was not fingering her plait. Bill was engulfed in the proceedings and Mel just cruised serenely around the cameras observing the magic of TV.

"I just adore this one Evan … and you will too 'cos I'm going to show the hard way and then my own delightfully clever little easier way. Bit of a cheat … but who cares?" With that Rory threw both hands up in the air in an extravagantly expressive manner. Evan stepped aside to avoid being accidentally knocked out. "It's just delicious and you'll love it … just like me." With deliberate ambiguity, Rory shot straight down camera 3 with a huge smile to the non-responsive camera. Rory had complete and utter control of all the action.

Evan was just about to ask what the base was when Rory started up yet again, this time to camera 2 which was the two shot camera. "The base has been cooked and, of course, you know you can get the recipe from my website. Back to the base, it's a puff pastry with a ring of choux pastry, baked. I always wonder why they called it 'shoe' pastry when it has an X on the end and spelt c-h-o-u-x?" Rory spelt the word out with a very deliberate X. "Oh, those French … they're a law unto themselves." He snickered as he picked up the puff cream balls or profiteroles as they are sometimes called.

Evan saw his opportunity as Rory paused briefly for breath and shot in with, "And these are made from the same pastry as the ring around the top here?" as he indicated the cooked ring.

"Mais oui!" confirmed Rory – it came out more like maize wee – a particularly atrocious attempt at French from a poorly educated and pretentious American.

Evan ventured, "I've always found this pastry easy to work with actually … quite simple." He indicated to a tray of the golden pastry balls.

Rory's expensive smile disappeared behind a set of very tight lips, as he asserted, "I wouldn't agree with that at all. THIS is one of the GREAT pastries and unless you handle it carefully, you will scramble the egg yolks. NO,

NO, not simple at all … but doable, when you have the touch," emphasised Rory.

Pretentious prick, exactly who does he think he is, thought Evan … I've never had anyone disagree with me on TV. Never. How should I handle this? As he contemplated, Rory took over the cameras again. Bill was keeping up somehow and was happy with the camera work.

With his eye on his monitor, Rory was in control and the show's Star was getting a rude lesson in having a segment stolen from under his very own nose. And yes, there it was, another little pinch! You perverse, egotistical bastard, thought Pettersen.

"… and now, the Crème Chiboust for the filling," purred Rory as he began stirring the lightly golden paste in the bowl.

Evan promptly interrupted with, "Rory, I always thought the filling for this dessert was that classic pastry cream – Crème Pâtissière."

With a look that would melt Maggie Thatcher's cool, Rory corrected in a patiently patronising tone, "Well yes, that is quite a common mistake, but NO. This IS the cream, Crème Chiboust, invented by Monsieur," (again with the appalling accent!) "Chiboust himself … and it is different to Crème Pâtissière because it has a rather delightful Italian meringue whipped through to finish."

He shot camera 1 an adroit, another-one-to-me-the-true-genius smile.

"Now, that's a perfect consistency," he continued, still stirring the light golden filling to camera 1; Jonesy was working overtime. "… pour it into the pastry base." With that, he lifted the bowl up facing camera 2, (no bases of bowls to camera for THIS star), and with an exaggerated up-down movement and a spatula worked the last of the crème out of the bowl.

"Oh, I just love this creamy goo, don't you darlings?" he cooed to camera 1 as the filling tumbled from the bowl. "…and Evan, I'm sure you'll know this. Crème Pâtissière is used in sooo many ways! If you added gelatine to the Pâtissière cream, you would of course create that stiffer filling we like to call Crème Bavarian."

What is this guy … a walking LaRousse Culinary Dictionary? Evan was feeling incredibly frustrated and caught the eye of Mel who was smirking. She gave the 5 minutes signal. For God's sake, could he really take another five minutes of Queen Rory?

As Rory moved the base around for camera 1, Evan felt another bolder pinch on his leg. Clever prick, as he knew the camera was on close up and so could not capture the little "love" pinch. Evan moved away a little from Rory; he was definitely between a rock and a hard place because, if he moved any further he would be out of shot and his body language would be saying – NOT INTERESTED … NOT INTERESTED! That would not be an acceptable way for the host of a successful national television program to react.

Evan, to his credit, managed his own illustrious smile and dived back into the segment – just in time to receive another lesson from Rory.

"And now you can see just how easy it is to stick these gorgeous little puff balls to the rim … simply by dipping into the caramelised sugar. Sit them on top of the ring … I mean, really, how easy can it be? Simple … now, that is simple, Evan … don't you agree?" What else could Evan say but, "Too right, Rory. Whatever you say," – but just a tinge of sarcasm crept in. "And …" was as far as Evan could add before the American took over – again!

Rory smiled for the studio cameraman who was taking still shots for the publicity department – he didn't miss a beat. "Now all we need to do is drizzle this caramelised sugar syrup over the balls and wherever," (quick, cheeky grin), "but just before we do, I'll pipe the Crème Chantilly over the filling. Now, I am using a special St Honoré tip for the piping bag … and if you can't find one of these … don't worry darlings, just use a swirling piping tip … the teeth on this St Honoré tip are wider than the average one… , and with that he shoved the tip up to camera 1 for a close up.

"On that Jonesy, on it!" Bill demanded into Jonesy's headset. Jonesy was. "Bloody beautiful," declared Bill as a dribble of cream dripped out in slow motion. The shot was perfection.

"Now that's done …" said Rory, "let's do the sugar sauce drizzle … like this," and the spoon loaded with the luscious honey brown sauce, drizzled over the balls giving them a bright glistening glow. He did this to great effect, with his left arm outstretched behind Evan – just as any Diva would when delivering her final high C in an aria. The drizzling was repeated until the star was satisfied with his grand finale. It did look absolutely incredible and Phil knew Facebook would explode with recipe requests when the segment went to air on Friday week.

It was a winning segment. A true winner.

"Oh my, this is so gorgeous, Evan. I adore the scrumptuosity of this darling dessert … don't you?" Evan was puzzled. Scrumptuosity … what on earth did that mean, he'd never even heard the word before. A slightly bewildered "Yes" was all he could manage before the pompous poof continued.

"Now, my lovelies, I told you I would make it easy for you, didn't I? Well, what would you say if I told you I have the most divine Tiara Chiboust cream for you in a powdered form and all you have to do is add water, and whisk. How easy is that!" – followed by more waving of his arms and seductive looks and smooches to the cameras. The lenses loved him and from somewhere could be heard a lone applause for five seconds.

"Well, that is my surprise to you all. It's in shops tomorrow and you've seen it here first on The Gourmet Game….r u Game?" he near shouted. "Yes Evan, and here's another gift from Tiara just for you and I know you're gunna love this one too!" By this stage he sounded like a typical US shopping network salesman. Tiara was his brand, which made and distributed all his 'stuff' as he called his money making enterprises.

Evan was silently praying this disaster would end. He was completely flummoxed, but managed, "Well, how marvellous is that. Thank you, Rory. I can't wait for this dessert to hit my taste buds and … Yes, I am Game … are you?" He sent his signature smile to camera 3 but omitted the wink which he felt could well be taken out of context considering the underlying connotations of much of Rory's contribution to the segment.

"But before I go, Evan, let me leave this with you." As he said this, he picked up the orange ball, or orb, that had been sitting amongst the herbal décor on the bench.

"Thank Christ that's over," snickered Spikey, "all that fucking queer needs is a tiara … like a real queen!"

With remarkable synchronicity, (how did he do that?), Rory popped the lid of the orb and there, perched in a nest of golden silk, was a tiara!

"Evan, this little gift is for you to pass on to a viewer of your choice! It's a personal gift from me to you and your simply divine audience!" he exclaimed to camera 1 accompanied with another of those huge cheesy grins. Jonesy was almost choking on his laughter and Spikey stood with his mouth agape, completely dumbfounded.

The fade out theme music started to fill Evan's ears and he realized that the segment was finally over. Mel confirmed this with her nod and gave Rory the wind up signal. The smirk was still glued to her lips.

The sound was killed and the lights began to dim on set as Rory and Evan were having a parting conversation and the hero shot of Gâteau St Honoré was spot lit, and the credits began to roll.

Mel, as floor manager, declared a wrap of the week's shooting complemented by the usual cheers and applause of the crew. Simone recorded the time of the segment; shit, 11 minutes and 48 seconds, the longest she'd ever seen and she was pretty sure Evan had felt each second with agony. Phil passed Mel, confirming all was good and disappeared in search of the Overham entourage.

The kitchen lights were dim now and the studio overhead lights came on with the Lucia lights.

Evan turned to farewell Rory. He was gone … ignorant prick! At that moment, his eye picked up the movement of Rory and the Overham minions as they proceeded royally past Simon's kitchen, where he was busily cleaning up before hitting the production meeting for next week. Evan watched in amazement as Rory flittered by and shook Simon's hand, slipping his business card stealthily into Simon's palm.

Zoe chased behind to thank the star, only to find she had become invisible and was ignored by them all. Thanks for fuckin' nothing she muttered to herself as she wandered away from the re-grouping studio. What about that goddam tea she'd spent hours sourcing and the fuckin' over-priced hand-towels? You have got to be kidding, she thought angrily. She still had to justify the outrageous expenses to the finance department … that'll be fun – NOT!

The Overham Queen and entourage were gone. Evan was shaking his head still in disbelief – gone with not so much as a goodbye. No thanks, just gone. His mind returned to the pinches and like the proverbial bolt of lightning from the blue, it struck him that Rory had not been hitting on him at all – just distracting him, putting Evan off his game, while he stole the segment. And how were they ever going to cut that one long segment into two to squeeze in the ad breaks?

The real object of Rory's lascivious attention was Simon. Go figure!

CHAPTER 3

A Barbie For Barbara - A Stalker's Delight

It was twelve days since Rory's astounding visit and the mayhem it created was just about under control.

To add insult to injury, some joker had uploaded footage from the director's overhead camera of the cheeky Rory playing with Evan's right leg, onto YouTube. An investigation was instigated to determine who the culprit of this mischievous little deed may be. After all, a congenial set was one thing, but smart ass pranksters forgetting their place in the TV scheme, was quite another!

Rory, that unabashed and lascivious queen of the kitchen, at least as far as the lucrative US market was concerned, had over two decades of TV experience. He knew his way around a studio quite well enough to time his 'little pinches' as a perfect distraction to Evan that enabled him to steal control of the long, fascinating St

Honoré Gâteau segment. A minor coup de grace for Rory's ever needy ego!

Unfortunately, Rory had been quite unaware of the overhead camera, monitored solely from the director's booth and controlled by an assistant. This camera operated continuously and was really useful for a close up shot as needed.

From this camera angle, it certainly appeared that Rory was playing with the leg of the very handsome star of the Game. The footage had now gone viral, much to the consternation of the Network's management hierarchy. Nige, who lived by that old adage of any publicity, is good publicity, decided to ameliorate the drama by letting it play itself out.

Seeing its own sales opportunity, the print media had weighed in with front page questions regarding Evan's sexuality. The gay community was overjoyed that these antics were beamed across national TV and all social media. The Network's public relations machine had gone into immediate damage control. Phillip Williamson, the Game's public relations man had practically lived with Executive Producer Phil Watts and the crew as they tried to figure the best spin to put on this potentially threatening situation, to no avail. Extraordinarily, all the excess publicity did nothing but lift the Game's ratings to an unprecedented high.

Phillip was heard to mutter, "Go Figure."

The 'love pinches' saga, as it had been christened in the media, was creating a win-win situation for the Game.

It came down to an ineffectual shrug of the shoulders and a decision to let the storm ride itself out, for Phillip. Of course, there were the obligatory press releases showing Evan and his stunning wife Lex – but no shots of their three children. Evan was extremely protective of his children and did not want them dragged through the publicity circus – damn that, whinged Phillip to himself!

Lex, in her inimitable fashion, dismissed the whole thing as a nonsense that had been blown up to ludicrous proportions. Several guys, who were definitely hetros and friends of Evan, laughed the whole incident off with statements like "stupidity personified" and "ridiculous show business stuff".

It appeared that the incident was causing no real harm to the network, so Nige was happy to stay right out of it. The Sales team were quite euphoric as they handled the increased enquiries to advertise on the Game and requests for product placements.

Phil, the over-active executive producer was ecstatic with the ratings and the increased revenue as the kudos settled in her general direction.

Not a single word was heard from Rory Overham since his return to the US. Having launched his latest Tiara sensation, instant St Honoré crème filling, he had long forgotten he'd ever visited the set of the Game. The creamy filling was falling off the shelves into shoppers' trolleys. All good, all round as far as Rory was concerned and, of course, he had not heard of the uproar his antics had caused.

Naturally, no one at the network thought of what the Pettersen children were enduring at school. Lex, sensibly and with the sensitivity of the caring mother that she was, had pulled the kids out of school – a few "sick days" was best, she felt. The taunts from the other kids at school had been extreme initially but, as Lex had predicted, the over-reaction to the viral YouTube and TV footage would soon be forgotten.

Somewhere, soon, another nonsensical drama would erupt and the press would be off following the next scoop leaving yesterday's drama to yesterday.

Such was life in the media.

Through all this kerfuffle, Simon saw a lot of Phillip, who was being very attentive. Philip was amazed to learn that Simon had dinner with the Overham crew before they departed for the US. The always elegantly attired, gay 48-year-old public relations man wondered if Simon might, perhaps, be gay. Maybe, it was wishful thinking.

Simon was straight … right? That minor problem did not stop Phillip from hankering after the attractive chef. He's a good looking young hunk, thought the smitten media savvy gent. Could it be? Well, he'd certainly had time to become better acquainted with Simon during the melee and found he liked him even more. How can I ask him on a date, Phillip quizzed himself one day as he left the studio. He'd just have to do a Scarlett and think about that one tomorrow – for now, there was another press release to go out to the turgid printed press.

What Phillip did not know was that Simon was indeed in a process of contemplating his personal life, or lack thereof, more specifically. Simon was a profound, self-contained guy who superficially appeared perfectly content in his own internal world. Given that Simon was an only child this behaviour could be expected.

Simon's parents had been small general store operators in the outer suburbs and he'd adjusted to being alone as a child. He'd always been a loner at school with very few close buddies or friends. He'd had several girlfriends without any sexual implications and his father would goad him about how good looking some of them were only to be told definitively "we're only friends."

His father would walk away disappointed, especially as his son grew to 177cm tall with not overly broad shoulders. He was fine in stature with delicate long fingers that were surprisingly not bony, given their length. His long hands were an extension of his non-muscular forearms.

His eyes were distinctive and intriguing as the irises were indistinguishable from the pupils. They were a dark circle of intensity in the clear sclera. His complexion was Mediterranean with light brown facial skin that could possibly be described as Lebanese or North African. His high cheek bones suspended under his fascinating eyes were accentuated by a reddish hue, almost as though they were lightly rouged.

His blue black hair was wavy, not curly. As a child he had grown it to shoulder length which had aggravated his father while bewitching his mother. She loved it and would run her open fingers through it whenever she could with tender caresses; his soft, thick hair was as close to girl's hair as she would ever know. Simon was the only child she would ever have and she doted on him – she was unable to carry any more children, at risk of dying. Both she, and her husband were well satisfied with their single offspring and he was adored.

Simon progressed through his school days without excellence. He was average in all areas of study except in social studies and home economics. He and two other male students existed as a solitary island of emerging masculinity in a sea of female cookery students.

This early foray into cooking allowed his exploration of a world that would eventually devour him and lead to a career he was sincerely passionate about. Simon had a destiny to cook as he had an ideal temperament and a natural passion for cooking and kitchens.

He did not finish secondary school but fell into a kitchen at fifteen and stayed to complete his initial studies in cooking. Simon was picked up by Evan Pettersen at nineteen and mentored by Evan in his flagship Mangereire, whilst he also undertook further gastronomic courses.

Simon was consumed by cooking and it became his life. He rarely thought of anything else and the friends he made were invariably from the same business. Consequently, the girls he dated were also cooks and while he had been attracted to the idea of dating, it always felt like a removed or remote experience. Nothing stirred for him sexually until he met Fleur.

Fleur was a patisserie chef which was an area Simon was inexperienced with – he aspired to be a patisserie chef of Fleur's calibre. At this point he was far too busy with his emerging career to even contemplate taking on another course and so he live vicariously through Fleur's adventures. Their dates consisted of creating a pastry or dessert as a prelude to sex and Fleur proved an avid teacher in both her areas of expertise.

For Simon, this was an all-consuming period of his life – the shared passion of cooking followed by bedding made for complete enjoyment and at twenty-one he thought he had found paradise. This promptly turned to hell immediately Fleur mentioned marriage and children. The very thought of having children was not adhering to Simon's future plans for cooking and kitchens. Fleur and he parted without acrimony.

Simon's dating and sex life went into the wilderness as he progressed up the career ladder with Evan and his expanding businesses. Evan became ever more reliant upon this talented and patient chef who was a born organizer and was totally unflappable.

Simon had delved into the world of Buddhism and found that the basic beliefs and precepts he encountered on these initial skirmishes were incredibly beneficial to him in this crazy, spasmodic world of cooking. In summation, at twenty-eight, Simon may have been considered somewhat naïve where life skills were concerned but highly advanced in his gastronomical experience and expertise.

Little did Phillip realise but his secret lust for Simon was to take an interesting turn; however, for the moment, both these men were embroiled in the repercussions of the Overham experiment.

Evan had been left totally bewildered at the furore and was still reeling at his loss of control of the segment. The fallout for recipe requests on the social media sites had obliterated the previous record. Zoe, the producer who handled the Overham segment, was overjoyed and felt like saying "I told you so!" She'd had a battle to get Overham on the show in the first place and then a further ordeal to placate the finance department over the substantial extra costs involved in fulfilling Rory's "requirements". However, there was a definite hesitancy where her colleagues were concerned when discussion was initiated regarding the next international Star. There would be no rushing to make the availability to appear on the Game an actuality!

So it was business as usual in the production office with shows to be planned and recipes to be decided. Segments to be scrutinized and meetings with sponsors and advertisers to be attended and product placement negotiations finalised – business as usual.

Additionally, the network had decided on a sure fire, if somewhat cynically motivated, publicity stunt raising funds for a young mother who had been left destitute after her husband and father of their 5 children had died tragically in a car wreck. Usually, this sob-story stuff was the grist of other programs in the network mill. However Nigel, as benevolent despot, had decided that given Evan's current high profile, it was timely and appropriate that he host a fundraising barbecue. The guest list would include family and friends of the grieving widow along with winners of various competitions to win an invitation to attend.

The winners would be rubbing shoulders with Stars of the network.

Nigel and sales whizz kid Phoebe Strong knew they had hit on a winner. Advertisers and sponsors would donate products and services to be used and auctioned off to barbecue attendees. It would be a public relations slam dunk.

The actual planning of the event was to be handed over to Phil Watts and her crew. "What … you want us to do this fucking thing for you? You have got to be fucking kidding! I'm not a fucking event co-ordinator; I'm a fucking executive producer! Get the fucking promotions people on it, they do fuck all else but socialise! We've got enough to do already … fuck you!" All of which was dismissed as another minor "Phil fart".

Consequently, the planning was taken on board and discussed at the production meeting that afternoon, where Phil was observed clasping her plait and chewing the tip – extreme anxiety personified.

Given no other option, Phil and the team got down to planning exactly how to make this fundraiser viable and exactly how to publicise the event. After several meetings, plans were under way and Evan was kept abreast of the situation by PT, his trusty PA and PR man, Phillip Williamson.

Evan had some experience in this arena having appeared as a guest star and performing cooking demonstrations on a couple of telethons and he lent a somewhat naïve sincerity to the event with his willingness to do his best for Barbara and her brood.

With prescience, the star realised that there was something missing. What was that something special that would give the supporters of the Barbie for Barbara bigger bang for their bucks? What would be the huge draw to get a humungous mob to this Barbie? He noted that all the usual attractions were in place. Barbecue points selling sausage and steak sandwiches with the profits going to the "cause" and a large number of sponsors' booths which would be manned and selling their products were all organised.

A number of entertainers were benevolently providing their appearances at no charge – naturally there was an implicit understanding that if they failed to do so they would no longer be offered the lucrative appearances they enjoyed at the Network.

Still, something was missing. What was it that the Barbie for Barbara was lacking?

Evan put in a call to Phillip Williamson. With no answer, he left a voicemail message asking Phillip to call ASAP. Evan had an idea.

As he hung up, PT approached him in their tiny office at the restaurant with a bunch of letters in her hand.

"Hey, what's up PT?" Evan asked as she placed the numerous handwritten documents in front of him.

Joanna started slowly on this mid-week morning, Thursday, known as hump day; over half way through the week.

"You may remember, I've shown you some of these letters from a Felicity Johnstone. We've christened her your stalker …" A smirk appeared on PT's face as she continued, "She wants you to meet her. In her last letter she states that you should be doing more for charities than you're doing now AND she wants you to know that you should pick up your act. She thinks you should enlist the aid of the Pope in helping out more because she knows you are CONNECTED … as she puts it."

Evan glanced through a couple of the letters and noted that the tone had changed from her original letters professing her love and wanting him to divorce his wife so they could be together. Her demands were becoming rather more emphatic – what a nutter! His memory was further jolted when PT laid the personal photo of his stalker, the one that had accompanied the marriage proposal, in front of him. She was quite a delicious looking redhead with huge knockers who appeared tallish and was probably in her late thirties. She was a very attractive woman certainly, but there was a sense of deviousness emanating from her eyes.

Evan had decided to ignore Felicity and relegate her "faux" adoration to the file labelled "part of being in the business". After all, he'd received any number of requests, with many and varied promises of what he could expect to happen to various parts of his body, if he was interested in sharing a bed. Wasting your time babe, he thought.

Evan was not to know that ignoring Felicity was the worst thing he could do. He had not recognised that she was an attention seeker – he should have, given her letters and her appearance. All that dyed red hair and those huge tits screamed out look at me! Look at me!

She was built to attract attention. Her particular type of look came with some work. Felicity had grown up with TV as her babysitter as both her parents worked and she was the ultimate latchkey kid. She did not mind, she and her two siblings were used to this way of life. Without a great deal of input from her parents as she grew, Felicity's attention identified with the glamorous stars she constantly watched on TV and the television's parental influence underpinned her emerging personality.

Living in the inner city, the normal precautions that children were given about staying indoors and not answering the door to strangers were enforced. Felicity was not especially attractive but tall for her age and wore inexpensive reading glasses. Her mousy brown hair hung lacklustre to her shoulders without a hint of a curl or kink. It was ordinary hair which seemed to match her personality and future. Her parents were poor and with a family of five, what was going to save her from mediocrity?

As she saw no redemption from her ordinary life, she became immersed in the lives of her TV family, especially her favourite stars in Days of our Lives. They seemed to have mostly ordinary lives, as hers was, but despite this dreariness these beautiful people were always well dressed and coiffured.

That was the way to go. The female Stars knew how to marry well and manipulate their men. It seemed so easy – all she had to do was change her appearance and attitude. She determined that to do this she needed to leave school and find herself a job. Her parents disagreed even though it would mean one less child to support through school and insisted Felicity complete her secondary education.

School was a pain in the ass for Felicity. She was a fair enough student excelling, if at anything, in mathematics and French. Perhaps a strange combination in which to achieve, but she did. In an act of utter rebellion she ditched school with some difficulty and moved into her first job as sales assistant in a boutique clothing store in the middle of the city. She was able to walk to work, which saved her some funds. With extremely strong motivation to achieve, she was frugal and her parents were lenient with her financial contribution to household expenses.

She was very much in the background at the store until the owners could groom her, which they had decided was worth persevering with the effort. Felicity toned her body, not by going to the gym as she would not waste money on that extravagance; she walked and did the exercises she found in an illustrated girlie mag. They worked, and with her no nonsense eating habits, an emerging beauty took her place in this exclusive boutique specialising in designer apparel.

When she had first appeared with her fiery red hair, her employers had been shocked, but realised their young employee was achieving a "look" and would prove a suitable hanger for their wares. The "look" met Anthony Johnstone as she approached her twentieth birthday. He worked in IT and was rolling in money – which was exactly what she could fall for. Felicity Mary Anderson became Mrs Johnstone in a simple family wedding, and so began the Days of our Drearies.

Fortunately, Anthony was a boob dude and was happy to pay the exorbitant sum the top plastic surgeon demanded for his work. Anthony was in love and would go to great lengths to maintain peace with the object of his affections.

Felicity refused to consider children, this body was too costly to put at risk. Her loving husband thought differently and practised procreating most prolifically and satisfyingly – hopefully one day, there'd be children.

Ten years disappeared and Mr Johnstone finally acknowledged the futility of this one-sided partnership and asked for a divorce. Felicity came out on top with the bulk of the disposable money and assets. Anthony felt wasted and used, devastated that eleven years of his life had been a sham, he moved to the other side of the country.

Felicity, now in her early thirties had long since moved on from the ritzy boutique that had given her a start. Loyalty was not her strong point. She was now a fashion buyer for a well-respected and over-priced department store chain. She rarely saw her aging parents and never her siblings; she had reinvented herself and the past was best forgotten. Her life was now everything she desired and equal to anything she'd envied on Days of our Lives or reading the social pages of the Sunday papers. She was a complete woman and casual sexual liaisons suited her far better than intimate relationships. She knew she was stunning and the red hair now had a name; she owned it exclusively. It was part of the package that Felicity Johnstone had become – a very successful package.

She rarely drank alcohol, so as to preserve that honed figure she prided herself on, but this Friday night she'd dropped her leash and consumed far too many Cosmos, her poison of choice. After a gratifying cab ride home (she did enjoy the power of you can look, but not touch!), she switched on her vicarious world; her obsession with her alternate reality had intensified as she had aged. On a late night talk show there appeared her Adonis, the man she had waited for her whole life. OMG who was he?

In her inebriated stupor she was glued to the screen waiting to hear his name. Evan Pettersen. WOW, what a honey – what a smile. She felt the wetness seep between her legs. She slept well that night, amid sweet dreams of the one who would be hers.

He was hers, what she deserved. She had to have him. Consequently, she began her research into the life of Evan Pettersen. She had not previously seen him on the box as work interfered with daytime viewing. Felicity began her campaign in earnest, with letters declaring her love sent to his network office and filling his Facebook page. There was one minor obstacle on her rocky road to true love that the TV insider mags repeatedly threw her way; apparently her man had a wife and family that he adored. "We'll see about that!" she told herself, "If I can't have you, Evan my love, there's no fucking way you can, Lex!"

Evan, naturally, was oblivious to what was around the Felicity corner and what she had in mind. If he'd had any inkling he would not be heading the Barbie for Barbara fundraiser that was about to enable Felicity to connect with her would-be lover.

It was around this time that the letters changed tone and PT became seriously concerned for her boss. Though not particularly intuitive PT sensed enough to recognise this woman was obsessional and could only prove a danger to Evan. The demands of the eccentric author of the letters had changed from coercing and coaxing to belligerent and bullying.

PT convinced Evan that it was time to take this particular stalker seriously and he picked up his mobile to ring the network's security office.

"Security – Ted speaking," said a jovial voice.

"Hi Ted. It's Evan Pettersen … how you doin'?"

"Fine sir. What can I do for you, Mr Pettersen?" was the brisk and businesslike reply.

"It's Evan, Ted … and I need your advice please. I've been getting letters from a Felicity Johnstone for a while now. I took them as a joke, a prank at first – but they've become more regular and a lot more insistent. I'm just not sure what to do. What do you think, Ted?"

Ted took control, saying, "Mr … eh I mean, Evan, can you send copies through and I'll appraise them. We deal with these nutters regularly and know how to gauge the seriousness of any threat."

"Not a problem … I'll fax them straight through. Hey Ted, thanks so much. Appreciate it, buddy," replied Evan with relief.

The landline rang as Evan was instructing PT to send the letters and photos through to Ted. It was Phillip Williamson returning Evan's earlier call, "Can you hold for a sec, Phillip?" Evan asked.

"PT, please fax copies of this stuff to Ted in security. I've got Phillip on the phone."

PT disappeared to expedite this request with her usual efficiency.

Evan returned to the call, "Phillip, I feel we need more for the Barbara Barbie thing. It's lacking a certain oomph. I wonder if we could get a car from Brendeen Motors – maybe a nice new C class Merc? One we could give away as a lucky door prize?" Evan frowned in concentration as he waited for an answer.

"Evan, can you leave it with me while I get some ideas from Sales? I'll see what Phoebe has to say. But, I do think you're right about the big day. It needs something and this could be it. Good thinking, sir. Gotta go."

"Just one more thing Phillip, before you go. I've been receiving some harassing and stalking mail from a Felicity Johnstone and I've spoken with security. She may be harmless or she may be a raving nutter. Just giving you a heads up and I'll let you know what they say. Okay? Oh, and thanks for returning my call, Phillip."

The morning was evaporating quickly but in a quick summation of the Barbie event, the celebrity chef felt all was starting to come together and with still two weeks before the big day, they were on top of things.

The restaurant was starting to fill for lunch and he looked through the bookings on his computer screen checking for VIPs or regulars. If there were none, he could devote his time to the recipes for the coming week's shoot and also for the looming cookbook that his publisher was harassing him about. Why did he commit to 200 recipes? The radio station was screaming for him to do new publicity shots for his upcoming debut.

The reservation list showed a couple of regulars and Daisy Fairbairn, mistress of the leading property developer in the city. She, and her guests, drank their fair share of DOM champagne and spent like there was no tomorrow. Yep, he'd be out there and make her extra welcome at 1.30 when her party arrived.

Taking a sheaf of recipes from the appropriate file, he began to peruse them while the steady verbal volume in the dining area became more fervent. Service was shifting into top gear. Evan signed off on the recipes for the Game and attacked a pile of appetisers for the cookbook. These were a little more work as Simon and the food stylist had supplied them for his approval. Naturally they were recipes that he had inspired but the hard part of creating and testing them came under Simon's job description. Where would I be without Simon, he wondered.

The tricky part with recipes was getting the balance right; balance between proteins, cooking methods, colours and appeal. So many considerations to take into account when putting a cookbook together. This was the largest compilation he had ever attempted and as his publisher assured him, size did matter.

Evan ploughed on until his alarm notified him it was "show time". He bolted out of the office, adjusting his super smile as he hit the tables. He smooched his way around the room much to the delight of new customers and regulars alike. The consuming nature of celebrity was one part of what made this restaurant hum. The vital part was that he knew what he was about and after the smooching was done, he'd be in the kitchen to work where needed for the evening's prep and service. It never stopped in this business and thank God for that as the other option was bankruptcy!

The big day for Barbara had arrived. The Merc from Brendeens had given the publicity team something to sink their teeth into. The Game was topped and tailed with advertising promoting the "Win a Merc" at Barbara's Barbie; the network had even allowed a few ad slots during prime time news.

The organisers were organised, the sponsors had been incredibly generous and it was full steam ahead for this event that would make thousands of dollars for Barbara and her needy offspring.

Ted had assured Evan that the "Felicity alert" was in place and that he need not worry about her, should she turn up.

Happy throngs milled around the sponsors' marquees and booths. The Merc was sitting on its light blue plinth – with a growing crowd of potential winners admiring their sexy new vehicle. It was so easy to enter, simply fill out the form with name, phone number and email address. More entries for the bulging databases of the Game and Brendeen Motors!

That's my power, thought Evan, I make this happen. He hastily corrected himself; no, that was the power of the Network. He reminded himself of rule one – never believe your own publicity. He silently acknowledged the sensational job Phil Watts and her crew had done in bringing the event together. Speaking of Phil, there she was with her plait in a bun, a sure sign that she was at ease, at least as at ease as the frantic executive producer could ever allow for herself.

Evan often pondered on the good fortune that had sent her his way, given that she was TV royalty, after all. She had proven her worth time and again over the past years in this crazy business and had worked with him in a genuinely friendly way, growing his presentation skills and boosting his personality to Star status.

The big day was in full swing.

On centre stage, the morning host, a brassy but adorable middle-aged woman, was holding court with her adoring fans. Approaching sixty, Isabelle Jenkins looked fabulous and her magnetic personality was given free rein as she recounted stories and introduced various guests. She thanked her last guest, the resident fashion expert, sashayed to centre stage and swung the mic from its stand. After a theatrical twirl, she nodded to the network's musical director and launched into her rendition of the raunchy Peggy Lee hit "Fever". The crowd sat mesmerised by her performance; very few in the audience were aware of Belle's singing ability. It was a well-kept secret that she had been a cabaret performer in London for many years.

It was nearing time for Evan to make his appearance, re-creating a couple of dishes from his upcoming recipe book. He entered the marquee that was serving as green room for the visiting celebs and network hierarchy and also as minute kitchen for his prep to be done. Simon had chosen simple but effective dishes. He had begged out of attending but had sent an able assistant for Evan, and all the ingredients for both dishes were good to go. Sound tech Max miked Evan and he donned his apron. He looked superb with his hair and make-up by Marj, "Please call me Marjorie." The vibrant aqua shirt was just perfect for him – and the day. He was ready to be brilliant – show time!

The ever effervescent MC introduced Evan with gushingly overworked superlatives. The fans went crazy as he walked to his kitchen bench with his usual sense of ownership. His smile took over and he winked at a few members of the applauding audience and paused deliberately, waiting for them to calm down.

"Are you ready to cook?" and the audience erupted once more with wild applause and wolf whistles.

He almost screamed, "Let the Game begin...are you game?" They screamed back in affirmation as Evan guided a stream of peanut oil into a preheated wok.

The emerging fish dish was a take on a Thai beef salad. As the fish strips sizzled away, he mixed the marinade that would saturate and seep into the fish strips as they cooked.

He was speed-of-sound quickness with his knife as he rendered the vegetables into the desired shapes. All the salad vegetables were placed into suitably arranged stainless steel bowls.

As he cut the cucumber, he took stock of the audience and smiled. Naturally, he winked at someone close to the stage. As he panned around the audience, she caught his eye.

Felicity Johnstone!

OMG, she looked perfectly delicious. Her patented red hair piled on top of her head, a bizarre bird's nest arrangement. Her huge knockers were lightly tanned and displayed with no hint of modesty.

Not missing a beat, Evan kept on with his wizardly knife action and his patter. The fine strips of cucumber were ready to be added to another salad bowl. He reminded the audience that these fine strips were called "julienne" as he sprinkled them into the bowl.

The fish strips were finished and sitting in the marinade. He flipped the strips with great agility – everyone in the audience wished they could imitate that movement. He milked the moment reminding the fans that it was better to flip them like this than to stir, as stirring would break the strips.

He proceeded to the salad dressing making special note of the finely minced ginger, achieved using his trusty microplane. The shaved lemon grass followed along with the many other essential Asian herbs and spices that made up this dressing. He especially liked the aromatic and tingly acid effect of lime juice.

Those few drops of Sesame oil made all the difference he emphasised as he gave the dressing a final whisk and poured it over the combined salad ingredients with an elevated swirl. He assembled the fish salad with great effect as it was projected on the huge screens around the grounds and each side of the stage.

While he tried with remarkable concentration to focus on the task at hand, his peripheral vision was drawn repeatedly to Felicity. Her micro-mini skirt exposed her lightly tanned and well-shaped legs. She sure works out, he could see. She changed legs in a wide sweeping movement, as she crossed one over the other. He could have sworn she wore no knickers. Did he have his own Sharon Stone in front of him? Was he about to live "Basic Instinct"? Had he seen right? Had he?

With great difficulty he returned to the business at hand. "It's time to bring this baby together. Are you game for these exciting flavours? Are you game for the chilli slices?" He paused for their loud approval before adding the chilli slices to the salad.

With a final splash of coriander and crushed roasted peanuts, Evan presented the completed salad to the applause of his adoring fans. "Bet you're game to try this one at home…are you game?" After further screams of agreement he moved on to his simple dessert.

"This is one for the kids, big and small …" he kidded. "All you need is this … vanilla ice cream and a few bits and pieces." More screams and nods as Evan began to whip cream with a sponsor's hand held electric whisk. He flashed that killer smile and winked at a child in the front row – everyone thought he was winking at them in the front row.

He didn't notice Felicity's departure until a few minutes later. Where was she? Why was she here in the first place when security had told him she was on top of the alert list? In an intriguing way, he missed her. Did he want to meet her?

The dessert came together quickly and was acclaimed by the mob. He finished to thunderous applause and more whistling. He was about to vacate the stage to make way for the next segment, hosted by the network's gardening expert.

However, just before leaving he introduced Barbara and her brood of five.

"Barbara, we know we can't bring back your husband, Geoff. But we sincerely hope that today's gathering will help the healing process. There are so many of us here from your Network 3 family and thousands of viewers have turned out with love. Our very best wishes to you and your family." Barbara welled up but held it together long enough to say a simple thank you. Sincere and sorrowful as she wrapped her arms around Evan.

A blaze of camera bulbs exploded. Eventually she left the stage with her children clinging to her sides. Evan thanked all involved in the amazing event and assured them that the money raised would be presented to the family as soon as it could be tallied.

He strode to the marquee, ready for a coffee and some water. As he approached the coffee point, Felicity appeared from nowhere.

"Hi gorgeous – why haven't you answered my mail, you naughty boy!" Her tone was sultry, teasing, tempting. Up close, the delectable stalker was even more alluring than her photographs suggested. She almost purred. But he was in deep shit, and he knew it. How the hell did she get in here?

"I thought we had replied …" he mumbled.

"No. No, I haven't seen anything from you but I would love to see a whole lot more of you." She grabbed his crotch with decided enthusiasm. "I knew it would be big and you'd have big balls too … I want you. You've gotta fuck me!" She continued to manipulate his cock and balls.

This was a nightmare! It reminded Evan of an extremely bad seduction scene from some "B grade" movie. How the hell am I going to get out of this, he wondered? She shivered and clawed at him to get closer. Was that possible?

He tried to maintain his calm as he said, "Hey, Felicity – I can't do this. You know I have a wife I adore. I know I told you that in a letter. I'm sorry but …"

Her smiling countenance turned to a rather ugly sneer as she continued, "I don't give a fuck about your loving fucking wife! I just want a bit of you. This big bit …" she intensified her grip on him, "you need to fuck me and you need to help me with my charities. That's not too much to ask for what I can give you, Evan. I love you so much."

The besieged star noted the crazed look in her eyes – there was no depth to them, just blackness. Ugliness. Desperation. He was suddenly very frightened.

What the hell was going down here? Help! Where was security? A quick glance around the marquee showed everyone else deeply enthralled in their own conversations. No one had noticed his dilemma. He wanted to scream for help but thought how ridiculous he would look. Was he a man or a wimp?

With her hand firmly attached to his merchandise, the fiery redhead went for the big, tonguey kiss. Evan ducked and squirmed which inflamed Felicity's desire and intent further. She was stroking his cock but not achieving her desired result. That infuriated her.

"What's the matter with you? I never have any problems with men. Don't tell me you're a fag … no way! Come on … get it up bubba!"

With his hands on her shoulders and determination written across his handsome face, he shoved the lecherous female away from him, saying through gritted teeth, "What the fuck do you think you're doing? What do you think I am … some sorta slut? Get your fucking hands off me!"

This certainly attracted some attention from the crew, who sprang into immediate action. Phillip raced for security and Bill rushed over with Spikey in tow.

Evan was flushed with anger as he continued, "Get out of here and get out of my life. How fucking dare you try this on me … GET OUT!" Evan was shaking with disbelief and humiliation. He felt dirty and betrayed. There was no calm left in him and his flushed face had drained to a pasty pallor.

Then just as she had appeared, Felicity disappeared. The apparition had vanished.

He collapsed into a chair and called for coffee.

Ted from security arrived, looking shamefaced and said hesitantly, "Mr Pettersen … I am so sorry. I don't know what to say. I am so sorry."

Evan looked at Ted and spoke firmly, "No more fucking excuses. Understood Ted? I never want to see that woman again."

And he didn't. Well, not for a few months anyway.

CHAPTER 4

The Chef, The Restaurant, The Radio And The Publisher – Balance?

Driving home after his harrowing experience with Felicity the feline stalker, Evan contemplated the serious underestimation on the part of security in relation to the whole fiasco and determined that he would be rather more wary in the future. Lex would be really pissed off and so, discretion being the better part of valour, he decided it best that he keep quiet about the incident and prayed the "A Team" would consider it wise to do the same, for his sake!

Evan picked up his cell phone and rang the event organiser for a result on how much had been raised. While there was no final figure, they did let him know that the Barbie for Barbara had been an enormous success and they estimated hundreds of thousands would be headed in Barbara's direction.

The Network publicity machine had milked the event for all it was worth and yet more would come their way when the cheque, naturally outsized and glittering, was presented to Barbara on the Game.

Evan allowed himself a smile as he drove – Felicity absented from his thoughts for now – and reflected on the sea of happy faces that had filled the day. He pictured the massive array of multi-striped marquees and tents of all shapes and sizes where the masses had foraged.

These copious food stands had served everything from tacos, burgers and roll-up bars to the usual ethnic offerings of Thai, Turkish, Cantonese, Spanish, French, Italian and assorted others. Evan's own stand had sold a specially designed chicken fillet sandwich that had proved to be a tremendous hit. Of course, he had previewed it and shown how to create it on the previous Friday's show – a charming char-grilled chicken fillet with a gentle hint of Ras al Hanout, an exotic North African spice. Evan had been most explicit in his demand that the amount of spice used be minimal so the older children could experience the sandwich and not be turned off by the aromatic spice mix. This delightful morsel was complimented with combined salad leaves, grilled mushrooms and his distinctive tomato based dressing; it was an adult dish that would also appeal to the more adventurous older children – educating young palates was a passion with Evan.

There had been a huge array of beverage options too – sodas, smoothies, juices for the kids and, naturally, Alpha wines for the adults. The ingenious major sponsor had created a PR winner, releasing a cheeky sparkle for the day and calling it Barbie's Bubbles, with an ongoing percentage of profit from sales being donated to THE CAUSE. Kitsch, of course it was, but it sold like sausages at German Oktoberfest!

Evan's ruminations shifted to the grand prize draw, the Merc, and the jubilant woman who had thrown her glass into the air and jumped into her hubby's arms. As she was accepting her superb prize, she'd confessed that she simply had no idea what she would do with the BMW sitting in her garage now that she owned a Merc. Evan had shaken his head contemplating the vagaries of the gods.

The photographers had loved the ebullient blond as she draped herself in a barely passable Marilyn Monroe pose over the bonnet of her prized new status symbol.

All in all, it had been a great Saturday and the best part was still ahead, no restaurant duties tonight, straight home to Lex. He was quietly hopeful that, as it was Saturday night, the kids would be organised and Lex and he could spend a precious evening alone together. Call me crazy, but I'm horny as hell, he thought as he noticed the hardening stretching his designer jeans. What that delicious woman does to me – I should be exhausted not randy!

His contemplation of his rampant randiness led him back momentarily to the Felicity incident. He attributed his partial hard-on to the power he felt in having taken control of the situation himself instead of relying on a minder, as would usually be the case. So much was done for him and in this instance with Felicity, he had taken control personally and he felt happy and rather empowered – truly manly! Tonight he wanted some quality time with his luscious Lexy – as he called her in their most intimate moments. After all, the day had been a huge success, thanks to the whole team.

He turned onto the cement drive leading to the suburban home which many thought a little understated for a Star of his status. But it was their home, their three square feet of the universe, purchased long before the Game and the millions that had come along. Sure, Lex and he could afford a more expansive and expensive home, but they loved their family home which was quite spacious enough for their happy little clan.

He parked his car and entered the kitchen through the garage. A Chopin nocturne wafted from the living room and led him to where Lex was curled on the sofa reading. She looked up to Evan with a smile that beamed welcome home.

"How went the big day? I heard on the news that thousands turned up … well done, you! Did you enjoy it?"

He returned her smile and told her it was a fantastic day. In the current atmosphere, he definitely would not tell Lex of the Felicity incident. Now, it was Lex and him – no one and nothing else mattered.

"Yep, quite magical babe … and so well organised. Phil and Phillip did an amazing job. I'll find out later in the week just how much we raised and then we'll reveal the total and make the presentation to Barbara on next Friday's show. Well, I think that's how it'll go, just gotta wait on word from the powers that be. Tell you this much, my lovely one, we were bowled over by the turnout. Brilliant!" He moved through to the kitchen to get a mineral water, calling back over his shoulder with a definite note of hope in his voice, "Where are the kids?"

He thought how adorable she looked curled there on the couch, his sexy Lexy – as he called her during their lovemaking. He remembered again, as he had during his premature arousal on his way home, that it had been a couple of weeks since they'd made love. She always referred to their sexual adventures as lovemaking – never fucking or screwing. Lex, or Alexandra, was a lady and that was for sure.

"Out until nine … want something to nibble on before dinner?"

"I know what I'd like to nibble on …" he said most suggestively, "… how 'bout champagne?" He grabbed a bottle of Taittinger NV already chilled in the refrigerator.

She was there and wrapping her arms around his waist from behind. He arched his back and leaned into her, dropping his head down to meet hers. She softly nibbled his right earlobe.

"So who wants to nibble on what?" she teased him as her right hand reefed up his shirt so she could get to his bare, flat stomach beneath. Her fingers brushed lightly against his tingling muscles.

The cork came out of the bottle with a delightful pop and he pulled away reluctantly to reach for glasses. Lex dragged along behind as he led the way to the waiting loungers and both sank down with a glass in hand. Evan filled them and they toasted each other. He slid across to be almost on top of her and filled her opening mouth with his tongue. She playfully pushed him away and took a sip of champagne, then slid back to him.

Lex gave way to a passionate kiss and snuggled into her husband of almost 20 years. He felt so good – relaxingly so. He was inhaling and she smelt so inviting; he loved that scent of her, that "all woman" scent. He could never get enough of her. How good it was that the kids were out. Their near full glasses were gently set down so they could take on their imminent lovemaking.

As their tongues tangoed back and forth, their clothing came away with ease – how did that happen? Soon he had her right breast in his left hand and his free hand moving up her thigh into her moistening triangle. She spread her legs with a satisfied sigh, not wishing to hinder his gentle approach and the pleasure to come. He had his mouth around her aroused, hardening right nipple. Her left nipple rubbed against his dark chest hair. She moaned ever so gently as she stroked his erect cock.

They could kiss like this all night – they loved kissing each other. What was not to love? For them, sex was a very real celebration of their love for each other and always would be. Their hands moved around the contours of their bodies and they collapsed gracefully onto the floor with Lex on top of a prostrate Evan. She felt his virulent erection massaging her lower stomach and gyrated onto it as she bit his lower neck. He shivered with pleasure as she slid down his body tonguing him as she moved ever nearer his rampant cock. She concentrated on his lower abdominal muscles with her silky, languorous tongue. He lifted his muscles to her and she met him with her tongue and mouth.

As she swallowed him, he opened his eyes to watch her in action. He was trying to stay still so she could suck him, but it was impossible to lie still with what was happening to his increasingly impatient cock. When he thought he could take no more, he pulled away from Lex and rolled her over. Her sweet salivary mouth found his and she forced her tongue deeply down into his mouth. She was sighing and pulling his head onto her mouth as they entwined and rolled around the carpeted floor.

As old fashioned as it was, Evan slipped into Lex in the full missionary position. She thrust her hips to meet him and he moved into her with tantalizing thrusts. Her moist opening gripped him greedily and she arched her back to meet him. He was all the way inside her before he started to slide slowly, teasingly in and out of her. Very soon, they found their rhythm and she folded her legs around him. She had no intention of letting him escape and he had no intention of going anywhere other than more deeply inside her.

He bit her earlobe and she scratched his back in response to his increasingly powerful thrusts. Perhaps, the scratches were a little too harsh as he threw his head back – would there be broken skin? Who cares – just let their passion run its course. Their bodies slapped loudly as their movements became more vigorous and their gasps more ardent. Reward was near.

"Come with me sexy Lexy. Come, I'm so close." Tell me something I don't know she would have said but she was too completely into his body speak to utter a word. Her groin met his with a vengeance and they both knew climax was seconds away.

"Come Evan … come! I'm almost there … come with me baby." She screamed at a pitch that made him grateful they lived in suburbia and not some high rise. It was all the encouragement he needed to give an almighty thrust and release his exploding juices into her. She gasped as she sent her climax on its way searching for air to refill her emptied lungs. They sank into each other with ever decreasing thrusts.

He pushed his hair back from his face and then softly brushed hers from her lightly perspiring forehead. There was no need to assure each other of how good it was – they had experienced this chemistry right from the first time they'd come together. Lex left for the bathroom and he watched, admiring the endearing bouncing of her buttocks. He realized that Lex was one of those women that would age like fine red wine as the saying went – lucky her … and me too. He stood with his still aroused cock and walked to retrieve the champagne bottle. He topped up their barely touched glasses with delicate sparkling wine.

He was sitting cross-legged on the floor supported by the lounger as she returned smiling with love and relaxation. She gazed at his now dormant dick and wondered how that flaccid flesh had been so rigid mere minutes ago. She took the offered glass and sat down beside Evan, snuggling into him.

They sat together in unashamed nakedness, each knowing how truly blessed they were in each other and their perfect life.

The gentle lightness of being was enhanced by another Chopin piece and their slightly raspy breathing.

Perfect!

Evan woke next morning to a day bathed in sunshine, made even more special by the fact that he had a cherished day off. The happy lovers had retired shortly after the kids arrived home just after 9pm. The ever hungry brood immediately raided the fridge for snacks which they took to their rooms and a quiet calm descended upon the house. Evan, still randy, had tried it on with Lex for a "return bout" as he called it when they hit the sheets. He was unsuccessful but consoled himself with the thought that he was often gratified in the morning. He sank into a deep sleep with no thought of Felicity disturbing his tranquillity.

The happy, sated chef rose early, as was his want, and checked the revenue report from the previous night's trading at the restaurant on his computer – a good night with excellent sales. All achieved with neither he nor Simon in attendance. He recognised once again the value of the training and enthusiasm he put into his business. He had a brilliant team.

He wanted to discuss their future direction with Lex. Sure, all was going well but it was a fatiguing way of living, not debilitating, but definitely tiring. Or, maybe it was just this morning after such a full-on day yesterday. He'd been thinking, recently, how he could change his successful life and businesses. He wanted a better balance between his business and home life; he longed to spend more time with Lex and the kids who were growing up fast. He wanted to see more of them before they fled the nest.

Charlotte was completing her second last year at high school and the twins were powering along. They were about to celebrate their 16th birthday and Evan felt he was missing out. Needless to say, Lex did a superb job as a virtual single parent and never complained. Nor did the children – it was just him and his perpetual pondering. Was he dissatisfied? Did he want to move on? To where and to what? It all seemed ideal now – why was he even contemplating change?

He loved his life as a chef and felt complete satisfaction in his work. He considered himself incredibly lucky to have chosen a career that he loved and indeed, that loved him back. He wanted nothing else than to be a celebrated chef with his thumpingly good restaurant, Mangereire, which had supported his family very well for many years now, even before the notoriety of stardom. That little voice he carried in his head kept reminding him – if it ain't broke, don't fix it! Right? Right.

With Mangereire, he had not hunted accolades – the only accolade that counted was regular and returning bums on seats. Happy punters. The modern Provincial style dishes on offer were well received. While these traditional dishes may have lacked a certain flair exhibited by some of the other renowned chefs around town, his menu gave him a very solid business. The trend of nitrogen freezing food items and creating something that looked like an apple and tasted like shrimp had never held any attraction for Evan. His philosophy was sourcing good, seasonal produce and creating food that allowed this produce to shine; and this philosophy had served him very well, thank you! The French, Italians and Spanish had been cooking this way for centuries and it worked for them. Evan especially loved the ideal of knowing the region of origin for produce and also for the structure and name of a cuisine. Every now and then, he allowed variations on the menu to let his younger chefs strut their stuff.

He ticked the restaurant off his worry list. The next item that was constantly nagging was the offer from a high rating radio station that wanted him to pilot a show for foodies. This show would incorporate wines from Alpha with the Game's wine presenter, John Smithton. Ugh! He loathed the wine segment on the Game but it was undeniably popular and certainly created excellent revenue for the network.

Radio? He was confident his voice would be fine, but how would he find the time? Would it be another case of creating the right team to make it happen? There would be production meetings here also, and could he really ask Simon to take on another project in his already hectic schedule? When did Simon get time off? What if he had a family? Evan contemplated how impossible his life would be to manage, if not for Simon.

Totally impossible!

Evan fussed back and forth with himself and finally decided he should ask Simon and Lex how they thought it could be done. The sponsors and advertisers that backed the Game were more than willing to consider this venture across the airwaves with their Star, who they considered to have the Midas touch.

Oh God, he thought to himself, that damn book for Marquis. Marquis Books' boss, Hermann Booth, was as far from couth as one might get; you could say he was downright pushy and crude. He had a unique style that could be best described as abrasive, but he produced books that sold, with a team he terrorised. He had attitude – and he was pushing Evan for his next book.

200 recipes! Why had he signed that damn contract! He knew that he, with a little help from Simon's team, could get the recipes together but it was not a simple process writing a cookbook. The recipes had mostly been chosen but the selection still had to be balanced. The test cooking had still to be undertaken followed by the re-writing and re-testing of unreliable recipes. Then the photography, which he could hand over to a food stylist and photographer – that Hermann insisted be used – and then the corrections to the book before print. He was wearing himself out just contemplating!

And then, after the book was printed, came the really hard part of the deal, the promotion to sell it in the overcrowded market of cookbooks by celebrity chefs. Was it profitable? Sure, but shit there was hard work in making that profit. Don't I make enough money already, he questioned himself? Is this pure unadulterated greed?

All this crap and he was supposedly trying to create balance in his life. Take a memo to self, you silly over-worked bastard, no more cookbooks! But, in his ever over-analytical fashion, he wondered if he might be looking the golden goose squarely in the eye, or simply having a day when he wanted to be a nobody and just enjoy his family, forgetting about tomorrow? Maybe that was it, and perhaps he should just accept his talent and enjoy the fame and riches that accompanied it.

Lunch was approaching and Lex was rattling around in the kitchen. Lex was more than a good cook and ruled supreme in the kitchen at home, which suited Evan perfectly as it was the last thing he ever wanted to think about.

He sauntered into the kitchen neatly dropping the dead champagne bottle into its correct receptacle as he passed and asked Lex what he could do for her.

"Lay the table and call the kids, please." The aroma of cheesy macaroni wrapped around the kitchen, so deliciously homely – just right for Sunday lunch. He thought of the big roast lunches his mother had insisted on every Sunday after church. Oh boy, what a ritual that was, but he guessed he'd loved it at the time.

With the salad and warmed bread rolls on the table, the kids meandered in, their steps quickening as they collided with the familiar aroma of cheesy mac – a particular fave.

Evan asked what they'd got up to yesterday. They had not been to the Barbie for Barbara because of the possibility of intrusive behaviour by the media. Evan and Lex had made a serious decision at the outset of his media rise that the children were not to be exposed to publicity crazy press photographers. Needless to say, the Network publicity team were less than ecstatic with this decision.

Charlotte spoke up first saying she had spent the time with her besties, not far from home.

Sarah interrupted her elder sister teasingly, "No, you weren't! You were with Alex. Go on; tell us all about your new boyfriend. Go on, Lottie."

"You know that's not true, you stirring little toad!" Charlotte combatted.

"Enough name calling, thank you. Is that true Charlotte? Were you with Alex?" Evan's interest was piqued, as Sarah knew it would be.

"No Dad, I was not. Promise! I can't believe she's doing this. Why, Sarah?" Charlotte looked daggers at her younger sibling.

A smirk appeared on Sarah's face and soon they all knew she was doing her usual stirring. It was a touchy subject given that Charlotte's parents wanted her to study at this important stage of her schooling and give "the boys" a miss. Dismissing young men from your horizon was easier said than done as an enquiring seventeen year old virgin!

When you looked like Charlotte it was impossible not to attract the attention of the opposite sex, regardless of age. Lex had attempted the sex and contraception conversation, much to Charlotte's condescension and rolling of eyes accompanied with, "Mum, we did all that at school about 5 years ago!"

Charlotte was around 170cm and she was truly striking. Her auburn hair highlighted her clear smooth skin. She would be a real beauty in years to come with a pale complexion against that hair and dark, perfectly curved brows and full sensual lips. She seemed even more so because she was totally unaware of her natural beauty.

For now, her parents' single desire was that Charlotte study and achieve good results.

"Sarah, now that you've had your fun, what did you get up to yesterday?" asked Lex as she spooned more pasta onto Seb's plate.

"Not a lot – me and Jessie went to Fiona's place and hung out."

"Would that be Jessie and I?" corrected Evan. She nodded and smiled back at her Dad in agreement, knowing she was his special little girl and quite indulged.

"You're quiet, Seb? What'd you get up to? Kick the footie?" Evan asked as he tried to penetrate Seb's reserve. Sebastian was going through that awkward teenage boy phase where Dads were "uncool" and really not to be talked to except in event of an emergency, usually involving a shortage of funds!

Evan had been somewhat wounded by his son's silent retreat; he was used to being adulated by his adoring fans, and it disturbed him to think that his own son did not seem to connect with him the way he had in earlier times. When he had brought it up with Lex, his fount of all wisdom, she had assured him that it was a stage he was going through and would emerge unscathed from in a couple of years.

Seb had his mother's complexion with a great mop of uncontrollable blond hair and vibrant aqua eyes that danced against his lightly tanned skin. At almost 16, he was 168cm tall and growing into his body. His shoulders were beefy and broadening, like his father's. While he liked football, he aspired to be a swimming champion, as his Dad had been.

Evan and Lex were blissfully unaware of the real issue behind Seb's retreat but the rollercoaster ride of discovery was an approaching storm on their horizon. Seb's grades at school had recently been slipping and he was having problems studying.

"Didn't do much. Hung out with Gav and watched a coupla movies," Seb offered with slouched shoulders and staring into his food.

"How was your big day, Dad?" asked Sarah with a mouthful of salad.

"Don't talk with your mouth full, Sarah. You know better than that!" Evan scolded; then proceeded with a

116

blow by blow account of his successful event, omitting, of course, the Felicity details.

As they were finishing up and asking the all-important question – what's for dessert – Charlotte said that all her school friends thought they only ever ate "fancy" food.

"Depends what they mean by fancy ... I'd say this meal your Mum has cooked is fancy to me 'cos I didn't have to cook it!" They all laughed as he continued, "Your Mum makes special meals for us that are nutritious and taste fantastic, if you ask me." A chorus of nods followed.

Dessert was Lex's specialty – Apple Pie made from scratch. Evan adored it as much as the children did. Lex would not part with her recipe for the pastry as it was her mother's, who had passed it on when she married Evan. In a world of haute cuisine, Lex had her own little treasure and she would guard it closely till she handed it on to her own girls!

Warm and ready to go, Lex served up the crunchy, green apple filled pie with pouring cream and silence reigned supreme at the family table except for the clatter of stainless steel on crockery.

Once they had gorged their way to contentment, the kids thanked Lex and began to clear the dishes.

"Just before you go, I'm about to have a chat with your Mum about our near future. Do any of you have any problems or worries you'd like to bring up? Anything you'd like to put on the table, so to speak?" Evan scanned them for any takers and hopeful of a twittering response to his little Dad joke. It appeared there were no takers, on either count!

Lex wondered where this had come from as he had not mentioned anything about this, apparently imperative, conversation last night during their usual post-coital chat. The kids dispersed as Lex and Evan headed to the lounge with their coffee. Lex wondered aloud what it was he wanted to discuss.

"It's just that times like today I know how lucky I am to have you all. I know I don't spend enough time with you and the kids, babe. I worry I'm not giving them enough of me. Look at Barbara with no hubby anymore and those five kids to bring up on her own. Look at us … we have it all and I can't help feeling guilty that I spend so much time away from you and the kids. Just guilt, I guess."

Lex listened intently conceding to herself that she and the children actually coped very well and besides, what was the alternative? After considering, she questioned, "Are you bored with what you're doing? Are you over it? After all, it's been a hectic six years, but I haven't noticed any waning of your enthusiasm. Your magnetism is still there. Is there something else on your mind, hon … fess up?" and she stroked his arm comfortingly.

"You know Lex; I really don't know what to do about this radio program. Like I don't have enough to do, but I feel I'm being pushed to do it … and this damned book – 200 recipes. Why the hell did I say yes to that deal? This morning, I checked the restaurant figures from last night.

They're fantastic. We could live happily on the restaurant alone. I guess I'm a bit tired of being pulled from pillar to post. I hate it! And like I said, I just loved being here for what went down today … being a simple family."

His eyes saddened as he looked at Lex and she pulled him into an embrace. Yep, it was time for her big mama hug. She said softly, "Perhaps it's time to take on that manager you've been thinking about so we can broker better deals and hopefully ease your workload. What about cutting back on the personal appearances?" Unfortunately, as Evan thought on this, he realised that it was the personal appearances that had already suffered. Evan wished they had not virtually disappeared due to his over-active schedule, as the cooking demonstrations were precious to him. Something had to give and he simply didn't have the time to put energy in that direction any longer, he had surmised.

They had discussed the idea of a manager many times but Evan continued to equivocate. "We'd pay a small fortune in commission to a manager and any increased appearance fees they demand for me, would end up straight in their pocket!"

It always came back to this and Lex would argue that they had any number of other specialists in their life, why not a manager. After all, there was the accountant, the financial planner, the lawyer, the executive producer, the assistant personal chef, the restaurant manager, the restaurant chef not to mention PT the PA. Why not employ a manager to ease the load?

The conversation inevitably stalled at this point. Evan said he was going to his gym – he'd installed it in the basement after it become impossible to attend his regular gym because of his adoring public. Between his gym and the heated, covered pool out back, he was able to maintain a fairly consistent fitness regime. Seb utilised the pool too.

He departed and that was, once again, the end of that conversation. She'd successfully cajoled her biggest kid and he was away – again.

CHAPTER 5

Uncool in the Coolroom

As he drove to the studio on the Tuesday following the Barbie for Barbara event, Evan mulled over his conversation with Lex after their intimate family lunch. It had got so far and as usual, he'd lost his way in trying to voice his nebulous ponderings regarding their future; one day they would have to come to some actual decision making and he wondered when that would be.

Sure, he realised he was sitting pretty right now and he still had a few months on his current contract which was up for re-negotiation prior to Christmas. At that time, he and Phil Watts would battle it out with network management over a new agreement. There was no reason why they wouldn't want to negotiate a solid contract as the Games' ratings were outstanding and the show generated real profit.

Nigel, the big boss and passionate lover of PROFIT, would be head haggler when this meeting eventuated. Currently, Nige was over the moon with the show's results in the only race that mattered, the ratings and profit stakes, won or lost weekly.

With that confrontation being months away, his ruminations returned to his son Sebastian and his withdrawal. Evan reminded himself to call his older brother Greg, who'd travelled this same road with his own son. Greg's son had come through these difficult years and was now powering ahead at twenty-two and surely it would be the same for his beloved Seb. Evan could not clearly define the inner prompting that left him concerned even as he tried to rationalise Seb's behaviour.

Greg did not live a great distance from his younger brother, but it seemed that they were so busy they rarely made an opportunity to catch up. Greg's IT business was booming and he was totally blown away by his success. His wife Katie was particularly fond of gloating over this success and the material trappings she enjoyed on the rare occasions when the families did get together. In fact, Katie's constant prattle about their architectural digest home and the matching BMWs they were now able to update annually, was a singularly important factor behind the intermittent contact between the families over recent years.

Evan dismissed further thought of the avaricious brother and his wife as he approached the studio and focused on feeling pampered, comforted and happy to see the crew. He parked his car and went in search of company, anyone other than Phil of course; being Tuesday, it was the day she had her fully blown "Phil's

Fart" attack. Evan needed not to see or hear this performance.

He slipped through the studio pausing as he saw his trusty right-hand man, Simon. A cheery, "All good Simon?" received a thumbs up from the handsome twenty-eight year old chef. Memo to self, thought Evan, get PT to find a gift for Simon's special day, he'll be twenty-nine in two weeks. He strolled down the hall to his shared green room and found PT there. As usual, Joanna was sorting through the studio mail and memos. He marvelled at her ability to keep those communication balls in the air and know where they landed and into which filing system.

PT nodded a good morning to her boss accompanied by her usual benevolent smile and headed to the coffee pot to get his first of many cups for the day. PT wished her boss, who she loved, would drink more plain water. He didn't.

"Can you get Simon a present from all of us? It's his birthday in a couple of weeks. You'll know just what to get." Evan thanked her as she delivered his coffee. She confirmed it was Simon's birthday in two weeks' time as she handed him a veritable mountain of fan mail. It constantly surprised him that he should receive this huge amount of fan mail, but he was grateful. A fellow network star had intimated, "It's when it slows that you need to start worrying, darling!"

PT agreed to source the perfect gift adding, "Will I get one from the crew and a separate one from you and the family?"

Evan nodded absently, deeply engrossed in the effusive missives from his adoring public.

Presently his attention turned to today's schedule and running sheet. Oh shit, that salty caramel mousse was up in the first shoot. He had a love/hate relationship happening with this emerging flavour combination. It was a dessert he'd talked through with Simon and had tried out as a special at the restaurant for a couple of weeks to gauge its popularity. It was Evan's habit to do this with dishes he was dubious of when they were to make a debut on the Game. This one had been a raging success.

It was an easy enough dessert but he needed to have some patter of the trend this dessert was establishing and in making it, he needed to emphasise that the balance between salt and caramel was imperative, or the result would be a disaster.

Apple season now and the roasted ginger apples to go with the barbecued pork cutlets was the feature dish for Wednesday's show. He loved this apple and pork combination, although he was pretty damn sure his mother would not have approved of his addition of the tangy, beguiling ginger flavour to the apples in her cherished recipe!

Evan was in two minds about young Will Hambers who was up today as second segment. He was known around the traps as the Prick on Pins, nicknamed for the legendary proportion of his appendage. He was a sensational chef who really knew his stuff and although Evan liked having him on the show he was a little wary of his popularity and ambition. Evan was fully aware that Will had made guest appearances on a couple of other cooking shows and been more than well received.

Will's personal appearances were growing in demand exponentially in relation to the legend of his dolphin like promiscuity in the sea of media opportunity. Besides being able to purchase the usual accoutrements at his shows, it was now possible to buy female undies to throw at his feet during his live cooking performances and they were inevitably the first item to sell out.

Evan needed to discuss this guest appearance with Phil to get a handle on just how far he should let the Prick on Pins go.

Looking at the schedule he guessed they would get through all this today; there were a number of pre-recorded "drop-in stories" and the big presentation to Barbara would be filmed tomorrow as the last segment for Friday's program. There was also an important segment with a British cooking sensation to be shot tomorrow after all else was completed. It was the only time the busy environmental cookery Star was available and Phil thought it was important she became a Games coup before some other show grabbed her.

Evan's only other concern with the schedule was the fact that there were three wine segments this week and he meant to have this out with Phil also. He loathed the wine segments with that supercilious twat, John Smithton. Evan had been unsuccessful in his attempt to have him sacked because he was the face for Alpha and the generated revenue carried much greater weight than Evan's whims. Frustrating, very frustrating.

Phil arrived at the green room and with three light knocks on the Star's door; she was standing in front of him. In six amazingly successful years she had never once waited to be acknowledged and given leave to enter.

"Congrats, babe, on the big Barbie day. How much did we raise?" she burst out, not bothering with any preliminary greeting. PT passed her the green tea she loved as she sat down.

"Not too sure yet. They're still working out final costs, but we should know this afternoon. And Phil, you did a sensational job – thanks!" He rose to top up his coffee.

"So, three wine spots this week – thought we had a food show here … so, what gives?" he said as his eyes narrowed and he grimaced his disapproval.

Phil's sigh was audible as she squirmed in the seat – why can't he give it a fucking break? Smithton's segments were going to exist as long as they created the revenue. Why can't he fucking accept it and just get the fuck on with it!

She replied with exaggerated patience, "Look, I know you don't like the wine segments but they rate and make the dollars, buddy … and to be honest, I'm a bit over this attitude of yours. Why don't you take it up with Nige, if you insist on banging your head against a brick wall?"

Evan backed down fearing he may become the brunt of one of Phil's moments, and being pretty certain he didn't want to experience it.

"Okay, okay … but you know I hate these segments," he whinged as he sat and took a gulp of his coffee before continuing in the same whining vein, "and Will Hambers's the second segment … what a way to start the week."

"Listen Evan, any time you want to take over programming, you're welcome. Let me just say, I am tired after a big weekend working and no break. I suggest you may be a bit tired too, so let's get on with it and get moving. You'll be fine with the Prick on Pins."

It had been Phil who'd created this sobriquet for Will, and she considered it one of her finest. "Pins" was a theatrical descriptor for legs and prick she thought more than apt, from what she'd heard. She knew he had a gigantic fan base and his social media following was also creating an international audience and so, they paid him to appear on the show whenever he had a spot available in his overcrowded calendar. She'd heard he could just as easily have chosen a career in porn as his sexual prowess was as celebrated as his culinary ability.

Phil rose to leave but paused as she was about to open the door saying to Evan and PT, "Is there anything else, boss? All cool?"

Evan waved her off agreeing all was good and watched her exit as he always did. Why could he never pinpoint what it was in that exit that he found reminiscent of his much loved mum? The vision was gone as quickly as it came.

While Evan faced off to Marjorie in make-up, Will Hambers had made his arrival. Everyone knew he had arrived, especially Mel the floor manager. She wanted to "meet" up with him badly and had spent many a pleasant daydream giving him one of her best, as she affectionately called her head jobs – she'd had plenty of practice and prided herself on her gift in this specialised arena. The goss had aroused her interest in Will and his legendary enormous cock and Mel prided her notorious reputation for oral gymnastics. Her prowess was an open secret in TV land.

She had shaken his hand by way of welcome, without bothering to look at his face. It seemed that his "package" preceded him, with its own persona and it was well dispersed and displayed in his tight tan trousers. In fact, his bundle was the first thing noticed as he approached with his exceedingly confident stride. He was imposing enough without the sexual advantage, at 184cm tall with masses of strikingly black hair, highlighted by his jade green eyes. At 34, he'd been married twice previously and was currently enjoying number three, his current wife of four weeks. Some claimed him to be a serial matrimonialist but he saw himself as being an honest man.

This process of self-justification was both interesting from a psychological perspective and questionable, as he screwed anything that moved. Females that is, only women. Men were safe from the Prick on Pins, much to the chagrin of many a happy fellow.

With the swagger he had mastered to accentuate his bulging crotch, Will approached Simon, who high fived the notorious guest. Simon could not help but notice how striking he was with his broad shoulders and chest to match. He also noticed Will's protruding nipples, rock hard and pronounced as they stretched through the sky blue cotton T-shirt that clung to his body like plastic cling wrap and that washboard stomach surrounded by its designer leather belt in his firm-fitting trousers. And then, as was usually the case, Simon's eye was drawn to the package.

It was Will's inclination to only inhabit light textured and light coloured trousers – no dark colours that might disguise the fact that there was nothing to crow about. If you've got it, you flaunt it – right?

Protocol had been adhered to in that Simone, official Games' meeter and greeter had picked Will up from reception but she barely made it to the studio before Mel took over with a lingering handshake. "It's good to see all of you again, Will," she smirked cheekily – Mel's idea of foreplay.

"Yeah … hiya Mel, good to see you again … you're lookin' hot, girl!"

Mel returned to the task at hand and noted that the basic prep was in place on set for Evan's first dish, the Salty Caramel Mousse. Those ingredients that needed chilling sat in the under bench refrigerator. It was a very trendy flavour combination and Mel was looking forward to tasting it. She noted that the hero mousse was beautifully decorated and sitting pretty in place for the final shot. Decorated with crushed, caramelised salted peanuts over whipped cream, it was positively pretty and with the right lighting would be picture perfect.

It was bound for an inundation of recipe requests – all extra cents in the network coffers and multiplied out the revenue from recipe requests was nothing to be sneezed at!

Simon had used extra gelatine in the hero mousse and whipped cream to "hold" them up. It was one less last minute thing to attend to in a hectic schedule and even the intense studio lights would not affect the hero mousse which was filmed now, as the finished shot; this would save time later on. The finished "shot" would be "dropped" in during editing of the finished show.

It was almost 9am and the quiet hum that a pre-shooting studio carries was being disrupted once more by shouting. The raised voice from the direction of the prep kitchen caught Mel's attention and she went to investigate. As she'd guessed, it was Will, dressed and ready to appear, with arms waving as he made a commotion. This was not particularly unusual behaviour for a chef as temperament and adrenalin combined in nervousness.

Mel knew she had a handle on this situation.

"So, what's the problem, Chef Hambers?" as she glanced over his prep for his Thai Prawn Salad, "what's up?"

Less aggressively now, Will presented the Thai basil and lemongrass which had offended his sensitivities by simply not being up to scratch. He wanted them replaced immediately and Simon was busy so there was no available help and what the fuck was he supposed to do?

Mel screamed over her shoulder, "Take over Mick. Come with me, Chef." She moved him away from the prep area as she flung a quick glance over her shoulder to make sure her backup, Mick, had followed orders. Simon breathed a deep yoga sigh of relief and mumbled some sort of mantra as he buried himself in the grilled courgettes for the Italian Vegie Salad that would be Wednesday's vegetarian specialty.

The diminutive floor manager escorted the irritated horn-dog chef to the cool room located just outside the main studio, as it was too large and noisome to be placed inside.

Will managed to brush sensually against Mel and she did anything but resist. They both knew what was to follow and were both silently congratulating themselves on this outstanding manoeuvre!

As Mel opened the cool room door the easily aroused chef lifted his apron and opened his trousers to reveal his grand prize. Mel involuntarily gasped as she gazed at the monster, what a challenge! She grasped his blooming cock with her hand as she shut the door.

Incongruously and rather ridiculously he looked her in the eye and asked what she was going to do with "it"; men are so fucking stupid she thought as she slid to her knees to show exactly what she was going to do with "it". He groaned as she enveloped his throbbing cock. She loved the power and control she felt sucking cock, she owned it and could make or break the little fella, and she was in seventh heaven with Will's Willie.

Naturally, he'd given himself over to instant sexual gratification and was panting all the right noises of encouragement, "Oh, yeah babe, suck on that monster!" Some discreet gagging was Mel's response as he pulled her head onto his now engorged dick with a rasping, "Come on babe, swallow me." More gagging was evident from the demonstrative floor manager as she swallowed a giggle thinking how fucking funny it was that guys all thought they possessed the biggest and best. Well, she guessed in Will's case it was a fair enough argument. And they all thought she was just waiting for them, well, they were not wrong; but she had them figured out and it was so totally, Mel in control.

Meanwhile, back in the studio, Max had his headphones on as did Bill, the director, who waved Phil over to her station and gesticulated wildly to get hers on too.

"Get every bit of this nonsense – record every little bit of it," she screamed down the cable to Max. "Bill, kill all other audio! This is private business and it's going to be great for business." She sat back chuckling softly as she listened gloatingly.

Professional men like Will Hambers really should know better; always remove the transmitter from yourself when you leave the studio floor. Obviously his dick had taken over and that quintessential professionalism had been abandoned. Yep, Will had left his mic on with the transmitter open and Max, Phil and Bill were privy to one of Mel's illustrious performances on the special guest star.

The pair had been absent some five minutes now but Evan was completely oblivious to the excitement in the cool room as Mick was now calling the camera operators into place and giving the five minute call. Evan had not missed Mel.

With the three headphones tuned to the cool room, the action end to this chilly adventure was approaching, according to the warning sounds emanating from Will who was full of gusto as he called further encouragement to Mel the closer he approached ejaculation.

"Come on babe, Oh yeah … I nearly near … suck my fucking cock, babe … that's it. Oh God, that's ittt!"

This was followed by a gasp loud enough to cause Max, Phil and Bill to remove headphones for a few seconds before returning to the residual heavy breathing. Reality and duty obviously poked its head through the lust filled fog as both Will and Mel started to insist they hurry back. Where the fuck was the Thai basil and lemongrass?

As Will adjusted himself he made a startling discovery. Holy shit! Fuck it all! His mic was on and he'd been sprung big time. Maybe, just maybe, no one had been listening in the studio? Oh crap, this was not good!

Probably not a good idea to let Mel in on his little oversight, he determined.

As they entered the studio, two sets of eyes pierced his own, letting him know that he was well and truly sprung. His smug mien vanished promptly, replaced by a crimson flush that no amount of studio make-up was ever going to hide. He was in very deep shit and he knew it.

Still thoroughly disconcerted, he took the herbs to Simon as quietly as possible as the run through for the first segment was underway in the kitchen. Once again, it was brilliantly sunny in the kitchen and Evan was warming up on the autocue and checking his prep.

All was good to go and Mel had resumed her duties as if nothing had happened. She had been absent for only eight minutes and she'd had some fun. She was also blissfully unaware of the impending shit that was about to go down!

The intro music saturated the studio and Mel called loudly, "Quiet on Set, recording in 30 seconds." The clapper board was noted on camera with segment and sequence, then she continued, "…and in 5, 4, 3" She pointed to Evan to take the show and his beaming countenance marked that the show was now underway.

"Hey, Good Morning and so good to see you again," and with another beaming smile into camera 2, he ran through the content of the day's program. "Here on the Game today … are you game to have a go at Chef Will Hambers's Thai Prawn Salad … I just bet you are! You're a game bunch and he is fabulous with Asian dishes, as you know." Bill called a change to camera 2 with his usual precision and professionalism and The Star of The Game continued without missing a beat. "We love having him here with us and we know you do too!" followed by a quick wink and another dazzler smile as he started to look at his impending dessert.

"How was your time at Barbara's Barbie?" he asked of camera 1 as he took his first bowl. "I had the best time and I was thrilled to meet so many of you. I just want to thank you all. You know, we raised so many dollars and it's thanks to you guys ... you gave so generously ... so truly, a great big thank you to you and we'll have Barbara and the kids here on Friday's show and find out just how much we raised."

A rather sombre Will Hambers took to the set but brightened to performance level immediately. Of course, he was a pro – but he knew his dick had brought him trouble again. How much trouble he would find out later when Phil confronted him. He had broken a cardinal rule and he knew it and wondered what the implications would be. Maybe, they would just laugh it off. However, he felt that Phil, the executive producer, was not that type of operator.

His segment was finished and it was a winner. He was so charming and handsome and sexy, really sexy. Twitter would be ablaze and Phil knew Facebook would be similar. Thank God PT looked after all that shit.

Will thanked Evan and the crew and withdrew with some of the prawn salad to his allotted dressing room.

After having his make-up removed, he was relaxed and tucking into the salad when three taps on the door meant Phil Watts had now entered his space.

She didn't bother with perfunctory greetings – just handed him a CD as she sniped,

"Quite a performance, Will. In the cool room, that is. Oh, and the salad segment was sensational too, but it's what's on the disk that I think you'll find most interesting. I certainly do. Would you like to hear it Will, or can you guess?"

She was relentless as he'd guessed she would be. What would she demand?

"Ah … no need to play it, I can make a guess. I know I left my mic open and I'm thinking that would be a cool room recording. Right?"

"Correct."

He glared at her, "What do you want? I mean, it was a simple little head job. Nothing more, nothing less – and a good one at that! Mel has a talent."

"Shut the fuck up, you idiot! Do you have any idea what I can do with this? I can leak it to every social media outlet …" she menaced, "… kiss your marriage goodbye, you fucking dickhead. What will your latest wife think after all those public promises you made. All that stuff in the papers about finally finding true love. What the hell must your previous wives think? What do you think the current Mrs Hambers will do besides finding a pair of giant shears to cut your fucking promiscuous penis off?"

Phil's face had turned a quite livid puce colour and her plait had been thrown over her shoulder to fall down her back.

Will immediately realised that she had him over the proverbial barrel as he remembered his current financial situation with two lots of alimony in play already – another one would be fiscally disastrous to him, to say nothing of his credibility.

He looked at Phil as he pondered his options. He had none. He was racing down shit creek towards the rapids and without a paddle in sight.

"What do you suggest?" Will smiled sardonically at Phil.

She gave him her best glacial glare as she spoke, "Here's the deal, Will. Eight more appearances on the current Game season and no fees charged. You will do an endorsement to advertise the Game. We can play it when and as often as we want across the network. Take it or leave it. It's your fucking career."

"Anywhere else, that would be called blackmail!" he looked at her aghast but she steadfastly returned her cool gaze. "What can I do?" he caved in with shoulders slumped and head drooping as he sank slowly into a chair.

Without pity or remorse Phil continued, "Here's how it will work. You tell your management that you've agreed to come on the Game, for no fee, for eight more appearances this current season. Nothing in writing – our own little private agreement, Will. I have the original audio tapes and I'll keep them until we finish this season. Deal?"

"Deal," he said softly and stood, ready to leave.

With a voice now dripping in sarcasm, Phil parted with, "Nice doin' business, Will – nice. See you real soon, you hopeless fucker."

In all sincerity she was thoroughly disgusted with him. She tried to understand her reasons as she stormed back to the studio. She was bemused by her outrage as she had seen so much crazy stuff happen in her career – this was just one more incident amidst thousands. Still deep in contemplation, she emerged back into the studio where Evan was in full flight. Here the 'make believe' was happening – the world of a better place, where pretence was all that mattered. Illusion was the winner and all that mattered.

What the fuck have I done, Will asked himself after the door had slammed and he began to pack his gear. What the fuck have I done this time? He was furiously trying to think of a way out of the deal he had just agreed to with Phil Watts – it eluded him.

Worst of all, he still had to face his management who were supposed to ratify all his arrangements and did not take at all kindly to having their commission depleted by their talent doing exactly what he had. He would have a hell of a time explaining this one away and more than likely, he'd cop a fine. Once more, he lectured himself regarding allowing his pride and joy to land him in trouble. Unfortunately, he kept forgetting that when his cock was engaged, his brain was not.

He picked up his stuff and headed for the door. Fucking amazing blow job, though. He smiled as he left the dressing room where his future had been decided for him. He'd be seeing a lot more of this room.

Back in the studio, life continued. Evan was preparing for his next segment still oblivious of the cool room incident and its repercussions. He noticed Phil and Bill together, huddled and talking low, but dismissed this as common enough practice. He went back to the set kitchen and Mel called for quiet in the studio as they recorded another segment.

They broke for lunch with the shoot going to schedule and Phil motioned to Mel to follow her. "Now, listen to me, Mel," Phil said as quietly as was possible – for her, "I don't know whether to sack you or thank you."

She held up the CD accusingly. "This is a recording of your performance in the cool room with donkey dick. The fucking halfwit left his fucking mic open and while he should have known better, so should you! Let me tell you that will be the very last time you ever, ever do that while you are here at work. That is, if you want to continue fucking working here." Phil turned on her heel and grabbed her plait as she showed Mel her well defined back.

As she did so, she said, "And you'll be seeing plenty of that Prick on Pins because I've just struck a deal. So, hands off the fucking talent, honey. Okay?"

She was gone and Mel was left smiling serenely to herself and thinking on just how good that blow job was, with not a hint of a blush.

Back to business and it was all in a day's work.

The day ended and Evan was going over some last bits of business with PT as he swallowed yet another coffee and she wondered how he ever slept consuming so much caffeine.

Three gentle knocks and immediate entry meant it was Phil – no guesswork there.

"A very good day, Evan, you're a star. Right on schedule. Well done, lover boy!" and she sat down in front of him. "We need to talk, Evan." And with that PT picked up a pile of fan mail and left the room saying she would return in half an hour.

"I do something wrong?" Evan asked, typically a little fearful of Phil.

"Fuck no, of course not. I had an email from upstairs. The dickheads want us to start doing advertorials during the Game. Adver-fucking-torials. Can you believe it? Like we don't support the fucking network as it is!"

He looked at her in disbelief, "What? Are you for real?" He stood up shaking his head and staring at Phil, dumbfounded.

She retorted, "Do priests fuck little boys? Of course, they're fucking for real!" THEY were senior management and Phil was pretty certain this suggestion had been put to

Nigel Herbert-Flyson by the Sales Department, and that Phoebe Strong was behind it.

"How can they do this to us?" Evan asked whiningly, "It'll make us just like 'Come Cookin'."

This second rate show was on another network and the Game had always considered themselves of a superior ilk. Certainly the ratings showed that to be true, but 'Come Cookin' still made heaps of money from advertorials, the cause of this debatable present predicament.

"Okay, then how do they suggest we do this, Phil?" he said, looking incredulously at his equally aggrieved executive producer.

"They've uncovered an emerging star called Ty Barnaby, so they say. No idea what rock the slime bag crawled from under, but we'll find out soon enough unless we can stop this fucking madness. What the fuck is the matter with them? Like the show's not jammed with as much legal advertising time as possible. It's a wonder we ever get any fucking segments in. Crazy, fucking crazy!" She chewed her plait between ranting sentences – a storm warning in any man's language.

"Where does it leave us, Phil? How do we stop this madness – how Phil?" Evan felt ill. They wanted to mess with his show after six years of ever increasing success and profit. There had to be a reason behind this move – a reason bigger than revenue, bigger than profit. He and Phil had to get to the bottom of this mindless threat to the Game.

CHAPTER 6

The Green Diva Arrives...Departs! Barbara Bubbles Over!

After an exhausting day filming, Evan was furious about the proposed advertorials that Phil had told him about that afternoon. Although not a fractious man by nature, this news had really taken him by surprise and boiled his blood. Have I failed? Haven't I brought in a huge amount of revenue to the network with the Game? What more could they want? There has to be something else behind this and he and Phil were going to get to the bottom of it. They would need all the information they could gather, if they were going to go head to head with Nige and the sales team.

Fuck it, he was just plain angry. Fuck 'em, he thought, fuck 'em!

He felt betrayed and had seen the magnitude of the disappointment in Phil's eyes as they parted at the studio.

The tiny creases around her eyes were not so tiny and her mouth was downturned. Her lips were thinner than usual and her plait was being tortured as they said their farewells for the night.

He wondered if she felt as betrayed as him, but thought that was hardly possible. She had been in the business for so long – surely she was impervious to hurt and betrayal. Maybe not? Evan had no idea just how jaded Phil was feeling.

First, there was Mel's performance with donkey dick. While she was fully aware that it was just sex, she felt there was a better place and time for Mel and Will's indiscretion. Phil took her role in a male dominated arena very seriously and professionally, and she had always liked Mel and even favoured her above others on the studio floor. Perhaps it was because the diminutive floor manager reminded her so much of her estranged daughter, Leeanne, but she couldn't allow herself to start meandering down that memory lane, it was too painful. She considered Mel's behaviour a personal slap in the face. As hard-nosed as she might like to appear, Phil had a code of ethical behaviour in an amoral business and she expected people who knew better, to adhere to the rules on set. Rap parties of course, were a free for all.

Then, that fucking edict from that turd, Nigel. She would have to sort that mess out too. Advertorials! "We'll see about fucking advertorials!" she snarled out loud as she walked to her Jag in the executive car lot.

Meanwhile, Evan had a call from the Mangereire. The restaurant manager called to let him know that a VIP was coming in for dinner and there was a problem with one of the "sous-vide" pieces of equipment.

Luckily, there were only two menu items that required this special method of cooking. He instructed the manager to make those two items unavailable for the evening and let her know he'd be there ASAP. Sometimes he was able to go straight on home after Tuesday's filming and Evan had desperately hoped this would be one of those Tuesdays, as it was going to be a huge Wednesday and he felt like crap.

On the way to the restaurant, Phil had phoned to remind him that the Green Diva would be in to do a special segment as she would not be available next week. She had to return home after the segment because she'd only made a flying visit to promote her latest book on green foods. Evan wasn't really all that keen on what he defined as the "wank stuff", but he'd been briefed by Zoe, the field producer, on how important this was on a world stage. He was reminded that it was, in fact, Zoe who had been responsible for the brilliant idea of securing that outrageous American faggot chef, Rory, for the longest twelve minute segment of Evan's life! How clever that perfidious little poof had been distracting him so he could steal the whole segment. Damn right, it had been another of Zoe's strokes of genius! Alarm bells were ringing once more for Evan.

On arrival at the restaurant, he adjusted his smile and entered through the kitchen which was in full swing with orders being hollered by the chef to all parts of the kitchen. To anyone else it would look like mayhem but to Evan the pandemonium was music to his ears and he knew all was well with the world. Madness, long may it reign supreme – it was that madness that would have the credit cards melting as the punters paid up.

He did not interrupt the flow by initiating conversation, but offered the head chef a wink and a smile on his way through to his office where he donned a fresh uniform jacket. He made a quick inspection of the sous-vide equipment and as he had expected, it was a computer glitch. He indulged in a private little bitch concerning technology and a restaurant manager who should well be able to call a technician on her own initiative. What did he pay her for?

Smiling, waving recognition and ducking between wait staff and customers to reception, he found the manager, who indicated to a table of VIPs. He explained the problem with the sous-vide equipment and told her to call the appropriate people tomorrow. She agreed, noted it in the diary and said she would send an email tonight, but not right now as it was frantic.

After checking the bookings for tomorrow's trading, Evan headed over to the VIP table.

The VIP was a regular who expected to be fussed over and for what he spent in the restaurant, Evan was more than happy to oblige. Each of the guests was introduced to Evan who graciously shook hands and smooched the guests as he knew he did consummately, working that famous smile with companionable pats on the back. After enquiring what the VIP and his guests were drinking, Evan ordered another bottle with his compliments and moved on with his ears ringing with his praises.

He mingled with patrons a while longer, enjoying the balm of his popularity before taking a quick look at his phone which told him it was 10pm and time for home. Gosh, it would be 10.45pm by the time he got there; so much for an early night! It rankled that the staff had not taken care of the kitchen issue – had he not given them enough leeway and persistently told them to be responsible for decision making on this type of problem. He realised he was a bit touchy and perhaps overreacting after today's busy schedule and the advertorial bullshit.

Calm down, he lectured himself. Calm down.

Dr Llewellyn Farnshaw was still sitting in Mangereire when Evan left. He was the VIP that the Star chef had been coddling, which wasn't strictly necessary as the good doctor was a regular customer who had been frequenting the smart eatery since its inception. He was a pleasant man and at 58, he inhabited the role of a successful and admired psychiatrist around town to a tee. Dr Farnshaw, or Lew as he liked to be known, had a booming practice specialising in the offspring of the rich and famous dealing with drug addictions and depression.

A cursory glance at Lew showed that he worked out regularly. His shoulders and torso tapered to a trim waist that was accentuated by the firm fitted slacks that were his preference. His salt and pepper mop of hair was curly and tumbled over his forehead, almost reaching his horn rimmed Harry Potter glasses. He felt these added a whimsical, "I've been lost like you" undernote to his professional appearance. He liked this "look" that he and his wife, Veronica, had designed for himself, which was a good thing because it took a ready supply of funds to maintain and most fortunately, this was no problem for him.

As he drove, Evan contemplated the doctor and his party and came to the same conclusion he always did after spending a little time with Dr Lew; he was a good man and it was always a pleasure to see him. Evan's dad would have known him as a good man – of the hail fellow, well met genre. Just wish I could have a restaurant full of that type of customer every night Evan thought as he beat his way home. He felt sure that Dr Lew came for the food and not his celebrity. Well … he hoped so.

The restaurant business was a tricky one and he often pondered what would happen if he was not so famous – would he still experience the success in the restaurant that he enjoyed now. After all, he'd had the restaurant long before celebrity eventuated. It was a question he asked himself continually and still had no answer to. He left it in the too hard basket and turned into his driveway.

Home – he felt his shoulders drop as he released the stress of the day. He wished he'd taken the time to attend the yoga classes that Simon had suggested and that kept him so centred and together. Oh shit, Simon's birthday, I must talk with Lex.

Lex was waiting up for him with a cup of coffee at the ready. He immediately told her about Simon's impending birthday. She gently told him to settle down as she'd already spoken with PT and had everything in hand and they'd be meeting for the traditional family meal. He should have known Lex would have it all in hand, as always. She also mentioned that his brother, Greg, had rung earlier expecting him to be home and could he return the call tomorrow.

They relaxed into each other's arms and after a quick "my day, your day" catch up they were in bed and asleep. Morning would come very quickly and yep, it was Barbara's big day and the Green Diva was in tomorrow.

He arrived at the studio and went in search of Simon to see how the prep was going. The schedule showed a relatively easy day with the big finale being the last two segments – the presentation to Barbara and the Green Diva.

Barbara and her five children would be in the studio with him and he would cook with them all. He'd decided to cook the chicken dish that had proved so popular on the big day. Whilst he'd cooked it once before on the Game to promote his stand at the fair, he wanted to show a variation that would make it even more appealing.

After greeting the crew he walked through to his green room and found PT already working, as always. Did she ever sleep? He confirmed that she and Lex had Simon's birthday celebration under control as PT headed for the coffee pot. As he sipped his coffee he went over Zoe's brief on the Green Diva, which was excellent and included questions he could ask while they were cooking on set, and the rest of the recipes for the day's shoot. Only seven segments plus the Barbara piece and then the Diva – too easy!

Strangely enough it was only now that he remembered the damned advertorials – he must talk with Phil and see what that fertile brain had come up with as a combat plan.

Feeling he had the day under control, he punched in his brother's number on his cell. Greg answered and after a curt greeting reminded Evan that he was an extremely busy man and this chat would need to be brief.

"Greg ... thanks but I'm worried about Sebastian ... he's gotten so quiet and that's just not him. I know you went through something similar with Zeb a few years back ...", but before he could finish his question, Greg was telling him there was no need to worry. "It's just teenage boys ... stop worrying ... gotta go," and hung up!

So much for brotherly advice. He wondered at times if Greg was still envious of him, a remnant of his success as a swimmer and hero of their father's affections? Perhaps he was right but Evan was still concerned about Seb's reserve and moodiness. He'd talk to Lex again, she'd have an answer.

Phil made her usual appearance at just after 8am – three knocks and there she was. She assuaged his fears regarding the British Diva and moved on to the press coverage that had been lined up for the presentation to Barbara. PR man, Phillip Williamson, had done a brilliant job and the coverage would give top publicity for the Game. She left assuring him they would talk about that crap from the head honcho later.

All was good on set and Bill, the director, was laughing – unusual, thought Evan. Mel on the other hand was most subdued, which was even more unusual. Evan had not been brought up to speed on the cool room carry-on. He would be surprised at the increased number of appearances that the errant chef would be making as the season progressed.

With Simon's typical preparedness, the segments flowed and there was harmony on the set. Even so, Evan was in the middle of the Sashimi of Salmon with Wasabi dressing when he noticed a commotion at the other side of the set. However, being aware of himself as the consummate professional he knew better than to let the disturbance break his flow.

Spikey was following Evan's every move and Bill was telling them how great this was looking. At that, Evan looked to his camera and flashed the huge smile and trademark cheeky wink that the viewers lapped up. "Got you again, you bastard," whispered Bill as he'd called the shot to Jonesy in anticipation.

Little did Evan know that the commotion surrounded one Joyce Humberton-Smythe-Fitzgerald, a minor aristocrat with the title of Viscountess and acclaimed internationally as the Green Diva. Due to her political allegiance, she spurned her titular nomenclature, as she was anything but a Tory. She was vociferous in her disagreement with the stand the Conservatives took on climate change and environmental issues, calling them murderers of the ecology at every opportunity. The British tabloids had labelled her a "fascinating dichotomy" after she'd publicly berated the Environment Minister as an "ignorant, capitalist heretic – an eco-disaster", and followed her everywhere hoping to break the next salacious scoop.

She was whisked away to her dressing room by Phil who'd barely managed to prevent herself from a most embarrassing curtsy. Joyce demanded Simon's presence in her royal chamber and Phil replied with, "Okay, Your Royal Highness." She was flabbergasted by the response of the erstwhile royal personage who told her in dulcet public school tones that she "didn't believe in any of that fucking nonsense!"

Phil located Simon, who was on set arranging for the grand finale. "Get around to Joyce's dressing room ASAP," she ordered, thinking what a let-down it was from Viscountess to Joyce, as Simon trotted off with notebook and recipes in hand.

Joyce, at 54, was extremely well proportioned and sported that iridescent English rose complexion that had obviously never been laid to baste and bake under a scorching sun. The statuesque Joyce was renowned as something of a beauty with natural blond hair pulled severely back from a face whose resultant skin was stretched smooth and begged to be caressed; something that rarely happened to this twice divorced and very independent woman. Joyce attributed her fine figure to her disciplined diet and lifestyle. "Of course, she never had children," the waspish matrons in her social set would proclaim as she left the room.

She was acclaimed as a superb cook and owned an extremely successful catering company in London, using only sustainable produce and products and natural ingredients. Her latest book – promotion of which was the reason for her appearance on the Game – featured her fanatical adherence to organic and sustainable products and produce in all her recipes.

Evan assumed that his famous visitor would be a vegetarian which was a subject he was not on top of as much as he could have been; being a dedicated carnivore he found vegetarianism pretty overrated. Soon he would meet the English gastro-goddess as she had been named in a magazine article.

In the meantime, the big presentation for Barbara and her family was about to take place. Barbara looked sublimely happy while the five children appeared a little shy with so much attention focussed on them as they were being made-up for the cameras. Simon had been dismissed by the Viscountess and was explaining what they were to do to help Evan during the cooking segment.

There was a collective goodwill on set. The children smiled a little nervously as they gazed in wonder at the last minute hustle and bustle of activity taking place about them. Barbara looked relaxed and pretty in the pale blue summer dress that she had worn on the big day. Her dark complexion and dusky eyes shone in an eternally surprised way.

Together with Evan, the network would be represented by Phillip Williamson who'd make the presentation of the cheque. After a degree of internal debate it had been decided by the network that it was best not to release exactly how much Barbara was about to receive. So the oversized expected cheque would not appear. Lottery winners often found a previously unknown range of family and friends when their winnings were made public and the network wanted to save Barbara experiencing this nightmare.

Barbara had wholeheartedly agreed and, at this stage, she had no idea of the size of the cheque she was about to receive either.

Mel called for silence in the studio and gave the thirty seconds call. At the silent 2 ... 1, Evan prepared THE smile and on Mel's point introduced the happy segment. There was a sincere depth to his brilliant smile and his excitement was palpable as he welcomed the viewers.

"So many of you Gamers came to our huge fundraiser for Barbara and some of you met her there. Hey ... did you have fun? I know you did, and so did I! So many of you told me just how much you loved my chicken burger. Now, with Barbara and the kids, I want to do a variation that I know you'll lap up! Are you game? And here's Barbara and Co to help out!"

The crew went nuts with applause and Barbara beamed as she introduced the children. Aaron needed some dental work, the all-seeing Phil noted. Evan explained what he wanted the children to do and they started. The cameramen were busy following as much as possible and Simon was on camera helping out also. It was messy but fun and when Simon handed the chicken meat to Evan to cook for the burgers, Evan commenced his patter with Barbara.

"Barbara, we know of the terrible accident that claimed your husband's life and in some small way we hope we can help ease your burden with this donation from your friends at the Game and Channel 3. How will you use the money, Barb?" he asked as he flipped the thin chicken steaks that had been steeped in a lemon and oil marinade – the sizzle was audible and Spikey captured the shot and the subsequent puffs of barbeque smoke. Evan's cameraman hung on his Star's face for reactions and that smile.

Barbara explained her substantial mortgage was the first priority and then maybe if there was anything left over it would go to the children's schooling. "Oh … and I could so use a new washing machine," she added, laughing.

The kids had now assembled all the bits they needed with a little of Simon's able help. The lettuce and tomatoes were sliced. Raw onion slices were avoided because of the kids; sliced pineapple and the special mayo that Evan and Simon had developed was prepared; the sourdough rolls were halved and so, all was good to go.

Evan and Barbara were both armed with serving utensils and it was time to assemble the chicken burgers. As they did so, the cameras captured the fun and rolled on as the kids tucked in with stray lashings of mayo dripping down fingers and chins.

Camera 2 focussed on Evan and Barbara in a wide shot as he said, "So, how 'bout we get on with it?"

Phil was enthralled and was feeling quite emotional at all this goodwill; it was a ratings dream come true, she could feel it in her bones. Evan continued, "Let's bring on Phillip Williamson, our man responsible for making the Barbie for Barbara such a huge success."

Phillip, looking very executive and dapper, walked on to shake Evan's hand and peck Barbara on the cheek, accompanied by applause from the crew. Phillip was a very handsome man, as any successful PR executive should be.

His smile eased and he became somewhat sombre as he began, "On behalf of Network 3 and all the sponsors, colleagues and viewers involved in the Barbie for Barbara, please accept this cheque as our way of acknowledging your great loss. We know it can't change what has happened but we really hope it will make a difference. That's what we set out to achieve … and we have done it." He handed the envelope to Barbara, who kissed Phillip and then Evan. Tears streamed down her face, (another ratings winner!), as she pensively opened the envelope with shaking hands. She stared at the cheque for a moment and grabbed for the bench in front of her.

Her face was the personification of amazement which turned to disbelief and then to almost hysterical laughter as she began hugging Evan with such gusto, it took the star by surprise and he, too, reached for the stability of the bench.

Bill, the director, was calling shots with vibrancy – there was so much to capture in this scene. Barbara finally calmed a little and almost screamed, "This can't be right … are you sure it's this much? Oh, my God – I'm speechless … but I want to say so much but …what? Oh, thank you all so very, very much … so many people to thank…"

The stunned Barbara wiped her tears and glanced across to Phillip, who was loving it all. He was close to tears also; he knew the public relations value of this exercise was enormous. Despite the cynicism with which he normally viewed such a media exercise he could not help but smile and hug the children, who were infected with their mother's exhilaration though they had no inkling of the hundreds of thousands of dollars handed to her.

Barbara gathered the children in a group hug and showed them the contents of the envelope. Their incredulous gasps assured the folks at home that this was a more than substantial gift. With his usual grand smile, Evan beamed at camera 2 and said, "So, there we are my friends … the Game strikes again! Remember, you made it happen just as much as we did here … without your support and company our big day for Barbara and family would never have happened … a great big thank you to you all!"

As the theme music started, a montage of shots from the Barbie day played as the Star finished the segment. The lights dimmed and Bill called for camera 2 to pick up a slow pan on Barbara and the kids in a huddle. Evan was all over the family as Simon and Phillip, standing very close to each other, observed the happy scene.

As all this heart-warming merriment and self-congratulation was taking place, the Green Diva was going through her preparation, which Simon had meticulously set up on a roll-on bench. She was determined to show all the organic and bio-dynamic produce and products she was so passionate about. She was accompanied by the constant hiss of an organic air sweetener – which smelt vile but she considered it "sublime" and gave it pride of place huddled next to the organic hand lotion and moisturiser.

The biography supplied by her publicist stated clearly that she preferred to be a vegan, but philosophically accepted it was simply not possible if she was to be the advocate of all green and sustainable foods she proclaimed herself to be. She acknowledged the value of proteins such as meat, chicken and fish, which was just as well since she sported expensive designer crocodile leather shoes, under her polyester slacks.

Joyce would cook a pasta dish from her latest recipe book, "The Green Diva Cooks – For You!" It was a simple dish that would allow her to ramble on about her eclectic products, many of which carried her own brand, The Green Diva.

Evan moved toward the wardrobe rack that held his shirt change. This shirt had been chosen to work with Joyce's segment on the following Wednesday's show; a beautiful turquoise matt finish cotton. The wardrobe department had made certain that no synthetic fabric would feature on his gorgeous body while working with Joyce. The Diva noticed as he stripped off to reveal the lean, broad shouldered torso that was fancied by so many women and definitely appreciated what she saw.

He slipped on the shirt as Max appeared to mic him up. The segment would require some movement around the kitchen and so, the boom mic operated by Marco would be needed as well. Joyce had been wired for sound already. Max had needed to use gaffer tape, that most indispensable tool of the trade, to secure the mic to her slippery sham fabric form-fitting top. The multi-hued designer top made her look like a rainbow on stilts and Max wondered that after all these years of experience she didn't know better and be more professional in her choice of clothing. Not only had it been difficult to attach the mic to the fabric, it would rustle when she moved. Such is the ruling class, he surmised, as he walked away.

Evan was being fussed over by make-up and a light shade of eye shadow was being deftly applied by Marj (Marjorie, please!). She fiddled with his hair. PT dropped by quickly to let Evan know that Simon would not be available for his birthday dinner.

159

Strange, thought Evan, but got back to the business at hand. Simon always had dinner with the Pettersen tribe on his birthday.

Phil escorted Evan to the Viscountess who was going through her assembled preparation with Simon. "My, you've done a super job. Brill. Thank you so much," she said as she patted his shoulder in royal appreciation. All words containing an "R" were accentuated by rolling the "R" – a device Joyce effected rather well.

Phil made the introductions as the minor royal and the Star shook hands and chatted very briefly about the upcoming segment. She was "Oh, so happy to be here … heard so much about the Game … an absolutely marvellous reputation the show had internationally." Evan wondered at that as the show was not sold overseas. Maybe, it was viewed on line. Maybe, that well-cultivated voice was talking a load of bullshit.

They moved toward the kitchen set as the crew repositioned cameras and lights and Joyce's bench on wheels was butted up to the main kitchen bench. She would be able to reach her precious products and promote the hell out of them on the Game.

The usual last minute flurry was underway as Mel took instructions from Bill who was on the studio floor. Shortly, he'd be secure in his director's booth. Marco, on boom, was climbing up into his seat above the studio. Phil was on the phone. Simone had her stopwatch at the ready. Cameras were being moved to position. Evan was getting last minute instructions from Simon as the day makers turned the kitchen set into bright sunlight. The Game's audience knew this scene so well.

Max was fussing around the roll-on trying to locate the constant hiss. He lifted the air sweetener to remove it but almost dropped it as Joyce told him in no uncertain terms to leave it exactly where it was.

"It can stay but it must be switched off – far too distracting," he said to her.

"We won't be able to smell it if you do that. Leave it on!"

"Honey, we make fucking television, not smellavision," declared Max with a chuckle as he switched the contraption off and relayed to Bill through his headset.

Bill was about to tell Evan about the air sweetener when Evan was interrupted by a sharp tap on his left shoulder. He turned to face an incensed Joyce brandishing a tub of margarine.

"What is this crap doing here?" she demanded without preamble. "It has to go … NOW!"

With that she hurled the tub over her shoulder whence it splattered over the studio floor.

Evan was taken aback as he'd had an impression when talking with Joyce initially, of a well-bred lady who would pretty much carry this last segment at the end of a tiring two day shoot. He recovered enough to ask, "What the hell do you think you're doing?"

With right royal pomposity she replied, "Do you have the slightest idea what having that shit on set with me would do to my career? Do you know what hydrogenation does and how injurious it is to one's health? To use it would fly in the face of all I stand for – my reputation and my philosophy on life. It is simply impossible to have that shit on set if you wish to appear with me."

Her face carried a royal flush and Evan was reminded of Queen Rory and his outrageous demands.

He saw Phil, plait in hand, in his peripheral view heading in their direction. The commotion had interrupted her phone call and she was desperately hoping there would be no drama at this late stage of an exhaustive day.

Evan took control. "You, Joyce, are a guest on this show. You have no say at all in what happens with our sponsors' products. After all, they are responsible for your being able to appear on MY show at no cost to yourself or your company." He gestured for a stagehand to replace the tub.

The Diva was having none of this and it became abundantly clear that, as a member of the ruling class, she was used to being obeyed. "It seems to me you are quite ignorant of what I am about. Do you know what I do? Do you realise what I represent?" was her acid retort.

Enough thought Evan. Enough … and he let fly in a way that was most unlike his personable self.

"Listen here, you high-flying hypocrite. What carbon fucking footprint do you think you incurred flying here? I know your products would have consumed huge amounts of fossil fuel in manufacture. You're covered in fucking polyester. Are your products totally sustainable? I think not! And you can cut that crap about your philosophies and your fucking reputation. Seems to me your main drive is selling your shitty stuff and growing your fucking aristocratic bank balance. So take your noblesse oblige and shove it right up your royal arse!"

For an instant, there was an utter silence. What would happen next? Phil stood where she was, plait in hand, surrounded by the crew, held in suspended animation.

"How dare you speak to me like that, you cretinous little man!" She screamed at the beleaguered star as she rose on her toes. She was fully adorned in her aristocratic mantle as she continued, "I will not be spoken to in that manner. I am a GUEST on your dreadful little show, you ignorant little man."

This name calling was heading nowhere positive.

"And you may address me as your highness," she continued, "Your ladyship if you must."

"Okay," Evan sneered, "How about your royal bitchship? The margarine stays and there is no negotiation on that."

Phil was most impressed by Evan's stance and the crew barely held back a cheer. Zoe was cringing and hoping this wasn't going to be a repeat of the Rory rout.

So far, it was Evan three, Green Diva two. Who would the next round go to?

The visiting star rose to her full height once more and continued, "So that's it, is it? Well, here is what you can do with your fucking little show – shove it up your own arse good and proper. It is quite obvious that you have no respect whatsoever for the environment and how we are killing it. It must change if we are to hand on a better world to the coming generations. Tell me at least that you feel some miniscule degree of guilt."

Evan showed his palm to her face, a mannerism copied from his beloved 15-year-old daughter.

"YOU may cut the lecture and your self-righteous fucking crap and get off MY show. Tell your slaves to come get your shit off MY set. Mel, kill the lights and Max, kill the sound. And you, you pretentious pretender, get off my set and never show your face here again."

He was furious. The last time he remembered being so angry was during the Felicity incident and wondered briefly if he had issues with women.

Joyce, the Viscountess, had departed in a decided huff, leaving her minions swarming over the set busily retrieving her "shit". Max ran after Joyce to retrieve his precious mic. He hoped she'd be sweet to him but guessed it was unlikely. He was absolutely correct – she was foul!

Evan retreated to his green room after congratulations from Phil on how well he had handled the situation. She was proud of him. He plopped into his chair and wondered what the hell was going on. He was totally exhausted. What gave this woman such a sense of entitlement that she could make demands on HIS show – HIS show! Just plain rude!

He went for a cup of coffee and realised there would not be any as he'd instructed PT no more coffee in the afternoons. Why had she listened to him? He roughly removed his thick make-up and splashed toner onto his face. He changed back into his civvies, grabbed his car keys and headed out of the studio calling his farewells and thanks as he went.

He left the network parking lot as he told Siri to call the restaurant. Almost immediately, the phone was answered properly and he informed the manager he would be there in fifteen minutes.

After completing the call, he told Siri to call Lex, whose earlier missed call he had forgotten to return. Her phone was ringing.

CHAPTER 7

The Game Goes Country and Ty Triumphs

Lex's phone call had not perturbed him, but little did he know that as he waited to hear her loving voice, his horrific day was about to take a turn for the worse. The Diva had only been the icing on the shit cake. Barbara and her kids had really affected him emotionally, more than he had expected. They were good people who'd been dealt a tragic blow.

Simon was not available for his birthday dinner. What was that about? Simon always had his birthday dinner with them. The advertorials and this new talent, Ty Barnaby – where is he from? What would it mean to the Game?

I'll get Ted from security onto Ty and see if he can find out more on this 'emerging personality' that nobody's ever heard of, Evan told himself as he drove to the restaurant feeling it was the last place he needed to be right now. It was a day that would not go away, no matter how he wished it would.

"Hi darling." Lex finally answered without the usual sparkling lilt in her voice.

With the tiredness evident in his own voice, he asked how she was. "Sorta okay. Hon, I'm worried about Seb now, too. He hasn't spoken a word to me or his sisters since he got home from school. I really think we need to do something." Her voice indicated the stress she was carrying.

"Yep, I know ... it's worrying me too. I thought I'd get Lew Farnshaw to have a chat with him, if we can get Seb to agree to see him. Maybe, this one has to be non-negotiable?" Concern echoed in his tired voice.

"Okay, can you arrange that, or PT? Or me?" Without waiting for an answer she continued, "Oh, and darling, I don't want to alarm you, but there is blood in my urine. Yesterday it didn't worry me because this can happen, but today it's more constant and it's not my time of the month."

Evan was quite uninitiated as far as secret women's business was concerned thanks to his loving but extremely orthodox Presbyterian family and a lack of understanding and fear of not having his anchor beside him caused him to explode and swerve to miss a car veering across his lane, "What do you mean, not alarm me, Lex? What does that mean? What the hell do you think I'm going to say ... Oh dear, we'll wait and see? For

Chrissakes Lex, what can it mean?" His anger subsided as he released his fear vocally.

She knew he was really upset when he blasphemed. "Honey, I can only guess, but I'll see the doctor first thing tomorrow. I guess I should have waited for you to get home, I can tell you're exhausted and strung out. I'm sorry to do this to you and don't worry, you don't need to come home right now." Lex went quiet.

Evan was immediately sorry and confused and started to apologise. "No, I'm sorry, I won't head to the restaurant, I'm coming home now," he insisted.

"Please honey; just go take care of things at the restaurant. I'm quite okay … we can chat when you get home. I love you."

"Alright, I'll be as quick as I can. Love you too, Lex." He accelerated off to his thriving eatery.

After solving a minor staffing issue, Evan was headed for home; the unnecessary visit, he deduced, had taken half an hour. Why the hell couldn't they solve that problem? He must organise a management meeting soon and get them more pro-active in solving small issues like this one, which was no more than a demarcation dispute.

He was thinking about Lex and the Ty problem. Was it really a problem? Maybe, he could use a backup and maybe it was time to bring on an apprentice for his TV role – maybe? He and Phil needed to get this one on the table at a management meeting with Nige.

First up in the morning, after he found out what was happening with Lex, he'd call Ted and get him on the case finding out whom exactly this Ty was. After all, Ted owed him after the Felicity debacle.

That would be his second phone call – the first would be to Dr Lew, the psychiatrist, about his boy, Seb. What was the issue with his, not so little, boy? Surely, it could be no more than a rite of passage.

It was Thursday morning. He'd sent a text to PT letting her know that he would be tied up for the morning and to handle things until he reached the restaurant. He phoned Lew's office and left a message for the respected psychiatrist to return his call. His next phone call engaged the services of Ted in the hunt for background on Ty Barnaby.

So far, so good! Now, to sort out Lex's problem, if we can. This morning she had said that there seemed to be less blood and not to worry.

"Are you kidding? How can I stop worrying? For God's sake Lex, get a grip. Please, just ring your gyno now and get an appointment ASAP," Evan said briskly. He almost never told Lex what to do.

"Personally, I think you're overreacting but to keep you happy, I'll call." She headed to the phone in the home office. She was happy that Evan had rung Lew Farnshaw's office as her anxiety over Sebastian was increasing on a daily basis.

Evan speed dialled Phil Watts and waited for her to answer as he poured his third coffee for the morning.

"Phil here," she answered in her habitual nondescript way.

"Hi darling – you okay?" Evan asked.

"Hon, so glad you called. Yep, everything is okay but we do have to deal with this Ty thing and the advertorials. I've had to give in to Nige about Ty, who I'm meeting tomorrow morning. If it goes as I think it will, Ty will be on the road to the country to do five segments. I'm sending Zoe with him and I've organised the OB crew." Phil seemed distant as she spoke.

"Do I have any say in this? Seems to have moved ahead very quickly … how come?" Evan was feeling quite vulnerable between what was happening at home and the sudden recognition that he was at the whim of the Network power player's will.

"To be honest Evan, Nige passed down an ultimatum and I had to give in. And, honestly, it will be good to get Zoe out of the office after all the shit she's in with that fucking bitch … the Princess, or whatever she is. I loved it when you called her your royal bitchiness, by the way. Good on ya. Hon, leave the Ty thing with me." And she was gone. Evan wanted to tell her of his upcoming conversation with Ted. Later.

He called Ted and asked him to look into this Ty Barnaby – find out as much as he could about him and his sudden appearance at the Channel 3 network.

With his fourth cup of coffee in his hand, Simon's number appeared on the screen of his cell phone. Of course, it was a favourite and popped up instantaneously.

Simon answered on the second ring, which was his typical johnnie-on-the-spot response.

"Hey buddy, how you doin'?" Simon could picture Evan's smiling face. They'd known each other for so long that he didn't need to be in proximity to know when that fabulous smile was working.

Simon said he was great and enjoying his day off. They laughed about the Viscountess and how Evan had dispensed her so peremptorily. So far, there'd been no backlash and she was the one who missed out as her Diva range had not received the coverage she'd anticipated. The Game would have no problem filling the space left by her disappearance. Again, they laughed as they talked about her pretentiousness.

"Simon, PT tells me you can't make your birthday dinner with us. I must say we were surprised when we heard the news." There was no smile in his voice.

"You know boss, I got caught between a rock and a hard place. Just had to take the invite I got out of the blue. Sorry Evan, can we do it the following week? I meant to get back to you but, well … I didn't." Simon sounded distracted.

"So, you're saying the week after your birthday – is that right? I'll see what Lex has to say and get back to you. You okay? You sound distracted. Is everything alright?" a concerned Evan quizzed.

"No problems, boss. Everything is good. Gotta go..."and the chef that made the Game work and played a major part in all of Evan's business had gone. Evan was dismayed at the abrupt finish to the call. Normally, on a Thursday morning, they would have a debrief of the past two days' shooting. Not today it seemed.

When necessary, things moved quickly in the TV business and Ty was introduced to Phil Watts the next day. He was a good looker that was for sure. His dark hair had blond highlights throughout and at 23, his eyes were clear and deep dimples indicated his happy disposition. His lightly tanned face and arms suggested to Phil, that he was a surfer. And yes, he sure was cute!

Unlike Evan, he lacked the broad shoulders that swimmers sported. He was tall at around 193cm, Phil estimated. He was pleasant and well-mannered as he'd stood when she came into the room and remained that way until Phil had seated. He also had a firm handshake. Nice, old fashioned manners were rarely seen these days.

Phil liked what she saw and realised that with those high cheek bones, he would photograph well and the camera would love him. As he'd be on the road, she would show him how to use pancake make-up for the camera to make the most of his cheek bones. Technical application of make-up was so important in TV. Phil asked him to get up and walk around the room. As he did, she noted he had great posture and moved with a little swagger that was inviting and sexy. Very marketable, she thought.

Phil browsed his CV and noted that he had done some amateur TV work. She quizzed him about his relationship with Nigel Herbert-Flyson, Network 3's CEO and he seemed a little evasive when he answered that Mr

Herbert-Flyson was a family friend. He usually called him Uncle Nige.

The cagey executive producer wondered if this was true. Nige really only had friends in the TV business but if she remembered correctly, he had discovered Evan in the country at some small town fair.

"Okay Ty, I'm going to send you to the country to do five stories for the Game. What about that? Think it would suit you?" He shifted in his chair with eyes squinted and young brow creased with perplexity.

"So soon? I wasn't expecting this to happen so quickly. When you say country, what do you mean?" He was definitely worried.

"I was told, Ty, that you were ready to go ... now. That's the word from the man upstairs. Your Uncle. I'm giving you our best producer, Zoe. She's working on stories now." Phil walked around to sit on the other side of the desk in front of him.

"Phil, may I call you Phil?" He looked up at her from his chair as she nodded her agreement.

"Thanks, Phil. You see, I know nothing about cooking and I guess it's a pretty specialised field. Are you sure I'll be good enough?" His concern seemed genuine.

"Well, here's the thing, Ty. You were 'given' to me, so to speak ... and I really don't know if you're any good or not. I haven't seen anything but your CV. But I have to use you and the best way is this way and hell, it will be your fucking baptism of fire. You know how to look down the barrel of a camera according to your CV … which also claims you're smart. So here's the deal, buddy, you're on your way to the country or you can fuck off out of my office and my life. How does that sound?" She tried to smile, but the attempt was unsuccessful.

Welcome to the world of professional TV thought Ty, with a cynicism rare in one so young! Grow up and just do it, said a little voice in the back of his brain.

"All set?" Phil asked, as she walked to the door, beckoning Ty to follow. "I'll introduce you to Zoe and she'll be all yours from here on in." She walked away and Ty followed behind like a lost puppy, but there remained a spring to his step.

Zoe was hunched over her desk with papers everywhere and a phone on loudspeaker. She looked up at Phil and Ty as they entered and told whoever was on the other end of the line that she would get back to them. She pushed back on her roller office chair and stood. There was no love lost between her and Phil but, as executive producer, Phil was her boss and that, as they say, was that.

"Ty Barnaby meet Zoe Hendricks," Phil said brusquely. "Zoe is the best producer in the business – second to me that is and you'll find that out, if you keep your mouth shut and do a fucking lotta listening. She'll show you the ropes and you'll learn. Zoe will tell me exactly how good you are Ty. And she will. Good luck buddy. Thanks Zoe." Phil told Zoe to make sure she showed Ty how to use pancake to make the most of his prominent cheek bones, then departed with a typical wave of her left hand and her brisk businesslike walk.

Zoe smiled. "Welcome to the wonderful world of television. I'm sure you've been given a lovely warm reception by her royal viciousness. It's not always like that around here. Or ... maybe it is. Just know you are about to work on a top show that's well respected in the business and, more importantly, makes mega bucks for the network. Ultimately that's what counts and keeps us on air and paying the bills. Phil cops no shit. Understand that and you'll be just fine, Ty."

She sat down and indicated for Ty to drag up a chair.

"Okay, here are some notebooks – you'll need to keep notes, some pens and pencils." She handed him the stationery as she continued, "I've got five stories and we only need four. So ... you ready?"

As she talked, Ty took in Zoe – she must have been a hot babe when she was younger. Maybe early thirties, perhaps a little older.

She spoke clearly and had a clipped accent which made her deepish voice sound sophisticated. Not at all warm – authoritarian. Her long blondish hair was piled on top of her head to reveal deliciously pixie like ears from which dangled pendulously long adornments. They had to be light as there was no obvious stretching of her ear lobes. Her top fitted her body and made her tits stand out – while they were not big, they were perfectly proportioned to her trim body. The grey wool skirt she wore was crinkled around her arse and groin as she was seated. He couldn't wait to see her buns and hoped that they sat out and up like her pert tits.

Ty was a sexual animal – he loved sex. Not only did he love it, at only 23 he was exceedingly proficient. In fact, at the co-ed boarding school he attended for six years, he was known as Ty the Triumphant. He would try anything on any of the willing female boarders and there were plenty of takers as Ty was both a looker and hung, or so the gossip went. After Ty read about David Duchovny's being a sex addict, he thought he could emulate the Hollywood star easily.

Zoe was saying, "…and then we can go to the asparagus farm. We could bring some asparagus back for Evan to use on the show, but we won't and we'll substitute with fresh stuff we'll have here. We won't be draggin' fucking asparagus back here. We can start the tomato story that afternoon. Next day, I've got a gun local chef to do a cooking segment using these special tomatoes that are usually canned." Zoe was pointing to a map of the area where they'd be located.

While appraising Zoe's potential, Ty had missed the other three story ideas. Zoe had suggested a mushroom grower who used an obsolete railway tunnel, a table grape grower and a lavender and rosemary farm. It was all double Siberian to him. Zoe asked what he thought and he replied that he would defer to her judgement, being the newby. The easy answer, considering he'd only taken in half of what she said.

"Okay … leave it with me. I have your email details here on your CV. That current?" She indicated the email address on his CV and he nodded in assent.

"We'll head outta town on Sunday afternoon and be on location that night ready to start shooting on Monday. I'll have all details and scripts to you by Saturday afternoon. I expect you to know what you're doing each day and we'll work on your thoughts and questions on the flight." She stood and began putting papers into piles. Ty just stood there looking bewildered.

"Something else? I got a heap of shit to do … why are you standing there still?" She was standing erect at her full 178 centimetres, looking rather exasperated and intimidating.

"Just not sure what wardrobe to pack?" he answered hesitantly.

"Look Ty, at this point, I consider you know sweet fuck all and as such I'm going to write the scripts with that understanding … okay? We're heading south so as far as packing is concerned, I would suggest some warm clothing, wouldn't you say? Plain shirts and not too city-fied." She looked at him scathingly as she continued, "Go home or wherever you live and get the Game up on YouTube and look at past shows so you understand what we're about. Google the stuff we have talked about. You don't want to look like a fucking halfwit when you're interviewing farmers, they pick up real quick. I will organise everything else we need including your flights and per diems. Now fuck off – I'm really busy."

177

He wondered what a per diem meant but was too awestruck to ask, so focussed on her hot arse as she turned her not unattractive back to him in dismissal. He was to find out that a per diem was a daily allowance to cover basic costs while travelling – very basic costs.

Evan's mobile rang. Lunch service had finished and he was entrenched in rosters, leave applications, superannuation payments and monthly invoices. There were new menu ideas and forward budgets to be digested and discussed with the external accountant. Oh, and that cookbook he was still prevaricating over.

He answered distractedly.

"Hi hon … it's me. You okay?" Lex asked.

"Sure."

"I'm just back from my local doctor, Danny. He says from what he can see in the urine sample, there's nothing to be anxious about. He's sending the sample away to pathology and I should have results by Monday. He's making an appointment with my gyno, Frank, for Monday afternoon." His wife informed him with not quite convincing confidence.

Evan liked Danny Levine, who was his doctor also and he'd also met Dr Francis Davidson, Lex's gyno who'd visited the restaurant and introduced himself with, "Please call me Frank – I loathe Francis." Pleasant, down to earth type of fellow had been Evan's summation. He'd also delivered their three children.

"So, I'll come with you to the gyno, Lex," he confirmed, without being asked.

"Thanks darling, I'd appreciate that."

Conversation over.

Zoe, her novice talent Ty and cameraman Oliver Munchsted had arrived at the small country city at 4.35pm and were now established in their hotel. Ty and Zoe had worked on the schedule, scripts and location during the one hour and fifty minute flight. As promised, Ty was loaded up with all the information Zoe had said she would email to him; he had immersed his brain in past episodes of the Game and read as much as he could find about lavender, mushrooms, tomatoes, asparagus and the peculiar table grapes grown in this area.

He was surprised to learn that asparagus was an ancient vegetable and the name originated from the Greek word for stalk or shoot. It was an aphrodisiac – he'd had to google that word, but made a mental note to eat a whole lot more asparagus! His reading also led him to the discovery of why his pee smelt strange after eating this delicious and nutritious vegetable which is a member of the lily family, along with onions and garlic. Asparagus contains a chemical called asparagusic acid which breaks down, once digested, into sulphur containing stuff. Strange, he thought, because asparagus doesn't smell of anything sulphur. He remembered back to chemical experiments at school producing rotten egg gas. Hydrogen sulphide, he smirked to himself as he recalled some of the boys who'd specialised in rotten egg farts. So delightfully disgusting!

Ollie, the camera operator would also act as sound man. Ty and Ollie had struck an immediate friendship when they discovered at the airport terminal that they supported the same football team and both body surfed women with zest. By the time they got to discussing various parts of their anatomy, the friendship was sealed.

Monday morning at 7am found them on a very busy asparagus farm; the picking had been underway for a couple of hours and the production manager, Jeff, was also the farmer. This well-tanned and crusty man would be their guide and interviewee. Ty and Jeff bonded very quickly.

Zoe had made it very clear to Ty that he must be liked out here in the country – no smart arsed city stuff. "You'll stand out as a wanker and they'll give you short shrift – so be friendly and smile as much as you can. Let Jeff, or any other interviewee, tell you the story and we can do reverses later." She noticed the look of puzzlement on his face at her mention of reverses. Later, later; she made a mental note to explain some basic jargon to her initiate.

Ty and Jeff had their microphones and transmitters attached by Ollie, who then took his camera further down the tram-tracks in the asparagus field. Jeff and Ty were to do a "walk and talk" down the tram-tracks, or contours used by the tractors that cultivated the fields.

When Ollie dropped his arm, it was the signal for the walk and talk to start. As resident apprentice Ty just stood, looking vaguely confused. Zoe rushed over and said as nicely as she could manage, "Watch Ollie, when he drops his arm, as he just did, he's ready for you both to start walking slowly towards the camera."

Take two.

Ty found he was totally engrossed in what Jeff was saying. He knew his script and what to ask at the appropriate time. However, they were at the end of the walk before all the necessary information had been gathered by Ty.

Zoe took Ty aside a little roughly hissing, "What's the fucking rush? You're in the country, numbnuts. You're totally enthralled by what this guy is telling you and you're trying to break the world record for the 100 metre dash. Take a fucking stroll in the country and enjoy this guy's company dickhead and slow the fuck down." She had said this in an exaggerated almost inaudible whisper so as not to embarrass Ty in front of Jeff, who'd obviously done this before and was not at all fazed by having to start again.

Take three.

It was a stunning morning and still only 8am. Zoe had decided that Ty did not need make-up and he was dressed for the part in a quietish blue and black plaid shirt that moulded very nicely to his trim waist; he'd tucked the shirt into well-fitting faded jeans and wore boots. The shirt fabric stretched over Ty's muscular arms. He certainly looked the part and his next take was a winner with Ty even managing to stop casually along the way to inspect the soil and asparagus stalks.

As all the facts were recorded for the interview, Jeff showed the appreciative novice three different varieties explaining that the American and British asparagus is green, purple is French and white is Dutch. The white stalks are grown by mounding the soil and mulch around the stalks to prevent the process of photosynthesis which would normally turn them green. Jeff continued on explaining that it is sometimes referred to as the vampire of the vegetable world because it never sees the light. Ty laughed sincerely and the camera loved him.

The morning was gone and Ty's first shoot, despite his neophyte status, was in the can so to speak. This is an old show business saying that no longer applies as it is all digital and not on a tape, but old habits die hard.

Zoe was happy and sent Ollie off to get some pick up shots while she sat Ty down facing the fields and explained what reverses were. She went on to show him where his eye line would be so it looked as though Jeff was in front of him being asked the questions. They'd seen enough of Jeff and asparagus, now they needed the reverse questions, some lunch which Jeff had kindly provided and they'd be back on the road. As Ollie approached them he yelled for "Quiet!"

Zoe put her finger to her lips and said nothing. When Ollie started to walk back to them a minute later, she explained that he was recording natural sound for the editing of the story. "It's called a natsound and it is so totally necessary for the editor when we get back to the studio."

So far, Ty's baptism of fire had not been so harrowing and Zoe acknowledged that he was a natural for camera (thank fucking Christ!) as she put a call through to Phil and let her know the good news.

Ty finished the story with a throw to Evan in the studio which would then allow the asparagus cooking segment to be introduced to complete the story. Ty was impressed by Zoe and her forward thinking and she in turn, was more than happy to compliment Ty on his first day, saying, "Keep this level of performance up kiddo and you'll make it! Tomorrow, we shoot tomatoes. Get some rest, it's another early start."

The next morning was another picture perfect day for filming and Zoe sent Ollie on his way to gather sunrise shots. The sun hesitantly blasted onto the landscape as it peeked above a small range of hills. Ollie was always awed by the majesty of sunrise and as such never had a bitch about the early start involved with achieving these shots.

Ty was dressed suitably in a blue-tan shirt and Zoe was impressed. As they drove to location with Ollie behind the wheel of the hired OB vehicle, the talent and the producer went through their proposed scenes.

They hit the location at 7.25am and were greeted by Terry Jazowski with a welcoming smile as wide and friendly as the surrounding countryside. The coffee was brewed and local Italian bread ready to toast. The toppings to go with the fresh local butter consisted of a homemade tomato jam and a tomato relish piquantly flavoured with chillies.

Terry was a third generation tomato farmer and his speciality was the Roma. He had developed his own variety which was a brilliant red beauty highly sought after for processing and canning. Slightly marked or spoiled tomatoes went to tomato paste production and he also supplied them to a famous cook who had developed a sun-dried tomato package that was currently in huge demand. These tomatoes were processed in huge ovens and the dehydration of moisture in the slow heat allowed the sweetish fruit to almost candify; when the tomatoes were quartered and doused with herbs and fresh local olive oil the oven produced heat concentrated the complimentary flavours of tomatoes, herbs and oil.

In the fields, Ty was surprised to notice how low the bushes were – virtually lying on the rich red soil. A mechanical picker scooped up the bush and some of the soil as it retrieved the tomatoes. He marvelled that this process was all completed by machines and yet the tomatoes were not bruised or damaged. Ty was fascinated as the bush was chopped and spat out the rear of the picker once the fruit had been shaken free and collected. In the following days the bushes would be ploughed back into the earth with fertilizer and other nutrients to replenish the soil.

The interview got underway with the harvester at work in the background. Terry was fantastic. He had a special look – Zoe was trying to figure what it was about him that was so interesting, as Ty quizzed him. His Slavic heritage meant that his tanned skin, combined with intense steel blue eyes that sat evenly above his defined cheek bones, made him especially easy on the eyes. His jaw was carved onto his face and his taut neck had no hint of developing jowls. His features, including his distinctive aquiline nose, provided a perfect mien that was composed and happy. The emerging fine wrinkles that creased the corners of his eyes somehow enhanced his appearance even further.

The tomato information flowed with ease from Terry and Ty had a real grip on the segment. Ty did his "noddies" beautifully. To do a credible "noddy", the interviewer has to look as though he is engaged with the interviewee though he is not present.

Zoe had instructed him on this essential technique. Ty would tilt his head to one side, straighten up and then nod in agreement – Ollie declared Ty's "noddies" worthy of a professional TV interviewer.

Shooting was completed quickly in the field as the rest of the segment would be the cooking of the tomatoes by a local hot chef tonight. Zoe had arranged the chef with a call from the network office and the tomato grower, who knew him well, was to be on hand at the restaurant to help complete the segment.

The crew took off for the mushroom tunnel. All was going swimmingly with no dramas and lots of laughs – as Ty relaxed into his role he revealed a delightful sense of humour with a suitable sense of wackiness that is essential to be a good TV presenter.

Arriving at the mushroom farm, Zoe discovered the main man would not be available till the next day, so she organised permission for Ollie to wander round with his hand-held for "pickup shots" that would come in handy for the editor.

Zoe gazed up at the sky and assessed that there was still plenty of light left for more filming with Ty. She briskly ordered him to change shirts – she had instructed him to always carry a spare shirt and trousers on location. He reappeared from behind a shed where he had changed into a delicately blue shirt that did wonders for his eyes and Zoe was forced to admit that he looked positively stunning, though she would never have said this out loud.

She handed him a script with the warning, "Ty, you need to be very careful not to spill anything on that shirt 'cos you're in it tomorrow. Put an iron over it tonight at the hotel. Here's the script you need to have down pat to do a piece to camera when Ollie gets back." She rotated, searching for a suitable backdrop for Ty to do his stand up. After finding the spot, she drew a mark into the soil for Ty to follow – no walking this time.

The sweating cameraman reappeared and they all moved to the marked spot which Ollie agreed would be excellent for the stand up.

Zoe positioned Ty with a warning not to move about too much and when she was certain he was word perfect with his dialogue, removed his script from shot. With a confident smile, he looked straight down the barrel and delivered a perfect take. "That was great, Ty! You've done this before, right?" Zoe beamed as she spoke. One take … excellent! If he can keep this up, he's going somewhere.

"Yeah, well a couple of times but not for real – just at college. You reckon it was okay … really?" Zoe responded with a simple "awesome" but decided on a second take for backup.

After packing all the gear, they headed back to the hotel. A quick refresher and Ty was in the shirt he'd worn for the tomato shoot. He was like a sponge soaking up Zoe's generous advice. He would tell her tonight just how grateful he truly was. On the way back to the hotel, she told him why he must stand still on a mark. Constant movement on a mark would mess up the soil and show how many takes had been involved - just a professional thing.

On the way to the restaurant, Zoe gave Phil a quick call to let her know how well it was all going. The touchy executive seemed happy, which was something of a rarity. Phil also told Zoe that Evan was a little distressed because his wife had seen the gynaecologist yesterday. Phil sounded a little troubled also – they really were great friends, Evan and Phil.

Lou (Luigi) Cantellani was the gun chef and owner of Rusticana – a lively yet rustic Italian style eatery in this local little city. He was crazy, in that he was always happy and would burst into song at random. The tables looked as though they were strewn at random around the large room and there appeared little order. This Tuesday night it was thumping with lots of loud music, laughter and children screaming spasmodically with joy. The place reeked of ambiance and good old fashioned fun and Zoe thought that many city restaurants would give their eye teeth for this sort of patronage on an early week night.

Zoe was embraced by Lou and kissed on both cheeks as he told her how bellissima she looked. Ty's hand was pumped with gusto and Ollie made a quick Italian greeting to which Lou grinned widely as he replied with a "ciao". Lou guided them to a table and ordered Prosecco "pronto", at which point the crew knew they were in for a big night. Terry arrived and was led to their table.

After a brief respite, the experienced cameraman was up and at it again. Zoe asked for ambient shots of the customers after which they'd meet in the kitchen with Lou, who was ready to do his piece.

Ollie wired Ty and the very excited and exuberant Lou for sound and followed them to the stove. Zoe was impressed with Lou's relaxed professionalism. He's a country chef, she thought, who is totally organised and ready when he said he would be, unlike so many of the wankers in their fancy city eateries who left her and her crew to stand around and wait for hours, as if she were waiting for an audience with the fucking Pope!

Lou was the epitome of precision. Even though this was a simple tomato, bell pepper and rosemary sauce, it was necessary to make him stop and repeat specific steps

– Lou was most gracious about this, benevolently smiling his acceptance. Zoe was also pleased to note that Ty was doing exactly as he'd been directed and was following each of Lou's moves with genuine interest.

Ollie's camera was focussed on a pot of boiling salted water readying for the dried fettuccine which would then be topped by the silky scarlet sauce. It was coming together flawlessly in Lou's loving hands. The pasta was thrown into the water with a dramatic flourish and Lou handed a wooden spoon to Ty asking him to stir to prevent the pasta sticking. He pointed out to Ty that this was the crucial time for pasta cooking and that a good cook never leaves his pasta.

"The pasta is cooked when it is cooked," he declared with dramatic effect, "You don't a wanna read the packet. You just watch Lou and learn." No one had ever accused Lou of having low self-esteem issues!

Ty was completely enthralled with Lou and loved every minute of what was happening and Ollie in turn was magnetically drawn to Ty. The camera loved his intensity as he watched and enjoyed Lou.

The tomato sauce was unctuous and thick and dredged with Italian parsley and rosemary - the green against the red hues made Lou's joke about the colours of the Italian flag completely appropriate. They shared their laughter as Lou seasoned with salt, pepper and a sprinkle of nutmeg explaining that every good chef has a secret ingredient and his dear Mamma had taught him this when he was just a boy.

Lou fished out a piece of fettuccine which he broke between his thumb and forefinger. He showed the broken end to camera and explained that you could still see that line of uncooked pasta. To get this shot clearly, it had to be repeated a further three times, before Ollie was satisfied.

"Al dente is whatta we want, Ty." Lou was looking at the young presenter with his head cocked to one side and with the steam from the boiling pasta water wafting about him so it looked quite surreal. "There's nothing more boring anda disgusting than overcooked pasta. Notta mushy, notta chewy – must be al dente! Justa right."

With his long tongs, he pulled out some cooked pasta into a chinois strainer and thumped the strainer against his hand to remove as much of the adhesive cooking liquid as possible. Without ceremony, he upended the pasta into the vibrant tomato sauce, accompanied by bravos and cheering from kitchen staff.

No psychomotor retardation with Lou, Zoe thought, as she watched the action with happy satisfaction. This is going to be a sensational segment.

With the coated pasta now in two serving bowls, Lou grabbed a hunk of lightly golden coloured cheese that had whitish specks through it and held it up to camera as he spoke, "This is the besta cheese we use for pasta, Parmigiano-Reggiano. Itsa the Parmesan cheese, but itsa special. Grate over the pasta lika this!" The finely grated cheese cascaded over the pasta dish with hedonistic harmony. "Itsa the only cheese to use. Okay? We never usa the muck ina the packet! Never!"

They picked up their plates and exited the scene.

The cooking scene complete Ty, Lou and Zoe joined Terry at their table where a bottle of Chianti sat beside the pasta they had filmed. This was just the beginning of the feast to ensue. The local printed press had arrived to get a glimpse of their beloved local star and to interview Zoe about the Game coming to town. Ollie would join them when he'd finished filming more of the restaurant in action.

Regional TV would join them at the mushroom shoot tomorrow and Zoe had arranged for Evan to do a radio interview from the network on Thursday, when the grape segment would take place.

Zoe was relaxed and ready for a drink. She knew about the special cheese Lou had raved about and had noticed on Rusticana's menu, the local tomato and Burrata salad.

She adored Italian cuisine and had travelled to Italy often. She loved Burrata which was usually made with buffalo milk into a ball of mozzarella then filled with cream and curds. The combining of this Burrata with tomatoes was a perfect culinary marriage, like rosemary and lamb or mint and strawberries.

At 36, Zoe had travelled extensively and was aware, when she visited Italy, to acknowledge the regional differences. She loved mozzarella and a cousin of this stretched curd cheese called Stracciatella and had often indulged in a roasted vegetable salad accompanied by this cheese in her birth city, which boasted a large Italian community. She laughed to herself tonight as she remembered it as a blackboard special in the northern Italian township of Bergamo.

She was further surprised and delighted when she was served a big bowl of gelato with asymmetric lashings of dark chocolate pieces, another speciality of Bergamo; this regional gelato was called Stracciatella. The Americans made a second rate copy of it that they called Choc Chip.

The feast was over and Ty begged out to catch up on some sleep ready for another early start. Ollie joined him but Zoe and Terry stayed on with yet another bottle of Chianti. They were deeply engrossed in conversation "*à deux*" as the other two departed.

Zoe was sure that Terry's ample lips were not botoxed as she stared at them lasciviously and leaned onto the table. She edged closer to Terry and was deep in conversation. Zoe was uncertain of the messages she was receiving from the tomato grower, but she hoped they were of a sexual nature. She was horny as hell and he was definitely a good looker albeit married with four children.

What happens on the road, stays on the road was the first mantra of TV land.

However, Zoe was in for a shock.

Whilst the nature of the conversation between Terry and Zoe was sexual and explicit, it was not what she was expecting to hear. Her ardent dinner partner wanted Zoe to know that he was trans-gendering. Oh, for fuck's sake, this was just her luck!

"What do you mean; you're fucking trans-gendering?" she said, a little too loudly.

He asked her to be a little more discreet as he went on, "I know it must look and sound strange to you, Zoe, and I'm sorry to unload like this, but it's not easy to find someone out here to talk about this stuff with. Can you just listen to me, please?" It was more a pathetically desperate plea than a please.

Oh, fuck it all – not exactly what I was hoping but why not listen to this good looking dude, who was about to become a good looking chick; she'd come across most things in the business!

With a good gulp of the Italian red wine, he went on to tell her that he was not attracted to men as he was not gay, but had always felt that he was a woman trapped in a man's body. How many TV docos had Zoe seen along this theme, but it did seem rather more unusual to be listening to this sexual conundrum in the middle of this rural city.

She listened sympathetically and guzzled more wine. Another bottle appeared from nowhere. Brilliant, she thought, all I need is to be getting drunk in the middle of a shoot with a novice presenter and in the company of a sexually confused guy I thought I'd be bonking shortly. How fucking crazy was this?

Only one thing to do – have another drink!

He informed her sotto voce that he had already started his treatment both medically and psychologically and that his wife knew and would support him as much as she could. His real concern was for his children and he was seeking advice as to how to handle the situation. She felt like saying how the fucking hell would she know? She was no expert in family affairs, let alone trans-sexuality. She figured her best bet was to shut up, let him ramble and get completely drunk.

She was pretty vague on how she got back to the hotel.

When her cell phone alarm screamed 6am at her next morning, she instinctively threw it, then prayed it had bounced not broken, she'd been lucky that way once or twice before. Her head felt like cracked peppercorns, her mouth drier that any beach and her mind still confounded by the news of Terry's secret. In a way, she felt complimented that Terry had felt brave and comfortable enough to share his news with her. On the other hand, she'd missed out on the lay she had thought was coming her way. She hoped she would not see him again during the next three days.

Although her head screamed, she would never let on to her crew. She'd used what must have been a litre of eye wash to rid herself of the red railway lines that criss-crossed the whites of her eyes and was glugging her third coffee when the crew assembled.

They were off to the mushroom tunnel. It was an easy shoot and Ty was on top of the interview. Evan would complete the segment with a mushroom terrine recipe that Simon had developed. Perfect.

The grower had promised them a shot of the mushroom spawning; this was how mushrooms propagate, he explained. Indeed, he was on hand to point out what appeared as a wisp of smoke, which was the spawning process. Ty rejoiced that he was not a mushroom – too impersonal, and no physical contact.

Ollie was really excited and said this would cap off a brilliant segment; he was known to enjoy indulging his artistic licence. Ty was happy with Ollie's decision, though Zoe seemed rather quiet and shortly they were on their way to the vineyard.

On arrival, Ty changed shirts and refreshed himself with the script. There was very little for him to do as Zoe had previously arranged for the grower to come to the network to do a "live" appearance about his grapes. Ty had to stroll through the vineyards, stopping occasionally to lift up the canopy of grape vines. There would be a cluster of the whitish green table grapes and he would take a couple as he smiled and ate them to show his appreciation of the outstanding quality. He then walked on with square shoulders, trim waist and exceptional arse to camera.

There was no comparison between these grapes and the wine grapes, the enthusiastic grower had assured Zoe and Ty. Ty was not at all sure about this as he thought all grapes tasted the same; however he had already learnt enough not to voice that opinion out loud.

Zoe felt she'd been let in on a state secret when the grower mentioned to her that he did, in fact, make his own wine out of these grapes and then distilled the wine for grappa. The very mention of grappa took Zoe back to a wild night with a hot Italian stud she'd hooked up with in Positano a few years back. They'd met in a small restaurant and bar in this idyllic setting on the coast, where she'd had a scrummy dinner and some wine before moving to the bar and starting conversation with the stud –a super stud as it turned out! After a number of grappas they had sung their way, arm in arm, to her hotel and enjoyed an outrageously brilliant sexual romp that she would remember with joy for the rest of her life.

She was wrenched back to reality as Ollie informed her they were ready for Ty to interview the grape grower. Still feeling very hungover and disillusioned, she limped along behind Ollie with her trusty notebook in hand and told Ty to go for it. He did; and while it was a simple piece on what grapes required to grow well, how they were pruned, etc., Ty handled it very well and with his usual enthusiasm. Zoe was more than happy to sit on the sideline and take notes.

When the interview was over, Ty said his stomach felt as though his throat had been cut and could they stop for a sandwich, or something, on the way to the lavender farm.

Zoe realised she had not eaten and wondered if some food might make her feel any better … she felt like absolute shit! It was nearly midday so something to eat and then on to the lavender farm, maybe just for some preliminary shots and a recce for tomorrow.

As they drove slowly through the bountiful bucolic countryside, Zoe was remembering the conversation of the previous evening in the crowded, noisy restaurant, Rusticana. She wondered whether she had been empathetic enough with poor Terry. With the post-alcoholic misery she was suffering today, she was feeling guilty about her reaction to his secret.

She determined to give him a call when she got back to the city. Terry's lips had intrigued her as she listened to his tale. She'd been all ears, but her eyes had been fixated on those sensual lips as she'd imagined them massaging her own in a prelude to sex. All of which was not destined to happen. What the fuck was she, Mother fucking Theresa?

She mulled over what would happen given that he was determined to stay here and continue to work as a farmer. How would he ever be accepted? How did he even begin to think he'd be accepted in this grass roots environment when he became a female but remained with his wife and children? The whole scenario was just too bizarre, even for Zoe who was pretty sure she'd seen it all. How would those kids go at school? They'd cop a whole load of crap from the other kids that was for certain. Just thinking about Terry and his future was playing havoc with her hangover.

Real life was so much more interesting than reality TV, she concluded as she closed her eyes for a few minutes, before they pulled up outside a local café. They piled out to eat and drink coffee and in Zoe's case, a lot of coffee.

The lavender farm was a stunning setting of undulating fields filled with the silvery deep green bush under the billowing mauve flowers. He could have been anywhere in Provence thought Ollie as he waxed lyrical once more. Behind the lavender fields was a deep purple mountain range, it really was an operator's heaven.

Zoe told Ty not to bother with a shirt change as Ollie would focus on set up shots of the sun playing brilliantly across the lavender bushes as they swayed to the caress of a northerly breeze. It was a truly sublime setting.

"Get it while you can," was the old TV adage that meant while the weather holds, you shoot the shit out of the scene, because you never knew what tomorrow's weather would hold.

The lavender farmers were an enterprising, retired couple from the city who'd created their personal haven – a farm that required minimal attention. There was a two bedroom B&B at the main house alongside a small retail outlet where they marketed their wares. This created a decent income and research and development for future products meant they wrote off a great deal of tax dollars on overseas travel to connect with other farmers of their ilk.

Zoe enquired after the owners at the shop. They were in town and not due to return till late afternoon. That did not faze her as the interview was organised for the following day. She and Ty were amazed at the range of cosmetic and therapeutic products on sale. Lavender was obviously a most versatile product.

Outside the shop, they discussed what they would do the next day and headed for a seat under a large, shady tree. Zoe was feeling slightly better, but she was a definite alcohol free zone this evening.

With enough shots, the indefatigable cameraman joined the other members of the team and they headed back to the hotel. There was enough time for a relax before dinner and so Ty donned his running gear and headed out for a 10km run around town and the adjacent hills. It was his first run in four days and he relished the anabolic rush he achieved running.

As he ran he reflected on the last few days and how much he loved the whole experience, so far. He recognised there could be a great career ahead if these last days were any indication. He found working the camera was easy and Ollie had been as helpful as Zoe. He had established a reciprocal love affair with the lenses. He valued the tuition someone like Zoe offered and wondered where it would lead once they returned to the city.

Back at the spaciously laid out hotel, Zoe was hiding under an umbrella, by the pool.

Ty joined her, claiming one of the timber poolside chairs. "Can I interrupt you?" Zoe opened her eyes and managed a half-hearted nod.

"Just wondering what's on for tonight and is it the usual kick-off time in the morning?"

She squinted as she looked at him. "Me, I'm outta town tonight – meaning I am dead, so you and Ollie do whatever you want. I need bed and liquids. Anything but booze. And yep, same time tomorrow morning." She started to lift out of her chair. "Ty, you're doing really well and thanks for your effort. Got a minute?"

"Sure, anything Zoe. What's up?"

"Nothing really, but I am curious to know what you want to do with this career of yours – we … I know so little about you. Where do you come from? I know your CV said a large country property … mainly beef cattle, but what are your parents like? How many siblings do you have?" She was pulling herself round to face him.

"Where to start?" he blushed at her interest, knowing what he said would undoubtedly go straight back to Phil Watts. "In all honesty, my folks adopted me as a baby," he began, with eyes downcast and furrowed brow, "…and I love them. I've known nothing else but their love. We lived on a huge property, a long way from here. Tell you the truth Zoe, I've had a really good 22 or so years. Jonathon and Penny, my Mum and Dad, have two natural sons also. Funny, isn't it, after they got me they threw two of their own, as Dad puts it." He laughed at his father's saying.

"Growing up on the property was basic, but we're old stock and there are certain rules one had to adhere to, and we did …" He was now sitting very correctly and the frown lines disappeared from his wide forehead as he continued, "We children had a governess for our early education and were then sent to boarding school at 12 – no options there. I didn't like the five years I put in there but it primed me for Uni and as you know from my CV, I'm really just out of Uni. I did well in the communications courses I took and so here I am … back in the country … and I'm really loving the experience too!" he concluded as he smiled at Zoe in the chair next to him.

"So, there you go …" Zoe started to rise as she spoke, "Thanks for that. Sure we'll find out more about each other as we travel along. Just a word from me to you – for what it's worth. You can have a big career with this lot, given your natural talent and your connections. Like having the BIG boss as a family friend is huge. So let me say this. Don't fuck it up with too much boozing and womanizing and just keep your ego in check … and the world's your oyster, buddy." With that piece of profundity, she departed.

Ty decided he'd go on the pussy prowl as he called it, got extremely drunk and told anyone who would listen that he was a TV star from the city … and yes, he scored a rough tart, but who cares? She was an enthusiastic fuck and that was all he wanted. He crawled back to the hotel at 2am and was up, dressed and smiling at 7am, which was call time. You can only keep that sort of pace at 22!

The news was not good at the lavender farm. The owners had been given bad news in town and had left to go to the aid of a sick relative.

"Damn it all!" Zoe cursed as she walked back from the lavender shop. At least she could be grateful this had not happened yesterday when her après alcoholic state would have made decision making difficult!

In a huddle, Zoe suggested they head back to town. "So, I'll call Phil and let her know the news. What I think we should do is get some extra pieces to camera that can be playing as intros to your interviews, Ty." She looked at him but went on without waiting for either his approval or agreement. "Given we don't know how they'll use you or the material back at the Game, let's get these stand-ups and walks, so we have them on hand, in case. Maybe some voxpops with the locals would work too."

As they started to drive once more, Ty asked rather shyly from the rear seat, "What's a voxpop?"

"Yep, should have told you. It's where you ask people their thoughts or opinions and they give 'em. Vox is from the Latin meaning voice while pop is an abbreviation for population … so, voice of the people. Got it?"

Ty was appeased and they headed to where they established the best coffee spot in town was and applied themselves to coffee and cake while Zoe spoke with Phil. With Phil's approval, they followed through on Zoe's plan. As they went to various locations that would suit each individual story, Zoe busily wrote the script. Ty read and memorised his lines and at the right moment Ollie captured each stand-up.

Ty had embraced a huge learning curve over the past four days and he was handling the camera brilliantly and delivering his lines with just the right amount of calm and conviction. He knew he was on his way.

The four days of concentrated shooting was declared a wrap by the producer, which meant the shoot was over and it was time to head in the direction of the nearest bar. TV crews had a knack for finding the best bars and best coffee places, in any town, anywhere. It was a natural and God given talent and this tired, talented crew of three were no different.

Tomorrow, they would return to the city and a totally different environment. For tonight however, they celebrate and talk shit. And why not?

CHAPTER 8

Ty the Unknown Becomes Known – The Celebrity Dinner Party

It was business as usual back at the studio whilst Ty was on location and creating a future with his first four stories. The buzz was out around the Game's office already that he WAS a talent. Phil was excited and felt that if he really lived up to the buzz he may be able to ease Evan's workload. In reality, how much say did she have in this option? The driving force was coming from the despot, Nigel Herbert-Flyson and if there was one thing she knew after so many years, Nige would not let sentimentality over his pseudo nephew interfere with ratings and profit – that had to be a major indicator of what Nige's gut was saying about the kid.

Meanwhile, Evan's request to Ted in Security to find out more about Ty Barnaby and his sudden appearance at the network had been met with silence. He called Ted to offer a gentle reminder that he was waiting for a response, which Ted had averred would be prompt.

It was Monday and Evan would usually have been taking care of business at the restaurant. Working from his home office he'd already appraised the four trading periods at Mangereire for the previous weekend and the place was heaving. As he enjoyed his second coffee he allowed himself a rather smug little smile, he was more than happy with the preliminary profit the software system showed.

Today was personal time and he was accompanying Lex to an appointment with her gyno, Dr Francis (call me Frank) Davidson. Lex was apprehensive. Blood in her urine had precipitated tests with her local doctor, Danny Levine. He had not appeared concerned by the results, but as both Lex and Evan still wanted clearer answers, they were making the visit to Frank who she trusted as a consummate professional after he had delivered their three children.

Eventually, they were shown into Frank's room where he welcomed them warmly and reassuringly. He was forty-five minutes late and Evan wondered how doctors got away with this tardiness – try that on in the restaurant game and watch the fireworks as customers go nuts waiting for their table or meals!

After enquiring about their general health, Frank got straight to business saying, "Lex, you have what is called Haematuria or simply put, blood in the urine. Basically it's a urinary tract infection. I can give you antibiotics if you like, or you can dose up with huge amounts of vitamin C which will flush it out. It's up to you. Either way, you must drink at least 1-2 litres a day of pure water – filtered tap water is fine."

Lex was relieved, but felt a little embarrassed at taking up Frank's time. He brushed the apology off, quite unperturbed; payment would still be added to the Hawaii holiday fund for the family this Christmas, he thought with alacrity!

With the weight of worry lifted from their shoulders, they walked elatedly to the car, and with a loving glance they suggested simultaneously that a nice little lunch was the order of the day. These moments were rare and while they drove to their local Thai, Evan went over his TO DO list.

That damn book! I need to call the publisher and the radio station and get them off my back. A weekly radio show, just one hour a week they said convincingly but Evan was more than aware that producing one hour of radio would mean one day out of his week. Seb was a major concern and he wanted to spend more time with him. The appointment with Lew Farnshaw was set for next week, as was the belated birthday dinner for Simon. Still unresolved, was the issue of the advertorial content management were trying to force into his show and he needed to call Phil to sort out how they would approach this disagreement with the suits.

Lex was relaxed and they settled into some fresh prawn rolls, the ubiquitous fish cakes with a green fish curry and steamed jasmine rice to follow. Evan was as relaxed as he would allow himself as they toasted each other with a chilled, crisp Pinot Grigio.

In such an incestuous environment as existed in the TV industry, it was near impossible to keep a secret but Simon had achieved the virtually impossible. He had not disclosed to anyone what he was doing for his birthday celebration. He'd surprised himself by taking up the offer of dinner with Phillip Williamson, the network PR guru. During some of the recent minor dramas on the Game, Phillip had spent time with Simon, as Evan seemed perpetually preoccupied. Simon was there for Evan and always had his back covered – a relationship that Phillip envied.

Phillip had recently become aware that Simon had joined the Rory Overham contingent (every member of which was as camp as the proverbial row of tents) for dinner and this information had planted a seed of hope in Phillip's thoughts. Certainly, there was no overt indication that Simon might be interested in his attentions when they spoke, in fact it seemed that all Simon did was work. He had no apparent social life and definitely no wife or girlfriend and had laughingly told Phillip he was married to his job. Phillip contemplated how many yet-to-come-out gays he'd known over his extensive career that used exactly this means of shrouding their true sexual proclivities.

The birthday dinner had been a huge success in Phillip's smitten eyes. Initially, he was surprised that Simon had accepted his invitation. Phillip had ticked the first box towards love or casual lust – he would follow whichever course was laid by the fates in terms of the potentialities of the situation.

Phillip had booked his usual table at a very intimate and exclusive restaurant which would afford him the privacy he wanted on this first outing with Simon. He hoped it would be the first of many and even allowed himself to fantasise that this may even become their special place. The dapper PR man was not fazed by the age difference and neither was Simon, it seemed to Phillip.

After settling comfortably into the banquette with their drinks, menu and wine choice were the immediate topic of conversation. Simon was impressed with Phillip's culinary acumen and so the dinner choices were made promptly along with a nice little bottle of Sancerre. Simon was not a big drinker but considering this was a celebration and in his honour, he thanked Phillip for selecting this expensive specialty French white from the Loire Valley.

Conversation flowed easily and with much gusto while skirting around likes and dislikes. Simon was no match for Phillip's worldly sophistication as his single venture overseas had been to the US (which locale one may refer to as gauche, but never sophisticated), whilst Phillip headed back to Europe at every available opportunity. He suggested to Simon that he would be pleased to show him around Europe when the time was right.

"I've always wanted to go to France – I love French food and the French accent ..." Simon admitted, "...I guess you speak French?"

"Only enough to get by ... and just like you – I have always adored France and French men too. I do adore them."

There was a pregnant pause. It was the first time that any Gay inference had been made by Phillip and he judged the much younger chef's reaction. Quickly recovering, Phillip added, "...and well, you can't help but notice how absolutely beautiful French women are."

The newly 29-year-old chef smiled demurely.

"Well, as you know, I've never been there so I only know from French people I've worked with. Phillip, can I ask you a personal question?" Simon hesitated as he watched Phillip's face to gauge his reaction. Phillip lifted his bright hazel eyes from his wine glass and smiled invitingly.

"Have you always been gay? Did you ever date women?"

At last it's on the table, thought Phillip. It was always an awkward moment and not unlike saying you love someone for the first time. The one who confessed such love first was always the most vulnerable. The elephant in the room was to be discussed, at last.

"Seriously, from the get go Simon, I was always into men. Never even took a girl out to the movies or any of that stuff. I got hounded at school, especially high school.

It became very obvious to all around me that I did not have a girlfriend and nor was I looking for one." Phillip's eyes hardened. Of course, his natural reaction was to ask Simon about his love life; he baulked knowing it may be too early in their friendship and might threaten Simon.

He was right, as Simon was still listening and was very happy to move back to travel again, leaving his personal life out of any discussion. He appreciated all Phillip shared of the marvels he'd experienced during his travels. It prompted the industrious chef to admit to himself that it was about time to re-invent his life – time to start living.

Sure, he had the money because he never went anywhere or did anything and he liked Phillip, with his easy going attitude and expansive knowledge. Perhaps, it was time to seriously think about some travel with Phillip? He had to admit, he was really enjoying his evening with this erudite and charming man.

Dinner finished and they departed unnoticed, or so they thought! Neither of them had noticed Phoebe Strong, network saleswoman extraordinaire in a huddle with a group of clients in a private room, but she had definitely noticed them.

Phillip drove Simon home. He got out of his sports car to say goodnight and to once more wish Simon a happy birthday. Simon went to shake hands and Phillip took Simon's hand as he pulled them into a man hug. With their hands still gripped and their free arms wrapped around each other, Simon still did not pull away or resist. They separated and Phillip leaned in to his dinner companion to plant a kiss on his cheek.

Again, Simon did not resist.

Stop now! Leave it here! Don't go any further! Warning bells were exploding in the older man's head. He moved slowly away from Simon and their hands dropped. Quickly and without any embarrassment, they agreed to meet for dinner at Phillip's large apartment the following week. They shared a laugh when Phillip assured Simon that although he was no cook, he was sure he could rustle something up. Phillip wisely resisted suggesting to the apparently eager younger man to bring a toothbrush.

All in good time.

Tuesday's shoot had gone really well and Evan had come to terms with Ty being on set to introduce his segments live. One today and one tomorrow, which would be the mushroom segment, and he was looking forward to presenting the mushroom terrine which had been incredibly popular at the restaurant, the trusted barometer for any dish to appear on the Game. With the required number of segments for the day completed, he was in the green room making ready to go home.

Phil gave her inimitable entrance rap and entered. He and PT were just finishing up on fan mail; sometime back, he'd agreed to be auctioned at a huge charity auction – he was waiting to hear what had happened. He would cook dinner for six at the lucky winner's home; he'd done this on previous instances with no problems and shitloads of great publicity.

211

"Can you make a quick meeting with Nige and Phoebe tomorrow evening after we wrap for the week?"

He looked up at Phil, "What for? Are they ready to talk about the advertorials, or has something else come up?" He pulled off his shirt as he considered the Wednesday night meeting.

"Yep, advertorials." Phil reached for her plait as she grabbed a chair. Evan stopped her, "I gotta go. Lex is waiting for me. We've got a real problem with Seb and I need to be there. We can catch up tomorrow between segments and nut out a plan. Okay?" He disappeared and she was left there with PT. Phil disappeared not bothering with good night wishes to the ever faithful Joanna.

Evan got a call from Ted as he was driving home suggesting they get together as soon as possible. "I think you'll find what I've uncovered very interesting Mr Pet … Evan." Evan was anxious for this information and hoped it would help them with the advertorial problem, with prescience he knew that somehow Ty and the advertorials were in collusion.

He had no idea of the bombshell Ted would launch tomorrow morning, but they would be meeting very early.

The mobile rang once more and he pressed for speaker as he heard Phillip Williamson saying hello, "That celebrity dinner gig has come in, Evan. On Saturday night at that charity function, you went for twenty-one grand. Wow, Evan – an all-time record they say! Good for you – you Star, you!"

"Wow ... awesome, Phillip. When is the dinner ... any suggested dates?" He panicked a little as he spoke because he really had no idea when he was going to fit this one on his agenda.

"No dates yet, Chef. I'll get something going during the week and email it through to PT. She'll take care of it for you. Okay?"

That was that. Another personal appearance where the restaurant would organise the food. He'd take a waiter from the restaurant along also, everything would be sorted and it would be fine. He took a deep breath and turned on his music as he eased back into his driving seat.

No more phone calls, please.

Evan sat hunched over a bowl of Shepherd's Pie with Lex snuggled beside him. The TV was on but talking to itself as the two lovers ran through their own thoughts, both tired and apprehensive.

Finally, Lex spoke, "Is it us? Have we messed up with Seb? Do you think it's us, Evan?"

He looked back at her in perplexity, "Maybe, Lex. But how? Where did we fuck up, Lex?" She stared at him in shock – it was not like him to cuss like that. Obviously, he was just as confused and concerned as she was.

"I don't know hon, I just don't know. He was such a happy kid and now, these last few months ... hell to live with ... no communication ... he only talks at all to me when he's forced to ... and I know he's no more forthcoming with you." As she spoke, her eyes welled with reluctant tears and she hastily grabbed her husband's hand.

She hesitantly mumbled, "Do you think it could be…" she looked at the TV screen but heard nothing as she was overwhelmed by her thoughts. Could she say it to him? "…do you think he could be on drugs?"

He took his hand from hers and wrapped both arms around her drooped shoulders pulling her tightly to him. It was an intimacy that said I love you and somehow, whatever happens, we'll get through this together. This intimate cuddle lasted until they both looked into each other's eyes with the recognition of not knowing. They simply did not know. God damn it all.

Neither Evan nor Lex had any notion of what drugs they might be contemplating. Evan accused himself of ignorance as he floundered through a restless night with Lex's gentle breathing lulling him to some degree of relaxation that he needed desperately.

The alarm shattered the peace of early morning and they wrapped their arms around each other, resisting the order to get out of their bed and face whatever followed. As Evan showered and shaved, Lex went down to make coffee. She looked at the microwave clock. It was only 5.30am. Why on earth was she up? Because Evan was up, that's why. He rushed through the kitchen and grabbed his insulated coffee mug and departed with a swift kiss.

What's his hurry, she wondered as she strolled back to bed.

Evan was first to arrive at the small, awakening café and ordered himself a black coffee. Ted soon followed, looking bleary eyed and flushed.

"Mornin', Evan." He sat down with a large manila envelope in his right hand which he placed on the table in front of Evan. He called the waiter over and ordered coffee. "You need to look at that. It's in your hands now and I have never seen it. Do NOT ask where or how I got this, but the guy who got it from the government department owed me big time and he's come up with the goods."

Evan opened the envelope tentatively and pulled out the official looking documentation. It was the details of Ty's birth parents. "Holy shit!" he exclaimed so loudly that the other patrons were staring in his direction.

He dipped his head and read through the document once more. He could not believe what he was reading. It certainly explained Ty's mercurial rise in the cut-throat competitiveness of television. Now that he had the information, he did not know what to do with it. He was astounded at what he'd read and needed some time to decide with whom he should share this shocking information.

They finished their coffees in disjointed and hesitant conversation, carefully avoiding any further mention of the contents of that envelope. Evan paid and they departed separately.

Evan put a call through to Phil on the way to the studio and asked her to meet him urgently in his green room in fifteen minutes. Phil was never late, for anything.

As soon as Phil arrived, Evan dismissed PT on a mission to locate Simon regarding a minor recipe change. As soon as PT had closed the door, Evan thrust the manila envelope in to Phil's hands demanding, "Read this!"

She quickly opened the governmental manila envelope and withdrew the documents. The top one appeared to be a birth certificate for one Tyrone Nigel Strong, son of Phoebe Narelle Strong. Father, Nigel Herbert-Flyson. Tyrone was given his mother's surname. Why?

Phil dropped the papers in utter shock. She looked with astonished disbelief at Evan who stared blankly back. A pin drop would have sounded like thunder in that instant.

"Well, fuck me!" Phil whispered. It was a startling discovery. Instantly, Phil knew precisely what to do with this explosive piece of information and it made perfect sense why Ty had managed such a high level entry at Channel 3.

Phil spoke again, "Evan, what are we going to do with this? Have you thought? I'm gobsmacked! I really want to think this shit through. That sneaky, fucking prick." She was, of course, referring to Nigel Herbert-Flyson, CEO of the Network. She wondered if Lynette, Nige's wife knew about any of this. She considered, and guessed the wife of forty-four years didn't but then Lynette was long-suffering and perhaps she did.

"You know, we have a huge shoot today and then the meeting with Nige and Phoebe this afternoon about the fucking advertorials. Let's get on with it and when we have time, think about what we can do now we know Ty's background." She stood and grabbed her plait as she headed for the door, passing PT on the way.

PT handed Evan the recipe with a note from Simon about the queried ingredient which he perused and nodded over. She also handed him a copy of the email from Phillip Williamson about the upcoming dinner for the society doyen who had outbid the competition at the recent charity auction.

The filthy rich woman was one Dottaya Bronstein. "See what you can find out about this woman please, PT."

He returned the email back to PT and rose to head for make-up and another dose of Marj – "Marjorie, please."

He knew he had to lose the preoccupation with the newly divulged information and hype himself in preparedness for an intensive day's shooting. He was a professional; he had to forget about what was going on around him and find that luminous personality with the famous flashing smile and killer wink.

In the studio, the predictable controlled mayhem was well underway. Simon was smiling confidently as he watched his friend and boss approach. They high fived and roughly hugged each other as Evan asked if they were cool for today's shoot.

"Of course!" was Simon's calm response, as always.

Simon had the prepared ingredients waiting on the bench, which would momentarily be flooded with light. First up today was a Jerusalem Artichoke Saffron Velouté. The hero shot of the soup was beside the set and the whipped cream that would sit on top sat beside it.

The day was up and running. Evan had retrieved that famous smile as the cameras began to roll.

"Hi there, and welcome to the Game! Hey, are you game for Jerusalem Artichoke Soup? Actually, it's a velouté … a velvet soup and I'm going to show you a really expensive spice. Can I tell you that one good pinch of it could buy a small diamond! Sooo expensive right – are you ready? John Smithton is here today. Sherries? Really? Let's see what he's up to."

Phil's phone buzzed as she watched on; it was Phoebe Strong from Sales (and she now knew what else, Phil thought with malicious glee). She moved out of the studio to take the call.

The advertorial showdown had been postponed till next week which was more than fine by Phil as it allowed her more time to think and plan. She sent a text to PT to make the appropriate change in Evan's diary.

Ah yes! There were interesting times ahead!

It was Saturday night and time for the $21,000 society dinner that Evan would cook for the esteemed Dottaya Bronstein. It was to take place at her mansion in a wealthy bayside city suburb. The mansion did not disappoint as

Evan drove slowly up the tree lined sweeping drive to the side of the house, where he had been directed there would be direct access to the kitchen.

The mansion was enormous and Evan wondered how many people lived in it. He guessed with a degree of irony that no matter how many inhabitants, there would be at least twice as many menials catering to each and every whim.

The side door to the mansion was open as he pulled up. A maid greeted him briskly and indicated for them to enter. The waiter chosen to accompany Evan was quick off the mark and grabbed a box of utensils. Evan followed him through the scullery to a huge kitchen equipped as well as one might expect in any up-market eatery. The car was unloaded and Evan was instructed to move the vehicle to another area so it was not visible from the grounds. Strange, he thought – such was the lifestyle of the rich and famous.

At this stage he had not met Mrs Bronstein – he soon would.

PT had carried out her research in usual explicit fashion and discovered that Mrs Dottaya Bronstein's parents had escaped Hungary during the Revolution in the mid-20th century. They had been an aristocratic family and Dottaya was born a few years after their arrival. With both parents dead she now claimed the title of Countess. Most local society folk thought it was all bullshit, but there were those, as always, that liked the idea of hobnobbing with pretentious people who carried obscure titles.

Her background revealed that the demised parents had owned a large department store in the capital city of Hungary. The rumour mill also had it that by the time they arrived here, they were penniless, but fought their way valiantly back to wealth through tailoring.

There were also other rumours that claimed the source of their immense wealth was heirloom jewellery "spirited" from the old country.

Regardless of earlier events, it was accepted by all that Dottaya had inherited extremely well and married an even wealthier Mr Bronstein, a property developer and family friend. In this part of the city it was known as a "good match" and two children followed closely. The couple were reportedly happy, according to the social pages of the media machine.

Mrs Bronstein was highly visible on the social scene and considered herself to be a significant philanthropist. She also had a reputation for being "edgy". Evan thought about this descriptor but could not come up with a concept for what it might mean. In the photos that PT had collated she appeared to be just another gaudy, flamboyant socialite whose age might be anything from mid-forties to late-sixties, depending on how skilful the scalpel of her plastic surgeon had been.

Evan was about to discover exactly what the descriptor meant.

He was peeling the tomatoes that would be used as the base for the salad course when the double doors leading to the kitchen swung open and a vision in jade green entered.

Mrs Bronstein was in the building! Well, in the kitchen, anyway.

The celebrity chef did a double take as she seductively swivelled her hips in a casual but defined saunter across the kitchen. Dammit, she certainly must have a great surgeon! She had been poured into her gown (Ralph Lauren darhlink, naturally!) that highlighted her curves and allowed her copious bosom to be flourished.

She offered a silky hand to Evan which he shook gently – how soft yet firm her hand was. The ostentatious diamond and pearl ring left an impression on Evan's fingers. Still holding her hand, he asked, "How do you do, Mrs Bronstein?" – and granted her his most gracious smile.

"I am very well, thank you Chef Pettersen. Good of you to come so quickly, after I paid all those thousands for you. It will be worth it, I assume?" There was a hint of sarcasm in her tone and Evan had to pull his fingers away, as she had them clasped quite tightly still.

"It will be, Mrs Bronstein – may I call you Dottie?" he enquired politely.

"Absolutely not!" and her capped teeth smile disappeared. "You may call me Mrs Bronstein – or Countess, but preferably the former tonight. This is hardly a State function!"

221

Mrs Bronstein quizzed him about the rest of the menu and he walked her through the dishes assuring her that he was most conversant with the menu she had requested.

When the Chocolate Marquise was shown to her, she swooned. She was overjoyed … until she saw the miniature pansies in the box with the rich chocolate dessert.

"What are those?" she demanded pointing to the fresh flowers.

He picked up the order form and showed it to her. "They are what you ordered when you placed your menu with us. They are to be scattered around the marquise."

"Not at all," she declared in her lightly accented voice. "I would never order trash like that on a dessert like this – violets perhaps, but certainly never pansies. Get violets, now." She moved away from the dessert in dismissal.

"That's not possible, Mrs Bronstein."

"What do you mean, not possible? Your impertinence is not acceptable, Chef Pettersen. I demand you get my violets!"

He was in a real pickle here and he knew it. He turned to her once more, gathering as much charm as he could muster, and engaging his best smile as he said, "I am sorry, it is simply impossible to get fresh ones, Mrs Bronstein. I can try to get hold of some crystallised ones from my restaurant, but that's all I can do." He rang the restaurant and told them to taxi the crystallized violets pronto to the mansion.

She breathed in deeply saying, "I have a proposition for you, Chef." She lifted her magnificent bosom to expand it even further. With the palms of her hands and in a downward motion, she smoothed non-existent wrinkles from her form hugging gown by brushing them toward her groin. She moved closer.

Oh hell, thought Evan, shades of Felicity the Feline. What have I done to encourage this, and what a turnaround from the demanding petulance of a minute ago?

However, what she said next came as a surprise to an already bewildered and bemused celeb chef.

"I have been speaking with Mr Bronstein and we would like you to come into partnership with us in a chain of restaurants to be named in your honour. We thought Pettersen's Palace in the first instance, but perhaps that is a little old fashioned, these days. What about Pettersen's Place?"

Evan was trying to come to terms with whether she could, in fact, be serious.

"What makes you think I would want to do that, Mrs Bronstein?"

"Why not? We have the capital and you have the name – it will be perfect. Our lawyer has mapped out an agreement and it will be sent to you later this evening. Perfect! No?"

"No, not perfect, Mrs Bronstein. I have no intention of going into business with complete strangers." He was very clear on that.

"Chef, please listen …" She moved towards him and he was forced to step back. At that moment the waiter appeared and Evan sent him straight back to the dining room with instructions to make sure all was set for the evening.

"Now, back to business. We must do this; it will make us all a great deal of money. You will find the business plan with the documents that are sent to you. Just give me some indication of your interest, Chef Pettersen." She was persistent; he had to give her that!

"What sort of cuisine do you envisage, Mrs Bronstein?" Evan asked to placate the forceful dame and give himself a little thinking space.

Her answer was well prepared and she described a menu not unlike what Evan had successfully created for Mangereire. She further explained that Mr Bronstein and she had visited the popular restaurant on a number of occasions and loved what he did; and this was the reason that they had come up with the grand plan. She absolutely adored the simple style of French Provincial. The accountants have prepared estimates on profits and profit splits and all this was laid out clearly in the documentation.

"And Evan … it will be so lovely to get to know you better. Don't you think?" She stepped in very close before stepping back at a knock on the back door.

"Excuse me," Evan said with some relief as he turned to the door which was being opened cautiously by someone enquiring, "Hello … anybody there?"

It was the cabbie with the crystallised violets and Evan doubted that he'd ever been so happy to see either crystallised violets or a cabbie before!

"Look Mrs Bronstein, I'll look at this proposition and see what my thoughts are … it's impossible for me to say yes or no on the spot like this. I'm sure you understand. Now, I really have to get on with your dinner."

She departed, espousing her last words of wisdom, "You must not let the opportunity of a lifetime escape!"

The waiter returned from the dining area to inform Evan that all was set and that the Bronstein sommelier would be pouring the wines and calling the shots. Lifestyles of the rich and famous!

The canapés were prepared and awaiting pre-entrance garnishing. The pomegranate and goats curd salad was to follow and Evan started on his signature pomegranate molasses dressing.

The duck breast with stewed cabbage was the order for the main course, a recipe for which had been sent to Evan and followed to the letter.

Evan had convinced himself he was too young to know what the next course was all about. However, the Bronstein sommelier graced him with an explanation. Sobranie Black Russian and Cocktail cigarettes and lemon sorbet with wafer biscuits were apparently a respected and ancient tradition of the old families and served as a major break after the main course. Evan had supplied the sorbet while the household had supplied the colourful cigarettes. He could not help thinking the exercise incredibly vulgar.

There was a flurry of excitement as the Bronstein's man entered the kitchen with a bottle of wine with a fabulous golden hue. He demanded to know how long the dessert would be as he wished to serve the special wine. Evan asked the name of the wine.

The haughty houseman slowly moved the label toward Evan and while the significance was lost on him he asked for the bottle or label to take with him for Smithton to view. The Bronstein man looked down his nose at Evan as he explained that Mr Bronstein would never allow an empty bottle to leave his home. Evan wondered what on earth that was about and reassured himself the sommelier at the restaurant would be able to give him an answer.

The sumptuous Chocolate Marquise looked delightful on the blue plates surrounded by the crystallised violets and would be served before petit fours. The end of the meal was nigh.

Coffee had been served and Evan was packing, ready to depart when a large envelope was delivered with a polite bow from the Bronstein man, along with a piece of paper with the name of the celebrated bottle of wine and a verbal message that Mrs Bronstein would be in touch.

He felt summarily dismissed – like some serf from a medieval castle. Who cared – he was satisfied that he had served a great dinner even though he was still coming to grips with the fact that rich people would spend that sort of money on a whimsy such as this evening and make outlandish proposals which, it appeared, he was expected to drop on one knee with gratitude and accept.

Evan had felt the meal the Bronsteins had ordered was far too rich and had wondered how they justified such extravagant dining on their Sabbath. Perhaps they weren't particularly devout, after all.

On the way home he received a text from Mrs Bronstein informing him that she would ring on Monday as she had something for him and he wondered what on earth it could possibly be. He would find out, all too soon.

All in all, he was left unimpressed with the Bronsteins and looked forward to his family day off tomorrow. He thought of Lex with anticipation, he always felt horny after a success and he was ready to jump Lex's bones – would she be receptive at this late time? He'd know soon enough.

CHAPTER 9

The Radio Show, The Publisher and The Advertorial Confrontation

After a rejuvenating Sunday at home relaxing with his beloved family, the famous chef, Evan Pettersen, was back at the office in his much awarded restaurant, Mangereire. He relived parts of his day off, after the successful and surprising celebrity chef dinner for the Bronsteins at their luxurious mansion.

He also relived parts of the conversations he'd shared with Lex yesterday in which they acknowledged how stressed they were about the impending visit to psychiatrist, Dr Lew Farnshaw, with Sebastian. While Lex and her husband were feeling all loved up after a very special sexual romp the previous evening, they were constantly beset with concern over the visit and the perceived problem that Seb was failing to deal with. He was increasingly and disturbingly quiet and no amount of coaxing helped him to interact with either parents or siblings. They had spent most of the day lounging around and cuddling, much to the embarrassment of the children.

Just lying around with Lex made him semi-hard and when she rolled over to put her head on his lap, he felt his cock engorge. Lex moved away saying laughingly that there'd been plenty enough last night and she was not up for an encore performance at the moment. And so, Evan returned to letting his mind wander, as opposed to his hands.

Evan contemplated the call that had come through from Mrs Bronstein as he was pulled up at the lights near the restaurant.

"Yes, Chef … it's Dottie. Thank you so very much for the fabulous work you did on Saturday night." She gushed, "I loved it all and so did my guests … and I want to see you to thank you personally."

Well, that's a bit of a change from "Call me Mrs Bronstein" on Saturday night when I asked to call her Dottie, thought Evan cynically!

"Kind of you to call, Mrs Bronstein."

"No, my dear, you must call me Dottie and I shall call you Evan. When can we have dinner?"

"You may call me Chef Pettersen. I assume that dinner is about your business proposal? Is that right?" He was trying to put her off, which he knew would be a challenge.

She rebuffed. "No … No Chef – let me call you Evan darhlink, please?" Evan noted how the accent became more pronounced as she put on her cutesy. "Tell me when to come meet you and where. I do have a little somethink for you."

"I'm not too sure this is a good idea, Mrs Bronstein." He stumbled over his words, knowing very well there was more intended than dinner and wondering what the "little somethink" might be. "I'm really busy right now with …"

She cut him off. "Don't be so silly and rude, darhlink. You can spare me an hour or two, one must eat! I will tell you … I will come to your famous restaurant. I read you work there, is that not so? I will be there on Thursday at 9pm, sharp." She hung up before he had any chance to respond. He tried to call back but her phone went straight to message bank.

Perhaps he should get his lawyer to go over this proposal.

The front of house team was setting up for lunch and in the kitchen pots were steaming, meat was browning for braising and chef was chopping leeks as he barked out orders over the musical hum of the food processors. Evan's world made sense again.

Evan returned to his office to find PT waiting. After the usual Monday morning greetings, she went for his coffee while reminding him, once again, that he was addicted to the stuff and needed to do something about that!

On his desk was a copy of an email response from the restaurant's sommelier regarding the special wine the Bronsteins had served with the Chocolate Marquise on

Saturday night. The memo explained that St Stephens Crown Tokaji 5 Puttonyos was a famous Hungarian wine from the Tokaj-Hegyalja region. This specialised wine was a sweetish one made from grapes that had the Noble Rot, which meant that the grape sugars had been concentrated by a fungus called botrytis cinerea. The wine was also known as the wine of kings and was highly sought after.

The description of the wine confused Evan further as it was quite beyond his understanding that a wine that was made from rotted grapes could be so famous and sought after. He considered this might be worthy of a segment for John Smithton in the future. While he was not a personal fan of the wine segment, he accepted that this may make an interesting story.

Hervé went on to say there had been instances of "identity theft" of famous wines in which the empty bottles had been refilled with a similar looking wine and sold at outrageously high prices and this was undoubtedly why the gentleman in question never released his empty bottles.

What the hell, he thought. At least I'll have something to talk with Mrs Bronstein about on Thursday night. What am I going to do about this proposal? What did she really want? People like Dottie Bronstein always wanted something when they said they had something for him; that much he was sure of.

The 98 emails that had arrived overnight included four from his publisher, Hermann Booth, asking him to get in touch – urgently! When coupled with the numerous text messages from Hermann, he knew it was something he had to stop pondering and procrastinating over – Hermann was added to today's "to do" list, in red ink!

He emailed his thanks to Hervé for the wine information and addressed a couple of more urgent emails which were mostly about TV stuff and … shit, there it was again, the radio program guy had flagged an email – again. He added his name to the "to do" list also – minus the red ink.

He then began his Monday morning debrief with PT regarding the week ahead. She reminded him, unnecessarily in this instance, of Seb's appointment on Thursday and Simon's belated birthday dinner, very necessary in this case, on Wednesday. He filled PT in on the Mrs Bronstein event and her coming to dinner on Thursday evening adding that it would be best if she blocked out table 28 which was situated safely in the middle of the restaurant.

Joanne Friberg, aka PT, handed her boss the recipes and schedules for this week's shoot. On top of this pile ad marked seriously in red, was an email from Phil Watts about a meeting tomorrow afternoon with Nige and Phoebe about their proposed advertorials for the Game.

Neither Evan nor Phil wanted these intrusions and they now had the information about why Ty had been introduced into the Game. They both felt quite smug at holding this trump bargaining card attained surreptitiously by Ted, the security guy. Phil would hold on to the information to be used as a last resort only – it was definitely below the belt stuff. She had another reason, which she held secret to herself. Phil was not above blackmail as she'd proved with Will Hambers, the Prick on Pins.

The Star told PT to call Phil and okay the meeting. He then put in a call to Simon.

"Got any problems for this week, Simon? Recipes … anything tricky?"

"Not really, boss…" Evan could hear his trusty deputy leafing through the recipes, "but maybe … look at that reduction sauce for the trout – cumin and red wine brown sauce is unusual for fish but with Rainbow Trout, it will be really good. Remember how popular it was at Mangereire?" Evan remembered and so why the panic?

"It's a lengthy segment. You've gotta skin the fish fillets … reduce the sauce, and pan fry the fillets. You need some patter. I'll put some notes together for you and give them to PT. Okay? Gotta go … another call coming in. See ya." Evan didn't get a chance to remind him of his delayed birthday dinner on Wednesday night.

"PT?" He looked around to find her.

"Yep."

"Remind Simon of dinner on Wednesday night … and can you email Lex to remind her too. I can't remember where we're going so can you put that into my reminders in my phone. Is it 8pm?"

"Sure is, Boss … and by the way Simon asked if he can bring a buddy … that okay?" PT looked across at Evan enquiringly.

Somewhat surprised, he asked PT if she knew who that buddy might be. When she replied that she had absolutely no idea, Evan shrugged and nodded in acquiescence. Typically, Simon would have been unaccompanied, married as he was to his job.

After the recipes for the show, he went through this week's specials for Mangereire.

One stand out recipe from one of his top apprentices caught his eye and he put it to the side to discuss with his head chef and the apprentice. Sea urchin was expensive and exacting technique was mandatory. Few restaurants offered it, but this recipe with the meat being used in a Japanese inspired warm, savoury custard was interesting to say the least. Evan encouraged suggestions from his staff and would cost out each recipe to establish the profit margin on the dish, which was essential to ensure the revenue kept rolling in and the consequent high profit amortised service costs. It also maintained the reputation of this very fine eatery.

A report of the restaurant's fiscal performance was next. Wow, what a great week it had been, yet again! Time for some bonuses he thought and placed a call to his accountant to discuss the bonuses and let him know he'd sent over the Bronstein proposal for his opinion. The accountant was unavailable but his assistant assured Evan that he would call back later that day.

As he ordered yet another coffee from PT, the clock ordered him to "frock up" for Showtime in the kitchen at Mangereire, and how he loved it.

With the outstanding recipe for the Sea Urchin Japanese Custard in hand, he paused to glance sideways at himself in the office door mirror, checked his dress, flashed his famous smile and grabbed his untouched coffee. He was headed for fun in the kitchen and the adrenaline had begun to pump through the celebrity chef's veins as he called for the apprentice responsible for the recipe.

Evan estimated the young apprentice to be about twenty. He sported sandy hair with blond eyebrows waxed to precarious shape. Evan wondered how long that waxing had taken as he shook the hand of Aaron Jepson who'd been apprenticed at the restaurant for a couple of years.

"Hey Aaron, this is a great recipe … have you tried it out yet?"

"Yes Chef, I have and the costings are spot on," he told his boss with bravado.

"What about production … and timing?"

"Chef, we can make twelve of them the first day to see how they go on the specials menu. I'll cook 'em off at around 11.30 and hold them in the bain-marie … and serve 'em with wasabi sauce. They can be done and ready to go." He certainly was cocky, which Evan always appreciated.

"All well and good ... but aren't you concerned about salmonella, holding them for two hours?" Evan frowned slightly as his eyes bored into Aaron. It was a legitimate concern with all seafood, and Evan was a thorough educator.

"Not in the bain-marie ... and the custards will have been cooked through." Aaron's former bravado dissipated and he shot a self-doubting glance to his immediate boss, the restaurant chef, who was taking part in the conversation.

He said, "Good point, Chef Pettersen. Aaron, I think we'd best be safe and cook to order. Have the sauce prepared – it'll hold. Have the urchin mixture done and the dariole mounds ready for cooking ... they'll only take ten minutes in a water bath ... especially if you're cooking off one at a time. If it looks as though you'll get a run on 'em ... cook off what you've got left and keep them. But only if they're really popular. Sea Urchin is too expensive to waste. Got it, Aaron?"

Aaron nodded enthusiastically and turned to go back to his section.

"Aaron?" Evan called. Aaron turned back to face the owner of the restaurant. "Thanks buddy. Great effort and keep it up. Want to come on the Game one day soon?"

The beaming smile assured Evan that was an affirmative and with that, Aaron dropped his head to hide the smile of self-achievement and embarrassment at being acknowledged by his BIG boss and hero so openly. He squared his shoulders and stepped jauntily back to his prep bench where he contemplated on his amazing day as he sliced the salad onions for lunch service.

Evan went with his head chef and talked briefly of Aaron's future, before taking his own instructions for today. While most people presumed it would be Evan calling the shots in the kitchen, he took whatever position his head chef placed him in. Rightly, Evan had established that there must be a full-time head chef that the kitchen staff knew, trusted and were willing to work for. This solidly sound arrangement made for a confident, well-honed staff and also let Evan off the hook when he was away on promotional commitments. It also contributed enormously in allowing the restaurant to operate as professionally and profitably as it did.

Evan had to admit that not being in the kitchen full-time robbed him of the control and timing that was essential to the smooth running of any kitchen but recognised that a star must pay a price. What a dream it was to have a kitchen that hummed in harmony – the normality of a kitchen at work usually appeared crazy to outsiders, it was something only a chef could understand and love. Today Evan was allocated to the sauces and plating on the pass. Usually the sauce would be the last item to be plated – usually, but not always.

When he was released from the kitchen, Evan did his habitual sweep of the restaurant to greet his clientele. That done, he returned to his office accompanied by a portion of the Sea Urchin Japanese Custard. Sales had been moderately successful on the first trial of this unusual dish at lunch service. He asked PT for a coffee and a sandwich to follow the custard. He was hungry.

The accountant had called back to okay a small number of bonuses and suggested a dollar value for the lot; he promptly passed this information over to PT who would get it to the bookkeeper. He then picked up his cell to call the publisher at Marquis, Hermann Booth.

"Don't tell me it's you … is that you Evan?" demanded an aggressive, gruff voice.

"Look … sorr…" was as far as Evan got.

"Is that right, you're fucking sorry after all these months of not being in touch. All I wanted to tell you is that I can make you a fucking fortune you son of a bitch and you've got the nerve to say you're fucking sorry. For two hunks of shit, I'd tell you to go stick your fucking head so far up your fucking arse you might start to see fucking daylight! But, I'm one of the good guys, so let's talk. I don't got much time."

Evan couldn't help but think that for a publisher he had an incredibly poor grasp of the English language and his PR skills were zilch. He considered hanging up, but in all fairness he had been quite remiss in not being in contact with his publisher. Especially when Hermann had already made him some substantial sums through the other books for Evan and the Game.

"Well, okay … what are your thoughts? I've got about 124 recipes of the 200 you want."

"Fuck that crap. I got a deal for you. I want ten books with thirty recipes in each; lots of images and it'll be called "Recipe Revival with Evan Pettersen". How's that grab you Chef?" Before Evan could attempt an answer, the immigrant German continued, "I don't want you to do a thing but go over the manuscript for each book – I'll send you the drafts. We'll do them in decades. Got it? Course you don't … 'cos I haven't told you!" It was as if he could see the confounded chef at the end of the line, looking particularly puzzled.

"See, the first one could be the Edwardian Age – 1900 to 1910. That was the age of romanticism and upstairs downstairs … an era of new and daring recipes hitting the tables. The young bucks with all the dough – the movers and shakers of their day. The next decade can be the war recipes from 1910 to 1920. Don't mention the Var!" he screamed with laughter at his own joke, before continuing, "You get it? You get it? Don't mention the Var … I'm German you know … well, we're used to this joke. Anyvay, you got no sense of humour."

Evan wondered how much more of his blustering publisher he could take in one phone call and the silence on the line must have alerted Hermann to this fact. "Hey, are you still there? You there?" he yelled down the phone.

"Yeah, yeah. Listen, I lost a great-grandfather to the Germans in France … so please, don't mention the Var, Hermann. I get what you want from me as far as the books go. Send me a new contract and overview. I'll sign the contract after my lawyer and accountant have had a squiz and we can get going. Change the dollars and we'll be good to go."

"Thank you Evan." The publisher was much more subdued and told Evan he would employ a group of home economists who specialised in recipe development to do the research and write the books.

Evan hung up then called the radio station to speak with the programmer, who was unavailable but whose voicemail assured Evan he would return the call. He picked up the past week's fan mail, PT's breakdown of the Facebook postings and perused her take on the Twitter messages received and sent. He sent a private blessing to his assistant whose grasp of social media had saved his arse time and again handling the load, not to mention the fan mail. Shit, it just goes on and on but it's just another part of being a Star!

Next he phoned Lex to see how her day was progressing. All okay, although she was dreading seeing Lew with Seb, no matter how crucial it was that they understand what was going on. She was excited about dinner with Simon and she, as much as Evan, was wondering who Simon would consider close enough to invite to the family dinner. Evan did not discuss the fact that Dottie Bronstein was joining him at the restaurant to discuss the proposal – he was stymied by what she had for him.

Next he called the restaurant chef to gauge his reaction to the Sea Urchin Japanese Custard and what he could do to boost sales – after all it was a good dish and

Aaron had done well. Evan wanted to nurture this young chef as his potential and enthusiasm reminded him of his own early days. After listening to his chef's comments he agreed and suggested fine tuning the seasoning which he would leave in Chef's capable hands.

Nearly 4.30pm and it was time to start thinking about heading back to the kitchen for evening service as the restaurant was well booked and then there would be the inevitable walk-ins to be juggled.

The restaurant extension rang and the restaurant manager let Evan know the radio guy was on the line. Okay, let's get this one over and done with, "It's Evan Pettersen … how are you Stephen?"

Stephen's voice was liquid and mellifluous. Evan knew his background as a huge radio personality, before buying into the radio network and becoming the program manager. Evan could listen to that voice forever and had done as a young fellow when the station had been his parents' favourite.

Evan could picture this charming man as he spoke with him – Stephen Johnstone was in his late fifties and his full head of hair was just beginning to grey. His face was virtually unlined, the only visible ones being around the dimples on both cheeks that demarked his frequent laughter. He was a happy and successful guy. Some of his more spiteful media competition rumoured that he'd been under the surgeon's knife but Evan gave no credence to the rumour.

Stephen had the good genes and positive outlook that enabled graceful aging, and having the millions he'd made through radio didn't hurt either. The station was undergoing a major overhaul and the new stars meant the station was experiencing a revival with substantially increased ratings and subsequently, swollen profitability.

Evan considered his reply to "ole velvet vocal chords" and resisted apologising after the reaction he got from Herman. "You know Stephen; I've got so much on my plate…" They both laughed in appreciation of one of Evan's better puns. "I just don't know where I'd find the time to juggle the show. I don't mean to string you along buddy, but what can I do?" Evan searched the ceiling for divine inspiration.

Stephen spoke as he contemplated options, "Well, I'm really disappointed Evan … we were so looking forward to working with you. Are you sure we can't meet up and maybe discuss alternatives?"

"Such as?" Evan sat up to concentrate.

"Knowing how busy you are, I had thought to have Jimmy Black front the show and you could make appearances with pertinent stuff you're interested in." Jimmy Black was a hack announcer who had been around the traps for years and had a gift for linking personalities in any show he worked on.

"So how does that work, Stephen?" Evan's interest spiked as he could easily get the material to talk about, after all he had a large range of experience and knowledge to call on.

"Simply put ... we would pre-record the show on a regular day each week. What we need is your name and the Mangereire name. Mostly, we would want recipes and we'd scrap the talk back idea ... and what else do you envision you'd like to contribute?"

"Honestly Stephen, I was thinking about doing nothing ... so, I'm a bit in the deep end here. Give me a few days to consult my team and I promise we'll talk on Friday."

He disconnected and immediately thought why not get Simon to do the radio show. He was more than capable. Why not start to promote this reliable and sincere young workhorse who had slaved with him for nearly a decade. Simon was very busy with work, frantic actually ... and what was the saying, "if you want something done, give it to a busy man"? Maybe, it was time to start building Simon's profile. Eventually, he may be able to take over from me, Evan hoped. I have to get outta there one day and today I would rather it was sooner than later!

What about Ty? Well, what about Ty – tomorrow night he, Phil, Nige and Phoebe would have it out about Ty. The night after, he would raise the radio program idea with Simon over dinner. Which led his musing back to who the hell Simon could be bringing to dinner?

Getting ready to head to the kitchen for service, he gave a passing glance to the emails, told PT it was time she was gone and donned his jacket and apron. The kitchen offered an invigorating three hours and Evan was energised as he headed in that direction.

All was quiet at the studio when Evan arrived next morning and he passed Simon offering a simple wave as he could see he was already up to his industrious elbows in it. Literally, as the major focus today was a sausage making segment and Simon was combining the ground meat content in the marinade. The black-haired chef nodded his head in recognition and bent back to the task at hand.

It was an hour before Phil Watts was due to make her usual Tuesday morning entrance with her generally anticipated imitation of a screaming banshee. Having made "the" appearance in which she impersonated the banshee with supreme dexterity, she was on her way to meet with Evan and plan their strategy for tonight's confrontation.

She stared down at Evan. "So, here's the deal." Phil was playing anxiously with her plait, as was to be expected, considering the enormity of the plot afoot. "We go in late. Okay? We'll listen to what they have to say. I can't imagine this advertorial crap can be about anything other than fucking dollars. If it's about Ty getting a foot in, he can do that well enough as a contributor. He did great stuff with those country segments."

She crossed her legs and sipped her tea as she looked at Evan for a reply. "Your call, Phil. I don't get what they're up to either. Crazy stuff!"

"We'll keep our little secret to ourselves." Evan had discovered that Ty Barnaby, the talent who'd been thrust upon them, was the illegitimate product of Nigel and

Phoebe. He'd been adopted and reared in the country. Was this spunky young man to be the replacement for Evan? How could they think that? He could burn water, for God's sake – but he and the camera lens together was an X-rated sex scene. HOT!

Phil had attempted to move the meeting to her office for a hometown advantage. It didn't happen; Nige was too much of an old pro to fall for that type of manoeuvre. The meeting would be held in the CEO's office on the second floor of the main office building. Phil's tactical late entry was designed to unnerve the boss who had a penchant for punctuality.

With the tactical play decided upon, the day's shoot got underway. It was a cool day which proceeded without hiccup until the very last segment. A technical glitch caused them to run on far later than planned. The gods had interceded on Phil's behalf, it would seem.

"It's about fucking time you got here. This meeting was scheduled for forty minutes ago. Where the fuck have you been goddamit? A man doesn't have all fucking night to wait around for the fucking pair of you!" He was fiddling with a Montblanc pen as Phoebe Strong looked on in silence.

Phil ignored Nige and sat down in front of his desk, leaving Nige still standing. "Keep your fucking hair on, Nige. Sit over there, Evan." Phil pointed to a chair close to her and next to Phoebe. Although Phil had been a little nervous this morning, a successful though tiring day's shooting had calmed her nerves and the plait hung limp. Unattended.

Phil and Nige went way back to the days when she was a kid brought into work by her all-powerful father who had been Nigel Herbert-Flyson's boss at that point in time.

"So what's this shit about advertorials, Nige? Surely, we make enough bucks for you as it is. Greed is a terrible thing you know, Nige. Dangerous – it brought down the Roman Empire, they say." She adjusted herself in her chair.

It was Phoebe who butted in with, "Oh, by the way, I saw Simon the other night at dinner. Nice company he keeps. Philip Williamson. They made a darling couple!" Her sarcasm could have stripped wallpaper.

Evan smiled benignly. "Yes, I know, I asked him to get some more stuff done for us on the PR scene. He said they had a good dinner. Did you enjoy yours, Phoebe?" That took the wind out of that bitch's sails, thought Evan. Not bad off the top of my head! Fascinating though and the plot thickens – wait till I tell Lex this one.

"Look, it's about trying to move things around on the Game. Six plus years of the same stuff, day in, day out. We need to shake things up," Nige said, as he squirmed unconvincingly. He was uncomfortable and his eyebrows kept lifting. I've got him on the ropes thought Phil who was an old hand at these TV land confrontations. What's he up to?

"Great, Nige, because we want some changes too. We're thinking of promoting Simon to do some cooking segments. The girls love him. We want to move the mix around and give Evan other things to do. And so, there really is no need to go down the advertorial line ... Is there Nige?"

Phoebe looked at Nige uncertainly. She adjusted the notebook on her lap and nearly dropped her mobile as she looked at the text covered screen. The near drop was not lost on Phil. Talk about sitting in the box seat – and Phil loved it, she knew she was going to win this one.

"I don't know about Simon ... he's your deputy, right, Evan?"

He looked at Nige innocuously as he said, "Sure is, Nige, and he's shaping up really well on screen. As Phil said, the girls love him. The Facebook and Twitter pages go crazy after his appearances. He's a natural." He looked to Phil who nodded her agreement. Nige looked at them both as he spoke. "So where do you want to use Ty Barnaby. I hear he's done very well so far. Correct?"

"Nige ... Ty as talent in a cooking show would make a great sports commentator. He's a nice kid, Nige – nice kid with a good talent, but he can't fucking peel a potato, let alone cook one. I took him on because you wanted me to, but we can't use him. You'll have to move him on. If you want more profit, move him out to sports, who can afford him. I really can't afford to carry him on the budget you've got me on." She turned her head to Evan and winked so Nige and Phoebe could not see.

Of course, Phil Watts, the enduring executive producer of the country's most successful and profitable cooking show had no idea of the grand plans that Nige and Phoebe had been plotting for their Clayton's son. Adopted, as Ty was, he had no knowledge that it was his birth parents sitting in this meeting with Phil and Evan. How could Phil and Evan guess that these two ex-lovers were planning to change the Game into a more informal chat show, with Ty as the host? Yes, there would be good cooking content, but more lifestyle and Ty would be perfect, or so his erstwhile parents believed.

Evan's contract would not be renewed at the end of the year.

As a consequence, Ty's profile would have to be given a phenomenal boost for him to take on the role. Appearing on the Game with its extraordinary popularity would be a very expedient way to build his profile. That and a shitload of public relations work from the network media machine would do it … or so they thought.

"So, here's the thing Phil…" Nige pointed the Montblanc at Phil as he frowned with a face lit up in a red flush of fury. "I want these fucking advertorials and I want fucking Ty to do them. YOU will make them happen and how the fuck come did I not know about you wanting to move things around on the Game?" He sat back feeling the power of the general who'd given a front line order.

"So, here's the thing Nige…" She moved forward on her chair and her plait was nowhere in sight.

"You can't tell me what to fucking do in my fucking show. So you had better take another fucking look at my fucking contract! What the fuck do you think you're trying to pull here? Tell me buddy and make it fucking good because I've had enough of this bullshit. Come fucking clean and tell me – what's it about?" She was stridently ferocious. "It's not about adver-fucking-torials is it? Why would you fuck with the Game when it's working so well for you and the network? What will the shareholders say when you start losing audience share … and PROFIT!" She was almost standing as a force to truly be reckoned with, which she was.

Evan contemplated what sort of lunacy had taken hold of Nige to mess with Phil, even if he was the CEO. Phil knew her stuff and had been around far too long to be intimidated and what's more, she could walk into any other network and start working tomorrow. A fact Nige knew only too well.

"What have you got to say? What?" Before he could answer, Phil stood and grabbed her notebook.

"Tell you what, buddy, why don't you have a think about what you want to do with my show? Put it on paper and have it on my desk by the end of the week. I'll look over it next weekend. Make sure you adjust the budget as well if you want these crazy moves and make it fucking good. Come on Chef – we're outta here. We've got eight hours of a fucking great TV show to shoot tomorrow and I'm fucking hungry." As she turned to leave she warned her theoretical boss, "If it ain't broke, don't fucking fix it!"

Nigel was confounded and couldn't believe he'd been upended; it was a very rare occurrence in his kingdom. "That went well," was all he managed as he looked to Phoebe, who had tears streaming down her cheeks.

Phil stormed away from the meeting with Nige and Phoebe. "Fucking little turd!" she spat out venomously as they waited for the elevator. Evan was profoundly puzzled as he contemplated that his was the only career at stake in this, the game of his life. He knew his confidante, Phil, and had learnt when a wise man kept his mouth shut in her presence. The meeting had established just how fickle was the light of a Star. He could be twisted and manoeuvred at their whim; he was no more than a pawn on this chessboard.

He was confused also about Simon and felt betrayed that he had not trusted Evan enough to say anything of Philip Williamson. He guessed that he'd find out soon enough and with tomorrow being another gruelling shoot, that was enough for now. He'd learnt the practice of thought compartmentalisation through Simon's mentoring with his Buddhism and meditation techniques.

Phil bolted to her car with not a word or gesture in Evan's direction.

Evan had no inkling of the surreptitious secret underlying Phil's behaviour toward Nige. It was a just reason, Phil considered, though its roots lay some three decades in the past. Ironically, Phil had been married at the time she made what she considered to be the greatest mistake of her life – a mistake that justified this love-hate relationship with Nigel Herbert-Flyson and allowed her to speak to Nige in a manner that would have any other subordinate fired on the spot.

The mistake was Leeanne and she was Nigel and Phil's daughter.

All was as usual the next day. Phil was in charge and ripping around the studio screaming to anyone who ventured too close, "Where the fucking hell is Mel?"

Melissa Goodman, the longstanding floor manager, better known as Mel or Oral Queen in recognition of her prowess and pleasure in oral sex, was the backbone of getting the show to air. Where was she? She had been more subdued than normal recently after an encounter with Big Will Hambers in the cool room and the tongue lashing she'd received from Phil.

Phil had called Bill Wiseman, the Games' director, who had organised a substitute floor manager within the hour. Still, it was not the same without Mel, she was integral to the "A team". Simon's prep was on set and the lights were bringing "sunshine" to the kitchen. Evan was licking his lips and preparing for his intro. He looked stunning in a light maroon, collarless shirt that hugged his chiselled torso and looked as gorgeous as ever.

The theme music engulfed the studio and the fill in counted Evan in after the clapper board had done its bit. First up this morning was a vegetarian dish based on pumpkin. The Asian aromas filled the studio and everyone was happy.

Everyone but Phil who was touchier than she'd been in years and sucking on that damn plait!

Evan arrived home and Lex was all ears as she listened to Evan and his vivid description of the day's shoot. While all had gone to schedule, Phil was not her usual buoyant self, which had meant he'd had to work a lot harder to bring the energy level up to that expected of the Game. That upbeat ambience was the signature of the best cooking show around.

The Pettersen family, minus Seb, was on its way to the restaurant and Charlotte and Sarah sat quietly in the back of the luxury car Evan drove. The girls, who had known Uncle Simon for years, were excited about the belated birthday dinner. Evan and Lex were disappointed, though not surprised, when Sebastian had refused to attend the dinner. He was as quiet as ever. Hopefully, tomorrow's session with the psychiatrist would sort out the problem with Seb.

Arriving at the suburban restaurant, Evan realised they were ten minutes late. Charlotte was taking longer to get ready these days and Evan accepted this as much as he hated being late for any appointment. After being greeted in a warm but non-sycophantic way, Evan's party was moved toward their table. Evan's smile became a somewhat strained one as he saw who Simon's guest was for this family celebration meal.

In deep conversation with the handsome young chef was none other than Phillip Williamson, the public relations specialist from the network. Simon was all smiles and looked positively exuberant.

Kisses and handshakes all round and introductions were superfluous except for Charlotte and Sarah who did not know Phillip. They settled into an uneasy conversation as the waiter distributed menus and took drink orders. The young girls were perfectly at ease in the eating out scene since it had been a natural part of the order of their lives since birth.

Simon eagerly opened his birthday gifts and gushed over the cashmere sweater Lex and Evan had given him (thanks, PT). Phillip looked on appreciatively and the girls waited in anticipation to see Simon's reaction to their gift. He was thrilled – the latest book from the French Kitchen and Chef Thomas Keller.

This famous restaurant was in Yountville in California's Napa Valley and although he'd not been there he loved the influences of this marvellous chef. Simon was not well travelled and it was something Phillip had suggested they remedy together. Yes please, was all Simon could say.

It took Evan and Lex a while to comprehend that Simon and Phillip had evolved beyond the work colleague scenario and this was no business dinner to them. Evan was a little shocked but put on his best front. Simon's gay? How come he'd never noticed in all these years? He kicked himself mentally for being so self-centred that he had not understood something so intrinsic to Simon's persona.

Soon, with a couple of drinks under the belt, the conversation reached its usual level of laughter and vivacity. Lex could not help but notice how tactile Simon and Phillip were and how intimately they seemed to know each other.

"So where did you go for your birthday?" Evan asked Simon. Phillip answered by saying that he had surprised Simon by taking him to a quiet suburban Italian place that he frequented. "They do the best mussels." He beamed a look to Simon.

"I have to tell you … I did know where you went," Evan said seriously. "Phoebe Strong told me last night at our meeting with Nige." This comment wiped the glow from Phillip's face, pronto. Simon, the innocent, totally missed the implication. "What did she say?" Phillip looked apprehensively to Evan.

"Nothing really, except that she had seen the two of you at dinner. I told her I knew and that I had asked Simon to work with you on some new publicity angles – especially for Simon." Simon searched between Phillip and Evan, and then cast his eyes down.

"We haven't talked yet, Simon, but I want you to step up and take on more segments on the Game and I want to know if you're interested in a radio show that Mangereire would back?" Simon's eyes shone as he looked back to Evan.

Lex interrupted at this point, "This is developing into a business meeting, Evan. I get to see Simon so rarely these days and I don't want to talk business. Surely you can go over this another time, hon?" Evan sat back, gently admonished.

"More to the point Simon, how long have you two been an item, if you don't mind my asking?" Lex looked innocently from Simon, then Phillip, to Evan, "You're obviously more than buddies."

Charlotte and Sarah looked at their food and then at each other. Adult conversation and they were not being sent away? They focussed ostensibly on their plates as they tweaked their ears. Evan was immediately uncomfortable – this was a chat he wanted in private with Simon, but as he began to interrupt he found himself on the receiving end of Lex's best don't-you-even-dare-try look and sank back in silence once more.

"In all honesty, it's been about two months …maybe a little less," Simon admitted quietly.

"Good on you, Simon!" Lex was jubilant as she had no problem with Simon being gay and wondered if he was just experimenting. She hoped the more mature and debonair Phillip was the right partner to experiment with. She knew it was not really any of her business, but she adored Simon in a protective older sisterly way and often worried about his all work and no play lifestyle hiding a deep loneliness. She also knew what he meant to Evan as a buddy and deputy in their businesses. Simon was flushed and Phillip demurely quiet. Evan had no idea what to say, but sat racking his brain for something innocuous as Sarah shattered the quiet with, "Are you guys going to live together?"

Sarah received mortified glares from both her parents, as she continued on in beautiful innocence, "Are you in love, Simon?" Out of the mouths of babes, thought Evan – it had certainly broken the quiet and Sarah had asked all the questions he wanted answers to, but was much too politically correct to ask.

"Not sure, Sarah, but I promise you'll be the first to know, once I do." He took Sarah's hand and squeezed it gently – he truly loved young Sarah whom he had known all her short life.

Conversation was taken up by Charlotte enquiring if Simon and Phillip would go to California to see Thomas Keller's iconic eatery. And so the evening continued in a more openly relaxed manner – a birthday cake that Evan (actually, PT) had arranged was brought to the table and they sang with gusto. Evan eventually picked up the check and all went their merry way.

The doting parents were keen to get home as it was an important day for them tomorrow; the nervously anticipated meeting with Dr Lew Farnshaw, the psychiatrist, would take place.

What a night!

On the drive back to Phillip's place, Simon sent a message to Evan thanking him for the dinner and confirming they would catch up with regard to the radio proposition and additional TV segments. Phillip pointed out to Simon that Evan obviously intended to build his profile and suggested that Stars don't give away their air time without a good reason. What was going on with that?

Phillip had no idea that Phil was trying to get rid of Ty Barnaby, nor was he aware of the background to Phil's machinations and her history with Nige.

Arriving home, Phillip poured a glass of Riesling for himself and a mineral water for Simon. They fell into the beige leather lounge and each other's bodies. Side by side they clasped hands and reflected on how well the evening had gone. Simon had been tentative about taking Phillip to the dinner but realised that it was time to be true to himself and had sucked it up. All in all, the evening could be called very successful and his relationship with Phillip was out as far as his adopted Pettersen clan were concerned.

That was important to Simon; he adored Evan and knew their personal friendship far outweighed their professional relationship. He was excited at Evan's suggested elevation in the business and had none of the suspicions that bothered Phillip. Simon described the depth of his trust and gratitude openly with Phillip and convinced him, for the present, to push his cynicism aside – and as Phillip's only desire right now was to be wrapped in Simon's arms, he did just that.

Simon was getting used to sex with Phillip and was relaxing into it and while it sure was different, Phillip was a generous, very experienced lover. He was patient with his novice and inexperienced partner whose few sexual encounters had been with females and had left him ambivalent.

Simon relished his sexual adventures with Phillip and tonight was no different as there was always a new move, a caress in a different part of his body that tantalised and aroused. Phillip had told him that his body was to be explored and he sure knew how to explore. Their tongues delved into each other's greedy mouths and their clothed bodies rubbed against each other. Phillip's hand was inside Simon's shirt, working his nipples while his tongue lashed Simon's. A guttural groan from Simon let Phillip know he was on the right track and the hard bulge in Simon's linen trousers was a further indication.

Phillip grabbed the bulge and massaged the erect cock. Simon loved it and thrust hard into Phillip's hand with expectant gyrations.

Leaving a trail of clothes, they worked their way to the bedroom – their forgotten drinks left lonely on the low coffee table. As they stood by the king size bed, Phillip roughly tugged Simon's boxers from his thin hips. He bent down and took Simon's hard cock into his mouth. Simon thrust forward knowing that Phillip was able to swallow his adequate cock. On his knees and with arms wrapped around bare ass, he drove Simon nuts with his magical mouth and Simon knew he was the beneficiary of Phillip's copious previous sexual adventures.

Simon loved it and rubbed his hands through Phillip's lightly blonded hair as he pulled his head onto his cock. When the young chef felt he could take no more and was about to prematurely explode into his older lover's mouth, he pulled out and dropped back onto the bed. Phillip eased himself onto Simon and immediately started rubbing their two cocks together in a sensually abandoned dance.

Simon slid further down under Phillip, letting his tongue roam over Phillip's smooth torso and stomach. When he got to Phillip's large cock, he felt its hardness and teased the crown with a licking motion. He tasted the pre-cum which he knew was quite salty and Simon liked salt! Soon Phillip could not help himself and began to thrust in and out of Simon's slippery mouth and while he was unable to take all of Phillip's cock, he compensated with a magic sucking ability. Phillip gloried at his eager lover's ability to suck cock, given he was a novitiate.

Phillip had smiled after their second, or was it their third, encounter when he recognised Simon as a natural cock sucker.

They were each about to explode. Simon knew from Phillip's reactions to his mouth and so he moved up under Phillip, who reached into the bedside table drawer and took a tube of translucent lubricant. He squeezed a generous amount on Simon's cock and stomach and then smeared some over his red-headed, brick hard cock and lowered his body onto Simon.

As they moved in a simulated fucking motion, their sexual energy was exhilarating. Phillip wanted so much to fuck Simon but knew it was premature and with some previous fingering knew that fucking was way off. He knew he could wait and that ultimately he would be rewarded with fucking this gorgeous virginal man beneath him. Patience!

With the mutual groping and thrusting increasing in pace, their mutual climax hung in the air; Simon's arching back and his perpetual groaning confirmed it. He moved down the body he was coming to adore and took Simon's cock into his mouth, once more. With a firm grip on the shaft of the lubricated cock, he masturbated it with his mouth and hand.

Simon could not hold back as he thrust into his lover's mouth and unloaded his cum. The explosion had initially taken Phillip by surprise, but he'd gotten used to it. He plunged onto the erupting cock and swallowed the saline reward. Simon was pulling at Phillip's head to lift him off but Phillip was having none of that and continued sucking Simon's sated dick. Meanwhile Phillip worked himself into ejaculation and let his load smother Simon's stomach. His whole body jerked in syncopated rhythm with his climax.

With mutual satisfaction, Phillip collapsed onto Simon and they kissed passionately and rubbed their spent cocks against each other. After showering, they moved back to bed and fell into satisfied sleep with Simon wrapped happily in Phillip's arms.

Thursday, and it was D-Day for Seb and his parents – Evan's mounting anxiety about seeing Dr Lew with Lex and Seb was palpable. Evan mumbled assurances to Seb, who remained stubbornly silent and unresponsive. After pleasantries were exchanged in the good doctor's spacious, wood panelled office, they seated themselves in the brightly coloured, velvet lounge chairs.

"So, how you feelin', Seb?"

Seb proffered no more than a reluctant shrug of his shoulders in response to the innocent enquiry from the psychiatrist. Lew smiled back at him and addressed the notes in a manila folder on his lap.

In an easy, relaxed tone, he said, "Seb, sometimes our brain acts a little differently to others and that does not mean too much, just as long as we recognise this difference … and generally, there is a way to fix up that difference … It is no disaster, let me tell you." He wished he could reach out to tap Seb's arm by way of reassuring him.

Seb sat immobile and relentless.

Lew referred to his notes once more. "As I look at the notes I have from your family doctor … and from talking with your mum and dad, I think you may well have what we call a Bipolar Disorder. It's not just one factor that causes this treatable brain disorder, but several." Lew was now very serious as he scanned Seb's face for a reaction. He then glanced toward Evan and Lex and took note of the tears welling in her eyes. Evan was deadpan and Seb moved uncomfortably in his chair, his adolescent mien motionless.

Absolute, crushing silence pervaded the doctor's office.

Ultimately, it was Lex who asked what was next and how they could ascertain that it was Bipolar. Lew explained that Seb's symptoms; the varying energy levels, unusual mood swings and poor school performance were some indicators for Bipolar Disorder, however he'd like to conduct some tests and suggested an MRI. He went on further, describing that this functional magnetic resonance imaging would show Seb's brain activity, which would be different than the established norm, if indeed, it was Bipolar.

Lew noted Seb's discomfort and rang for his assistant, who came immediately. "Seb, this is Anthea and she'll take you to do some preliminary tests … nothing that can hurt you. Can you go with her please and we'll be with you in about fifteen minutes." Seb stood – Lex reached for his hand. He lingered as she kissed the back of his hand and it slid from her grip. She reached to her handbag for a soft, receptive tissue to relieve her leaking eyes.

She reached for Evan and sighed, "My baby … my baby boy. What have we done?"

Lew let Evan comfort Lex for a few moments before continuing, "Lex, it's not as bad as it may sound. Firstly, we need to determine how bad his Bipolar is. There are different types and we know how to treat them with psychotherapy and medication." He was reassuring and reached out to Evan to comfort him also.

"Let me get some tests done with Seb, after which I can make a final diagnosis and give you a prognosis. From there I can recommend suitable treatment. I wanted Seb out of the room because there are some disturbing facts he doesn't need to hear at present. We can treat Bipolar very well these days; however you must understand there is no cure for Bipolar Disorder."

He let the information sink in to the distressed parents who looked glassy eyed at each other.

"Can this affect his twin, Sarah? Tell me, Lew, please, that it will not affect my little girl too. Please tell me that." Lex was desperately squeezing Evan's hand and raised the other in supplication.

"It's highly unlikely. Identical twins can have problems. You would have noticed some similar symptoms in Sarah, if it was the case, and you haven't mentioned any." Lex was somewhat placated and eased her grip somewhat on Evan's hand as she looked for his assurance.

Evan gave her a smile of encouragement as they rose to leave. A smiling Seb joined them and after they'd paid, they thanked Dr Farnshaw who promised to be in touch as soon as the results were available.

They headed to the car and Evan asked hopefully, "So, Seb, what do you say to your fav hamburger and fries?" Seb nodded with some enthusiasm and said, "Awesome Dad … and thanks for taking me to Dr Farnshaw." He jumped into the back seat with more zip than he'd shown in months – a good sign.

Evan reached for his phone to retrieve his messages. Amongst them was an urgent demand from Phil that he call her immediately. He pushed the return call button.

"Evan – Evan." This did not sound like one of Phil's tantrums, in fact she sounded terribly distressed. "Evan … we've found Mel. Evan…" Phil let out an anguished tearful sigh, "Evan … she's dead. Christ, I can't believe it, Evan, Mel's dead. Suicide. Her poor mother found her. What can I do Evan? What?"

He was dumbstruck and stuttered what comfort he could offer to Phil, promising to call later.

CHAPTER 10

The Contract Negotiation, Litigation and Loving – Game On or Game Off?

It was Friday morning and as Evan gulped his first coffee sitting in his office at home, he allowed his mind to drift over the week. Boy, what a week it had been.

While he was dismayed about Mel's death, he still did not know the complete story. He did feel sad that he would not see her again and he knew how much they would miss her on the floor. She'd been such a professional and always good fun. It was quite beyond Evan's comprehension that anyone would contemplate suicide as a solution to their problems. He wondered at Phil being so emotional about it, as it was really not like her.

What had happened with Dottie? After getting the family home and having a short respite with Seb, he'd headed to the restaurant which was both his work and his retreat, a safety net. After checking current emails and phone messages, he checked in on the chaos in the kitchen. He caught Aaron's eye as he moved on to the dining area, and Aaron gave a quick thumbs up to indicate all was good for him. Good young man – good worker.

He waltzed around chatting with regular clients and introducing himself to new ones before moving eventually to his table to await the buxom Mrs Bronstein. While going through some text messages as he waited, he sucked on a mineral water. In the back of his mind he was still appraising what it could possibly be that Dottie had for him. He ordered some bread and let his gaze wander around Mangereire. It was now twenty minutes past their meeting time. He called her mobile.

The message was, as it would be with Dottie, contrived and convoluted. Distinctive harp music played under a breathy Mrs Bronstein who invited you to leave a message which she would return as soon as she possibly could. How appropriate the message was for Mrs Bronstein, everything about her was complicated.

He ordered some calamari and was struck by how strange this scene was. Here he was, sitting in his own restaurant and possibly being stood up by Mrs Bronstein, the woman who'd paid a small fortune for him to cook a dinner at her mansion. His financial people had gone over the proposal for a chain of restaurants she'd virtually bull-dozed him with and they saw possibilities and this meeting tonight had been at her behest. Was this just another passing whim for a wealthy socialite who considered the time of other people of no consequence?

He finished the crumbed calamari, left the table for two and bid goodnight to the restaurant manager after signing for his calamari. No such thing as a free meal, even in your own restaurant – his accountant had drummed that into him from the outset of his successful business.

When he thought about it, as he drove home, he was happy to have escaped Mrs Bronstein and the uncertain deal. It was a novel experience being stood up, something that had never happened before and he still contemplated what it was that Dottie may have had for him and guessed he was now unlikely to find out. He thought of his all too brief conversation with Seb earlier in the day, as he'd held his son's hand and assured him everything was going to be alright and they would tackle Seb's challenge together. Seb had cuddled into his father in a way that had not happened for a long time and both had felt a renewal of that bond that is singular between father and son. My little boy – well, not so little – Evan thought, as he pushed his way home through traffic.

Back to earth, in the conservatory of his home and with his now cooling coffee beside him, Evan returned his thoughts to the week that was not yet over – please tell me nothing else can happen, what a turbulent time it has been!

The angry meeting with Nige and Phoebe had resolved nothing. Why had Phil been so implacably aggressive that night and where did she find so much bravado? To brave up to Nige like that – there must be something else behind her attitude. Evan was completely unaware of the undercurrents that existed in the relationship between Phil and Nige.

And then there was Simon's revelation. Where had that come from? He admitted that his gaydar was somewhat underdeveloped but introspection suggested that he was also so self-involved that he simply did not notice – or want to notice. Had he let Simon down?

His mobile disrupted his musings and he answered Phil's call, "Hey hon, how you feeling today?"

"Still frazzled, if you must know. Why the fuck did she do that, Evan? I don't get it … why?" Once again tears permeated her voice and because he still had no idea what he could say or do, Evan figured it best to provide the metaphorical shoulder. This was twice in twenty-four hours that Evan had heard the impervious Phil in tears.

As Phil sobbed, Evan admitted he did not understand how Mel could have taken this path of suicide. When Phil revealed the gruesome detail that Mel had hung herself, he sat bolt upright almost knocking over the now dead coffee from the table beside him.

"Tell me you're kidding … you gotta be joking!" Evan was genuinely shocked.

"Why the fuck would I joke about something like that?" she spluttered.

"Whether you know it or not, Evan, hanging yourself is very definite. You don't want to fucking be here when you do that!" Phil said through more tears and a paroxysm of coughing, "We did a doco years ago on youth suicide and that's one fact I'll always remember! You remember a band called Badfinger?"

Evan nodded and then said that he did.

"Mel had a Badfinger disc in the CD player. Evan, the guitarist from Badfinger, Pete Ham, hung himself in 1975. Babe, she really did not fucking want to be here…it was no cry for attention that went fucking wrong!"

There was silence across the line for a few seconds.

"Not wanting to be too practical at a time like this Phil…" he said hesitantly, "…but have you got a new floor manager lined up?"

"Yeah, Bill got that underway the minute he heard about Mel."

Director Bill Wiseman not only did the Game, but a number of other shows, including the news and he and Mel had been great buddies. He was as shocked as Phil about Mel's suicide but hid his distress well; after all, he was a man. And Bill was definitely a man of that ilk. After being a director in television for over twenty-four years and having been a cameraman before that, Bill had seen things a man wasn't supposed to see. The car accidents that left you numb even though the camera was supposed to be a barrier and the raw footage from countless war zones with bodies dismembered and destroyed, he'd seen a great deal. He would shed a tear privately for his dead little friend, Melissa Goodman, the best floor manager in the business.

Phil was telling Evan that all would be good for the next shoot and not to worry. She moved on to what to do with the advertorial situation. Evan hazarded to mention, "You were incredibly aggro with Nige … lucky to have a job, aren't you?"

"Don't you worry about me and Nige … I know how to handle that fucking little turd!" This attitude gave Evan a dawning realisation that Phil must have something on Nige that he was not au fait about.

"Phil?" Evan wanted to pursue the meeting and its fallout.

"Yeah?"

"You know I've got to negotiate a new contract in a couple of months … and I want to sign up again … you do want me to do that, don't you?"

"Of course I do, Evan."

"Well, I'm really in need of your help on this one. You know what Nige can be like and last contract negotiation with him was a nightmare. Will you help?"

Phil remembered only too well what an arsehole Nige had been during that period and now, instinct and experience told her that he was aiming to shift Evan sideways and she was not going to let that be the case. She wanted another three years for Evan, who was not only a great professional talent but also a decent and generous human being – he was her friend and she had so few of them.

She wanted to control her future with Evan and the Game, not Nigel – and she would.

"What do you think, Evan? Of course, I'm there for you, buddy. You and me – we're buddies and we're a team and we don't get dictated to by fucking little pricks like Nige and his cock-sucking whore, Phoebe-fucking-Strong! Got it?" The Star chef was glad he wasn't in Phil's immediate vicinity as she was in fine fettle today and he'd learnt that it was better to be physically absent during a tirade.

"Thanks Phil. Look I gotta go now … got to get to the restaurant." He'd thought about discussing the Simon/Phillip development but decided it would be better to wait until they could eyeball each other.

"Okay hon. Talk after the weekend … I know it's your busiest time. All good in the restaurant business?" He assured her it was and breathing a sigh of relief, ended the call but not without thinking just how complicated a personality Phil was. Why was she so extremely upset about Mel? Could it be that she missed her own daughter who she saw so irregularly? And her overt aggression to just about everyone, especially the big boss, Nigel, was frightening at times. I certainly have learned to live with her, that's for sure. There was no one in her life romantically and Evan thought he understood the reason.

He walked through to the kitchen where Lex was making the English breakfast tea that was her morning habit. After asking if he wanted another coffee she said timidly, "Evan," and with eyes averted from his seductive steely blue eyes, "Hon – I've got the bleeding back."

He was with her in a nanosecond with his arms wrapped around her as his gut wrenched and the passing thought flashed through his head – and I thought nothing more could happen this bloody horrid week.

"You're going to Danny as soon as you can, right? Can I come with you?" She pointed out that there was nothing he could do by coming and she felt she needed to confront this on her own. After all, it could be mid-life stuff and she was approaching menopause. She'd been thinking about this recently and noticed some of the symptoms. The power surges, a girlfriend called them – hot and cold flushes.

Evan pressed on, but ultimately acquiesced on Lex's insistence.

Evan prepared to leave for the restaurant after receiving Lex's assurance that she would let him know what was happening as soon as possible. As he walked out the front door, he heard the kids stirring. It was eight in the morning and another day was under way in the perennially frenetic Pettersen household. Long may that be, thought Evan prophetically, as he closed the door on his precious home.

The first of the manuscripts were waiting for Evan on his desk and PT pointed to them saying they'd been delivered by courier. Does anyone sleep any more in this crazy city? It was only 8.25am yet Evan felt like he'd been up all night. He was impressed with what he saw at first glance and told PT to get Hermann on the phone as soon as business hours commenced.

He filled PT in on the devastating news of Mel's demise and asked her to find out Mel's mother's name and make contact to see if there was anything she needed, besides TLC. PT took it on board and noticing Evan's empty coffee cup, she refilled it without comment. Once again, she evaporated to make things happen.

It was now a month later and some form of normality had returned to the set of the Game. While Mel was still missed, it was very much business as usual and the new floor manager; Gus Livingstone, was working out well. He'd come from another network and with a wealth of experience he adapted to the culture at Channel 3 very quickly. At twenty-nine he'd been in TV since he left secondary school and he loved the thrill, emergency and energy of television. Gus was married and had one "sprog" as he called his daughter, Dahlia. If he had further female sprogs, they would be named after flowers also.

Mel's death was still with the police and an inquest looked as though it would be held into the circumstances surrounding her death. Although there were no apparently suspicious circumstances, her mum wanted to be sure. So with the situation in limbo, everyone just got on with it.

Evan had noticed that Jonesy, whose bubbly personality was legendary around the studio, had been rather quiet of late. As operator on camera 1, he was Evan's cameraman and they worked together like rosemary and lamb. Evan wondered if Jonesy was suffering end of season slump or there was some bigger problem lurking.

Ernest Hemingway Jones was his full name, donated by his father who was fanatical about the famous American writer and held a few pretensions of the literary type. He was a local government clerk, said position providing him copious time to expand his mind, but he possessed very little ambition and retired after fifty-one years in the same position. However, he was extremely well versed in the classic tomes.

Jonesy, on the other hand, did not give a flying fuck about reading classics, which was a bitter disappointment to his mildly academic father, whereas he was the apple of his mother, Gloria's, eye. Gloria boasted proudly of her son's career in the glamorous world of television and could name drop along with the best; she knew all the stars on a first name basis despite having met nary a one! Familiarity breeds recognition was Gloria Jones's mantra.

Evan took Jonesy aside during a break and asked if he was okay saying he was a little worried about his gun cameraman being so quiet and could he help in any way? Jonesy deflected Evan saying he was just worn out and needed a break after a long season; he and his wife would veg out on a beach somewhere for a few weeks and he'd be fine.

Jonesy was anything but fine. He'd been having a furtive fling with Mel, who was ultimately protective of her single status and especially with Jonesy being married to a career ascending accountant in a major bank. Mel and

274

Jonesy found they had a great deal in common, to say nothing of the outrageously super sex they enjoyed – far beyond Mel's customary blow jobs and I'm-the-one –in-control attitude. She was a tigress and he felt like a tiger around her and so, they complemented each other in and out of the bed.

Jonesy had not anticipated the depth of his growing devotion to Mel. Devotion did not come into Mel's frame of reference – no way, was that a happening thing! After all, as she'd point out while they lay in post-coital cosiness, "You're married, you big dope!" and she would explode into a fit of giggles, much to his chagrin.

And so, the relationship had continued with Jonesy trying not to notice Mel's interest in other men. Though he admonished himself that he had no right to be, Jonesy accepted his jealousy and covered it well. Meanwhile, his wife was busily forging ahead with her career and did not seem to miss the constant sex that had previously been part and parcel of their life. She was happy and as they still engaged in the occasional fuck, it was a perfect arrangement, ostensibly.

Jonesy admitted to himself that he was lonely without Mel. He missed her and was confused at her having committed suicide. He hadn't seen it coming although he knew that she did have down times. She was always willing to please and smiled continuously – he'd entertained the notion from time to time that perhaps it was a bit of a front, maybe hiding low self-esteem.

Mel was dead and he was sad, and yes, sorry she was gone. He quizzed himself constantly about his part in her death – did he have anything to do with it? Did he fail to ask the right questions when they were alone? He agonised over these questions now that it was too late – way too late.

The sixth season of the Game was dragging along. Not dragging perhaps, but yes, that was the best description and there were another four weeks to get through. Phil knew it was time to get the incentive juices happening. Her demeanour changed entirely to the crew, although definitely not with management. She knew just how important these next four weeks of shooting were and she needed to raise the energy level – so, some suck-up was the order of the day. She was uncharacteristically polite and full of thanks for the team's work and introduced Rap drinks on set at the end of the Games' two day shoot to boost morale and bring the "A-Team" together again.

Nige's personal assistant had made the appointment with Evan to begin negotiation on his contract renewal with the fractious CEO. Given that Evan did not have a manager, he informed Nige's PA that Phil Watts would be accompanying him.

Evan was excited that there were only four more weeks until he could enjoy a short break before readying himself for the silly season at the restaurant. The Christmas party bookings had commenced and they were highly lucrative for Mangereire and after another highly successful 32 week season of the Game he anticipated a substantial end of season bonus from the network – he wondered if he really needed that extra dosh. Take it without question while you can get it was the mantra in TV land and then he remembered the upcoming school fees for the next few years for three children. Ouch!

Lex's health issue had been diagnosed as yet another urinary tract infection and Danny had insisted on the antibiotics with this recurrent bout – Lex had acceded somewhat unwillingly. Seb had been diagnosed as Bipolar and had accepted, at this stage, that he would be on medication – antidepressants. He knew he had the love and support of his family and so chose not to broadcast his situation at school, although it was noted by students and staff alike that he seemed to have returned somewhat to his former self. Somewhat, though not completely.

In the tiny restaurant office, PT managed to claim Evan's attention as she handed him his third cup for the morning – not quite 9am on this bright Monday morning.

"I've been trying to work this out and didn't want to disturb you. There has been some strong French movement on Facebook and Twitter and Phil asked about the increase of recipe requests online and emails from the south-west of France. It's really odd … she has no idea what it's about and neither do I … all I can do is process the requests … and that's not easy boss, because my French is so merdy!" She quickly explained to Evan that *merde* was French for shit – it was a joke, she said.

Evan blinked in perplexity and replied to PT that he'd contact Phil, before he buried his head back in the upcoming weekly menu specials and noticed two more suggestions from Aaron. He made a mental note about the value of mentoring that boy. It was going to be another crazy week.

He had no idea just how crazy this week would become!

Phil Watts sat in her office viewing the next season budgets for "The Cooking Game....r u Game?" when her landline rang – strange as it was normally her cell phone.

"Hi Phil, it's Sam here from Programming." He was an old friend and they had known each other for decades at Channel 3.

"Hey Sam, how they hangin'?" She lounged back in her comfy executive chair as she readied for a chat.

"Phil … yeah, good … well sort of. I need to see you – can you come to the parking lot … now?"

"What, right now?"

"Right now!" he insisted.

"The fucking parking lot? Okay, give me five."

She wanted to let someone know she would be out of the office briefly but her secretary had disappeared and Zoe had taken a week off due to a family emergency, so she grabbed her cell phone and headed for the parking lot.

Sam stood beside the star newsreader's flashy steel grey Jag. Phil nodded a quick greeting to her old friend who said, "Let's go this way so we can't be seen."

Sam did a quick check over his shoulder before he began, "Phil, what I am telling you now can get me fired if you say one word about it ... okay?" Again, he checked to ensure they were completely alone, "You notice Ty Barnaby around any?"

"No..." said Phil, "...he's on assignment with Sports. I didn't want him ... nice enough guy, but no good to me on the Game." Sam took a cigarette and offered the pack to Phil, who refused. She'd given up years before and only smoked a joint, now and then. She didn't mind a joint!

"Phil, he's not on assignment with Sports. He's shooting a pilot for his own show ... if it's a goer; it'll start soon as the Games' season is done. He's in the south doing a story on a transgendering tomato grower. Up north, he's got a yarn on a single parent with Siamese twins and then he comes back here to a couple who run a half-way house for runaway kids. He's a de-frocked priest and she used to be a nun." He drew deeply on his cigarette, turned his head to exhale and then turned back to Phil who was staring in wide-eyed, speechless, disbelief at him.

"It's going to be one of those sob story half hour shows and if it works, Nigel wants it to be a permanent slot, taking some viewing time from the Game." He breathed heavily, and took another tug on his cigarette.

Phil lifted her head as she pronounced each word staccato, "Tell me the producer is not Zoe Hendriks?" Sam nodded slowly that it was.

"I'll kill the fucking bitch. That fucking two timing…" Sam put his hand on her arm, trying to quieten her vocal gymnastics.

"And maybe, you won't want to know this either…" he hesitated and again scanned the area with nervous eyes. "Nige sold seven eps of the Game to a Jonathan Turnballs who intends selling overseas. I heard he's sold them already to a network in the south of France."

So he must have been successful and that, at least explained the arrival of the myriad French enquiries from cyberspace, construed Phil.

She took Sam's arm and stood to look her old friend in the face. She said nothing – they both knew this territory, how the biggest game was played – then took off back to her office. She needed time to think this through. She knew Nigel fucking Herbert-Flyson was fucking with her, she understood him only too well after the decades they had worked together, not to mention their regrettable liaison. Christ, he was the fucking father of her daughter and he goddam well knew it. She had fucking protected him all along and never disclosed a fucking thing to his wife, Lynn … mind you she had a husband to think of at the time as well, she supposed.

So, what was that little prick up to? She had to think – on her own, not with anyone else and least of all Evan who could not possibly comprehend this Machiavellian twist in events. She did, and she was a key player in the brutal game of television. She now wished for that cigarette, but found her plait instead, with its banded tip.

Phil knew that piece of shit, Turnballs, known in the business as "Snakeballs" because no one had a lower standard as far as ethical conduct was concerned. He would be perfect for this deception and she, and Evan (of course!) had been right royally ripped off! Evan was entitled to know the show had been sold and he was entitled to revenue from the sale of the eps.

I'll fix those arseholes, Phil muttered through her plait and nodded to herself – but it was crucial to remain calm.

The week continued and the two day shoot was excellent. Simon was not surprised to see Phillip on set more frequently, always on the pretext of wanting a word with Evan. Phillip always carried a wad of notes and a notebook as props when he invariably ended up talking with Simon. They did have lots to talk about (aside from their increasingly passionate love affair), as Evan's proposal for Simon to take on further segments and presenting the radio program had taken off.

Evan had to admit he liked seeing the two of them together, he could feel the respect and love that surrounded them and wondered if the rest of the team were noticing.

Evan was more than happy to leave the studio at a reasonable hour and head home on Wednesday night for a family catch up dinner. He loved these nights and it was so good just to be there with his darling Lex who had recovered from another recent bout of illness. How he loved her – he adored her. There was laughter all round and Seb was the centre of attention tonight as, for the first time in months, he'd topped his class in the latest math assignment.

The family was together again and that was all that mattered to Evan. He and Lex ultimately fell into bed and then into each other. Evan held her as they went to sleep and thought they must do this more often. Lex was a sublime lover – well, as far as he knew because his experience had been severely limited prior to Lex. Doesn't being happy with your wife count for something? It sure did and he congratulated himself as they drifted off.

Evan had no idea that in less than twelve short hours, that happiness was going to be tested. Severely tested.

It was quiet at Mangereire as he walked through to his office at the back and yet the restaurant smelt of people, it was not an offensive smell but he wondered at its uniqueness. He loved it – he loved everything this morning.

The day was his. PT handed him a coffee and stood back as she placed a newspaper in front of him.

"You've not seen this, have you?" she asked nervously. There, covering most of the front page of the sleaze filled newspaper, the Morning Star, was Dottie Bronstein.

The tear tracks down her cheeks were laced with mascara, her mouth sneering as she stared out to anyone buying the paper.

The headline read: "CELEB CHEF RIPS ME OFF FOR MILLIONS"

The name Evan Pettersen shot like a bullet at Evan from the lead in line.

He collapsed back into his chair in complete disbelief. So that's why she didn't turn up. Goddamn it all, he cursed. What the hell is this about? His phone vibrated in his pocket. Phil Watts.

"Hi hon … and yes, I've just seen it." He laid the paper on his desk despondently.

"Have you phoned Lex? Will she have seen the paper yet?" Phil was concerned for the impact on Lex and the family when they saw this destructive trash.

"No. PT just showed it to me. The thing is Phil … I have absolutely no fucking idea what this is all about." Phil was shocked to hear Evan; it was not often that he cursed.

"Evan, have you reached the part where she says you tried to seduce her there in the kitchen of her own home?" Evan was in such a state of shock that he could not speak.

Phil took control. "Okay, here's the deal, babe. We're in damage control babe – so zip your mouth and say absolutely nothing to any reporter that rings … and believe me … they'll be ringing. I'll get onto Phillip Williamson and the legal department at the station. Just DO NOT speak to anyone! And ring Lex this minute."

Evan knew the potential fallout of this headline and knew it would be a disaster if not handled properly. The Network was good at this sort of stuff – generations of practice!

He rang Lex. His incredible Lex, who after a moment's stupefaction, was her inimitable self and labelled the incident as part of the crazy world of Celebrity.

Naturally, after paying in excess of $21,000 for Evan's services at a charity auction, Evan had presumed the Bronsteins were rolling in dough and the mansion where he cooked for her and her guests did nothing to alter that misconception.

What Evan did not know is that they were seated on the bones of their respected bare arses and intended to sue him for a motza!

What the Bronstein plan had not taken into account was the fact that they would be suing the insurance company that housed his indemnity – and insurance companies fought back like a mother lion defending her cubs. It would be a battle royal.

For now, and with only two more weeks of the sixth season of the Game to complete, Evan's concentration had to focus on the show and his performance – and of course, the upcoming contract negotiation.

Next morning at the studio, Evan had checked in with Simon, who offered heartfelt sympathy. The Star was rather more rattled by crew, who averted eyes as he approached. He was shocked to think they would entertain the thought that he would somehow be involved in a scam and that he would even want to fuck a Dottie, when he had the genuine article at home.

Ironically, the scandal did improve ratings (no bad publicity in television, goes the saying!) – just as did the scandal of Rory Overham's appearance when everyone thought the visiting US Queen of the Kitchen was playing with Evan's leg.

The ratings soared and Nige and the rest of the suits were over the moon with delight. There was talk of a marketing survey correlating the relationship between sex scandals and ratings. It never got off the ground – after all why waste money on a survey when the fact was – sex sold. Finally, it was decided to view the event as fortuitous as it would fill in that precarious ratings hole over the Christmas period. Thank you, Evan!

He arrived at his studio office and reviewed the schedule for the day's shoot – nothing untoward and PT (who was suffering a minor meltdown with the extent of deflection she'd been doing with journos), graciously handed him coffee.

Phil crashed straight in with, "Don't worry about a thing. It's all under control. We'll get those fucking rip off Jewish pricks. Have a drink with me after the shoot – see you at Curley's." She was gone.

There were no major dramas with the shoot. A visiting chef threw a hissy fit because he got coriander and not cilantro; while it was a slight mistake, the reaction from the pedantic minor chef, was definitely over the top.

Phil retrieved the situation before Evan knew anything had occurred. She apologised and said there was very little, if any difference and the options were to stay and use coriander or keep up the bitching and go, never to return. He stopped the bitching in record time!

Evan was more than happy with his dishes and let his viewers know that the following week would be all about kids' stuff to get them ready for the encroaching school holidays. Naturally, delivered with that irresistible smile and wink.

He arrived at Curley's promptly, having phoned Lex to let her know he'd be home fairly soon.

His blond plaited boss had a glass of Chardonnay in hand and he ordered a mineral water.

"Now, this thing with Mrs Bronstein will get sorted. We're digging into her background and she's not as clean as you might think. We're finding some dirt stuck to the father, Mr Rockenbauer-Szabo. Supposed to have been a tailor, but how can you make that much money outta suits? There are more important issues around that concern you and me a whole lot." She took a firm grip on his forearm and moved closer to her Star.

As he sat sucking on his mineral water, Phil filled him in on the sale of the Game to a French TV network and the fact that Ty had been off shooting a pilot for his own program. If the pilot was successful, the Game would lose air time and that was not what either of them wanted. He was astonished when she told him of Zoe's traitorous behaviour.

He walked over to the bar and ordered another glass of wine for Phil and a double Glenfiddich for himself. He sat back down and looked at Phil with that little-boy-very-confused look that she knew only too well – in so many ways he was still a complete innocent in a business that operated on guile.

"What a mess," was all he could come up with.

"So, my friend, here's what we're gunna do. When we go back to meet Nige, I'll have all this on paper. I'll hand it over and we'll see what goes down from there. Okay?"

She dropped a few pages in front of him and told him to follow as she explained her tactics.

She described how she planned to restructure the Game to the following format. Evan would still be the Star and would do 468 segments for the season over 36 weeks; this broke down to thirteen segments per week which would vary in the schedule, depending on the content of the segments. She also intended to increase the number of appearances by Will Hambers, the Prick on Pins – as she had so aptly named him. Will was becoming quite successful after Phil had blackmailed him into regular spots on the Game, following his tryst with Mel in the cool room. She explained to Evan that her intention was to ease Evan's workload as she knew he wanted more time to explore other avenues.

She went on further to suggest 108 segments per season for Simon Hacknell. John Smithton, the wine guru, would do 144 or an average of four per week. The conundrum of Ty would be dealt with by 180 segments in which he would feature as "The Farmer's Friend". By the time Phil had finished with Ty Barnaby, he would know all there was to know about agriculture, horticulture and anything else finishing with "ure", including a segment on manure which was being processed on farms as biofuel. Evan gazed at Phil with veneration as she continued.

"Now, let's talk France. That fucking little turd thinks he's sold the Game without us knowing. Stupid dumb arse dickhead should've known I'd find out … here's what he's going to pay you for the Game in France," she pointed to a large six figure amount and Evan's eyes seemed to pop as he stammered, "Bbbut…"

No buts; Phil assured him that she knew what he was worth and she'd let that dumb fuck, Nige, have a little leeway bargaining here, if necessary. "Now, during season's break … here's what's going to happen." She picked up another sheet of paper and handed it to Evan. "I'm going to get Zoe to cut 200 ten minute fillers that'll feature segments from the current season and will have adverts included – a complete package the network will use as fillers. Got it?"

He got it and was about to speak, but Phil was in full flight and he allowed that he would be foolish to step in front of a bulldozer.

"So … you don't have to worry and this way, we have the Game in front of the viewers during a period they wouldn't normally see us. It averages about two fillers per day…" This meant that the fillers could go to air in the evening connecting to an audience who typically did not see him – the woman was brilliant!

The fillers would be free to Nige as, all said and done – the network legitimately owned the content.

"So buddy, all up this is what your new fee structure will look like for the next three seasons." She handed him a sheet of paper with one figure printed on it … he did a double take.

"…and when I wake up. What then?" He was beaming a sublime, but perplexed smile.

"It being as it is, Evan and that is what you're worth. And what the Game's worth. And that is what Nige is going to pay you." Phil had never sounded more adamant.

"He'll never buy this, Phil and you know it. Never." He dropped the piece of paper to stare her down – she did not flinch. He was in for a rocky ride at the upcoming meeting but knew he could not be in better hands.

He was incredulous over Nige's duplicitous behaviour regarding Ty, his illegitimate son. No doubt Phoebe would be present aiding and abetting his skulduggery. What sort of a way is this to treat a loyal Star? He silently admonished himself for his naïve thinking, after all was said and done, he knew this was a business that was completely lacking in integrity, loyalty and veracity – come on Evan, this is television – get a grip!

They finished their drinks and headed to their cars still discussing strategy for the meeting in two weeks.

A few revelations came to Evan as he headed home. Firstly, he was putting his career squarely in the hands of Phil and he wondered at his trust in her; but then Phil had nurtured and fostered him from the very first day that Nigel brought him to the network. Secondly, what the hell will I do if Nige completely baulks at what Phil is proposing? After all, she planned some significant changes to the Game and those changes would impact on programming at the network. Where will I go if he sacks me? I guess, back to the restaurant from whence I came, and that would not be all that bad.

What will be, will be. He thought of Simon and his spiritual beliefs and Buddhism practices. I wonder how his future will pan out, now that he's come out as a gay man. He contemplated how very odd it must be going for a grope of your bed partner and finding a cock and balls rather than a furry moist patch of flesh. It was too difficult a concept for Evan to currently contemplate.

The week continued and Evan was delighted with his performances and also a segment Simon did that received rave reviews in the electronic feedback. The Twitter and Facebook accounts went nuts and PT decided to put the segment on YouTube. The char-grilling of the sliced young eggplant was the secret to this Turkish dish, as Simon pointed out and then succinctly finished the rest of this simple, trendy dish.

For the rest of the week, the television and the restaurant business cycle followed its usual course for the frantically busy celebrity chef. He listened to the network's legal eagles regarding the Bronstein accusations and was at ease with their advice; and Hermann the German was keeping clear of Evan and leaving his deputy to work with Simon. Cool, too cool!

Zoe returned after her week off dealing with the "family emergency". On her desk was a brown paper bag awaiting her return. She opened it to find five ruby red tomatoes and a scribbled note that read: LOVE TERRY?? Oh, fuck me – she knows!

Her cover had been busted and she mentally kicked herself in the backside because she should have known that she could never get away with subterfuge in the gossip rich culture of Channel 3. What to do? Absolutely fucking nothing! Play it out and with any luck Ty's show will get up and I'll be an executive producer, just like that fucking bitch, Phil Watts.

The sight of the tomatoes drew her memory back to Terry Jazowski, the tomato grower she'd first met on her original location shoot with Ty. She'd lusted after him even though he was married with four children. What goes down on the road, stays on the road!

The confusing reality was that Terry had initialised transgendering and had commenced hormone treatment. He was, as he'd confessed to Zoe on their first meeting, a woman trapped in a man's body. Yeah, well okay, thought Zoe but such an attractive man's body to be trapped in – fuck it all! Working with Ty on the pilot for his show had reintroduced her to Terry and she'd found him more attractive than ever – what a waste of a good cock!

She picked up the tomatoes and moved them aside, knowing they'd be put to good use in her dinner that evening. Thanks Phil, she thought with sarcasm dripping like poison from Snow White's apple.

The proposed Bronstein legal action had simmered down since Phillip Williamson's feeding the media some realistic information and denying the accusations made by Dottie and her husband. Somehow, her confessions on TV and to anyone else in the media who would give her the time of day were not ringing true. Her acting wouldn't even make a midday soapie Phillip had told Evan and her storyline kept changing. Evan put that little drama out of his mind as he knew the network had his back.

What he couldn't push from his thoughts was his concern over the outcome of the meeting for his future. How was Phil going to pull this one off? At least he knew her motives were not entirely altruistic and she was fighting for her own survival too. Without the Game she'd be up shit creek without a paddle, right? True, even though she convinced herself she could walk straight through the front door of the competition and work, whenever she so chose. Phil loved the power and the pay that the Game afforded her.

Life goes on and worrying was not going to change the outcome of that dilemma.

He was enjoying reading the manuscript of the upcoming books and had arranged a meeting with Hermann Booth from Marquis for the following Thursday. PT diarised the meeting and booked the small function room at Mangereire, where they could spread out with the manuscripts.

Simon had to be involved given he'd had so much input with the basic recipes – ultimately, this project was his baby. Evan had relieved him of all restaurant duties so he could concentrate on the books and get material together to do the pilot radio show with Evan. The radio station was ecstatic that they were finally getting a piece of the Pettersen action and had dedicated one of their top producers to work with Simon and Evan.

On the home front, Lex was organising for a short break for the two of them at her parents' home in the country, just a few hours' drive away. The kids were doing fine and their end of year exams would be completed before their parents departed. Charlotte, Seb and Sarah each had plans with friends and Lex accepted this as part and parcel of growing up. Lex's parents would have a few minor gripes about the absence of their grandchildren, but they'd get over it, as they always did.

Evan was hanging out for time on his own with Lex away from the rigid restaurant business and the flashy flow of la-la land.

Hermann Booth arrived at Mangereire and was escorted to the function room where he laid out the contract and the first two books. One was on the Edwardian period (1900-1910) and the other the following decade, which would include wartime recipes.

Evan joined him and PT offered coffee. Hermann sat down in his chair with a thump (Hermann the German was generally described as rotund) and Evan sat a little ways down so they could spread out the manuscripts once Simon arrived. PT handed Evan a coffee and Hermann's contract with Post-it notes she'd placed on specific pages.

She asked if Evan needed her to stay. He did not, but asked her to come back with Simon when he arrived to discuss the books.

"So, vot are your problems?" Hermann asked as he looked at his own copy of the contract.

"No real problems, Hermann, except for the royalty percentage for books sold overseas … and I would like to own the recipe app. Those are the only minor points we need to discuss." Evan sat back to wait for the explosion he knew would follow.

"Minor points! Vell, mebbe minor to you … mebbe major for me!" He slammed the contract onto the table. Evan remained silently regarding the publisher who went on to elucidate that Evan had done no writing of recipes as Marquis had used the services of their own team of professionals. All Evan had to do was collect royalties and concession fees, the flushed publisher concluded.

"Und … now you vant more money. Is that the picture?"

"If it's that easy, Hermann, do the books without my name and photo on the covers and see how many you sell, or how few!" Evan was surprised by his own toughness.

He continued, "What I'm asking for is the same fifteen percent we agreed on with our last contract. That's all I'm asking for and you know you'll sell most of the books here and perhaps a few around the world … unless there's something you're not telling me."

Hermann looked away and then back to the contract.

Evan got it immediately – the bastard's got a deal going and he's not being honest. Typically, with the small unit sales overseas, the larger royalty percentage would not be an issue. However, if Hermann had made a deal already for larger sales worldwide, he would not want to pay a larger royalty fee to Evan. International sales and royalties were a pain in the arse to monitor and the author was at the mercy of the publisher's integrity – and that was highly dubious in most circumstances.

Hermann was demurring and Evan continued quietly, "Okay Hermann, out with it. Tell me, or I don't sign … simple as that."

The pudgy publisher admitted that he'd made a deal to sell fifteen thousand copies to a distributor in France. Evan already had a presence in France and guessed that Hermann knew about his show being televised there. Hermann admitted that he'd heard a rumour.

"Bullshit Hermann! You don't make a deal to sell fifteen thousand books into France on a rumour. You're not that stupid!"

Hermann smiled slightly at what he chose to take as a compliment and admitted he did know that the Game was showing in France and the viewers were lapping up the handsome chef.

"So, let's decide on fifteen percent with an audited review every six months. Sound like a deal to you?"

As flummoxed as he was, Hermann knew when he was backed into a corner.

"Okay. Okay alvedy … Vee shake." Evan shook the extended hand as he asked Hermann to adjust the contract.

"Now … the App, Hermann. I want that and the revenue from it."

Hermann was crestfallen and told Evan that it was Marquis who was carrying the risk here, given the book market where it was and Evan already had a great deal. Evan conceded he was right as hardcover books were giving way to e-books and recipe Apps – all the more reason for him wanting the App for the ten recipe books in the Recipe Revival series.

"Vot vould you say to a fifty-fifty split?" Hermann suggested to Evan, who did a very quick revision of his figures and realised that with the publishing deal and its associated perks, he should agree with Hermann. It was a good deal and now he had confirmation that the books were going to France, he would plan a promotional tour for the coming year. France – here we come, Lexie, my lady!

"Okay Hermann, let's do it! Amend the contract and I'll sign." Evan kept his deadpan visage though he was thrilled with the deal. "Everything cool, Hermann?" Hermann the German sat back and took an enormous gulp of his stone cold coffee. He gathered up the contract and pushed the manuscripts to the middle of the table. He gave a simple, but explicit nod of agreement.

Evan rose and walked to the door, opening it to beckon Simon Hacknell to join the meeting. He hugged Simon with a genuine smile for this man who was integral to the success of the Pettersen realm. Evan loved this man as a younger brother whose media career he wanted to mentor and perhaps have Simon take over from him when the time came.

Simon and Hermann exchanged greetings and Hermann informed them that Lee Nolan should be waiting. Lee, or Lenora, was the project manager for Marquis and, as such, had been Simon's contact within the organisation. They had agreed on most components of the books although they both felt the project held some challenges.

Simon checked, but Lee had failed to arrive. Hermann called her mobile and she explained she was just parking her car. She entered the room, giving Simon a quick hug and completely ignoring her scowling German employer. She apologised to Evan for her tardiness and they sat down to business.

Simon took over, saying that the two books were fantastic. The recipes were suitable for both books and he felt the second one, which included the WWI recipes would need padding as there was a dearth of good recipes from that specific period because of the scarcity of foodstuffs at that time. However, there was a plethora of super recipes from the earlier period which could easily spill over. He went on to commend the writers, who had researched the period thoroughly. There were images of the Prince of Wales, who'd been known as the Playboy Prince and would later become King Edward VII. He was renowned as a gastronome and the upwardly mobile society he mingled with experimented in the kitchen (and elsewhere!) as social rules were bent to suit the tactile needs of the emerging Edwardian Era.

Simon complimented the Marquis team on their thoroughness and Evan was impressed by how well Simon was managing this meeting. He thought how Simon had really come into his own since Phillip Williamson and their emerging love affair. Simon had more confidence, looked more mature and had lost his nervousness. He was a good man to be around.

In the Edwardian tome there were many recipes that had been vamped to current fashions and times. Mutton was replaced by Lamb; roasted Cod replaced by a local large flaking cold water fish and while oysters, game and offal featured heavily there would need to be some changes to suit current trends. Oysters, for example were now cost prohibitive whereas during the Edwardian period they were so cheap that they had often been used as a filler in dishes, Simon continued and offal was not as acceptable as it had once been so they'd only include a couple of dishes such as the lamb's liver and caramelised onion dish flavoured with Balsamic vinegar.

The book also featured some excellent afternoon tea recipes, Simon commented, with great photography. Hermann beamed at Evan – this book project was getting easier all the time.

Simon then suggested, "Hermann, we could consider releasing the first book on February 12th which would be the anniversary of Georges Auguste Escoffier's demise the celebrated chef of the Edwardians and arguably the first celebrity chef." Hermann liked the link and saw future PR possibilities immediately.

After some further discussion the meeting drew to an equitable conclusion. Evan congratulated Simon on his skilful management of the meeting.

Eventually, the critical day arrived and Evan and Phil met in Nigel's office. Nige had wanted Phoebe to be involved but Phil had railed against that proposition and threatened to bring Evan's legal reps if he insisted on the Sales Manager being present.

As it was, the three of them settled into an uneasy meeting. Nige began with a few compliments about the Game; he'd liked the Will Hambers appearances and was amazed that he had agreed to appear *gratis.*

"Why is that? I wasn't aware that he's a philanthropist," Nige asked suspiciously.

"That's what he wanted … he sees the value of a regular spot," Phil said with assurance. She did not bother to tell Nige that the arrangement was about to end – the year was up and their private agreement was over.

"So, what's up for next year, Phil? Evan?" Nige asked, feigning innocence. But innocence and Nige was an oxymoron – there was not a single innocent bone in his aging body! Phil passed the proposal that she and Evan had decided on across the desk, to Nige. She watched him read as she observed the all too familiar body language – arms crossed, eyes squinting and ears reddening. The classic Nige symptoms of anger and dissatisfaction!

Nige sat back in his leather chair, removed his reading glasses and took a swig of water from his glass before slamming it down and grabbing for his Montblanc which he pointed at Phil like the barrel of a Beretta.

"Are you fucking kidding?" he spluttered.

"No," Phil replied calmly while Evan sat impassive and out of his depth.

"What the fuck are you on about, Phil. This is a radical change of format … what the fuck are you thinking?" Nige raged. Phil had heard it all before from Nige and he failed to intimidate her.

"So Nige honey, how about you fess up what's going on? Where did Ty Barnaby disappear to with my top producer, who was supposed to be away looking after a family drama? Want me to tell you, Nige?" Phil sneered at the Boss she had neither time nor respect for.

Sheepishly, he admitted to the pilot for Ty. One-nil to Phil.

"…and when exactly did you intend to let me and Evan know about the sale of the Game to France?" She was on a roll, and continued, "…I know all about Snakeballs and his part in the sale. When did you intend to share some of the sales? Will that be part of our Christmas bonus? Come on Nige … tell us!" Nigel Herbert-Flyson had been right royally caught out.

What was he to do? Could he bluff and bluster his way out of this situation? He thought not as Phil was too savvy – he was her miscreant boss and she was wise to him.

"So you know every fucking thing don't you, Philomena … and what exactly does that mean? If you think you can get half of this fucking shit you've written, you're out of your fucking tiny fucking little fucking mind!" Spittle coagulated at the corner of his mouth and Phil took this as a sign to take a more astringent approach.

"Okay buddy, let's look at it. If you calm down and think seriously at my plan, it's a win-win situation for you and the Network … increased revenue … and an opportunity to move programming around to test a few new ideas. Ty can build a real profile within the Game and then move on to his own show … if he cuts it." She sat back in her chair and looked at her watch.

"Who the fuck do you think you are? No fucking way … no way in hell is this going your way, Phil! No fucking WAY!" Nige was adamant. Phil leaned to Evan and asked him to vacate the area for a few minutes, which he was very happy to do.

"So, come on Phil, tell me what you're up to?" Nige came to her side of the desk and was about to perch on the arm of her chair.

"Don't even think of sitting there, you little turd." She reached for two sheets of official looking documents. She'd tried sense and reason – now it was time for the big guns.

"These happened to fall into my hands … and don't ask how." She handed him the copy of Ty's birth certificate and adoption document.

Nige blanched and almost stumbled as he returned to his enormous chair. Nigel Herbert-Flyson appeared to shrink as he sat, staring dumbly at both pieces of paper.

"How'd you get these? This is completely illegal and I can have you for this, you evil fuckin…" Phil cut him off before he could complete the derisive descriptor.

"Did I tell you not to ask, fuckface? Suffice to say, I know a few people in the right place." Phil was in complete control now.

"Nige, you can go for me and report me to whomever you wish, but it'll all blow up in your face, honey. Once the board finds out that you're pushing for your fucking bastard son, they'll have your guts for garters. You remember the policy about nepotism? You should … after all, you instigated it after Dad gave me a job. Remember Mr Smarty Pants Chief Executive Officer?" Phil could be quite biting, even vicious, with her sarcasm when she felt the need and she was definitely feeling the need. "You had policy changed so no relative could be employed. Remember, sweetheart? And I really hate to bring it up, but how many board members would love to see the back of you, Nige. Most of them … give them an excuse, Nige, and they'll cut your balls off and hand them to you on a platter as they kick you out. Ever thought about finding another job like this … at your age? Oh … and what will poor Lynn have to say when she finds out about Ty … to say nothing of our own Leeanne?"

Nige could sink no further into his chair, no matter how he wished he might. Could it swallow him up?

Please? The meeting he'd been anticipating with relish had turned to shit, and he knew it.

"So, what's up for negotiation, Phil?" and butter would not have melted in his mouth.

"Not one fucking thing, Nige. Not a single item. The only thing for you now, is to decide when we start the new plans ... I'll get Evan back, shall I?" She was up and heading for the door.

"Hold on a minute, Phil ... hold on. It seems to me, you hate me, Phil and I don't think I deserve that. After all we've been through ... I mean, come on Phil ... you had a husband."

"And you had a wife, Nige. What did you think we could do? And no Nige, I don't hate you, I just get tired of being treated like a fucking halfwit. I mean ... how did you expect to get away with your fucking deceptions? I won't be treated this way, Nige. I deserve more – I bring you a top fucking show every week and now I'm about to bring even more revenue..." she shook her dropped head, "...will I get any thanks, unless I push for them? No fucking way! You'll take the kudos and leave me like a can of stale booze after a wedding." She reached for the door handle and opened it.

Evan walked back in, apprehensive for his future.

Nigel Herbert-Flyson stood to his full height as he said, "Congratulations, Chef. We have a deal!" He did not shake Evan's hand. Evan had no idea of what had gone down as he waited nervously on the other side of the door. He didn't need to – all he knew was his future was guaranteed for another three years – on outrageously huge money.

Phil had seen to that!

Coming Soon...

CRISIS CRUNCHED – GAME ON!

Evan Pettersen, the outlandishly handsome super star Chef leaped into the seventh season of his internationally known cooking show, "The Cooking Game....r u Game?" Propelled by passion for his TV show and his restaurant and the other aligned business, the 46 year old couldn't wait to front the cameras that adored him and to collect his humungous paycheck each week.

Philomena Watts (aka Phil) the feisty Executive Producer of the Game had negotiated Evan's sensational three year contract at the end of the sixth season with the horrid **Nigel Herbert-Flyson**, CEO of the powerful Channel 3 Network. Profit is his main driver and Evan's lucrative pay would rob him. That that fucking bitch Phil Watts had blackmailed him into the conditions for her Star was another issue. He'd have his revenge one day.

Emerging star, **Simon Hacknell,** arrives back from France to find his lover of less than a year has been disgraced as a thief; **Philip Williamson,** the Games PR man has not only is he sacked from the network but also has been sacked by Simon as his lover. **Simon** is devastated and buries himself in his labours for the Game, the radio show TABLE and in the century of recipes books for pugnacious publisher **Hermann Booth.**

At the studio where the Game is shot every week, the crew continues to change as the director Bill Wiseman throws a hissy fit and disappears – this precipitates unforeseen movement in roles as a cameraman becomes the director and Earnest Hemingway Jones becomes **Hem Jones,** assistant executive producer. The gorgeous illegitimate son of the conniving CEO, **Ty Barnaby,** is still clawing his way to Stardom; this chick magnet is scaling his way to the top.

Philomena departs for France and into the arms of lover **Laurent** leaving the way open for her nemesis, **Zoe Hendricks** to be appointed as her replacement. **Zoe** is overjoyed but is plagued with her transgendering lover's indecisions about his sex change. Something has to give and it does.

Mangereire, the Star's outrageously successful restaurant has its share of operational worries and is, unbeknown to the Star, the rendezvous for his daughter and her ardent would be lover, **Aaron Jepson.** At 16, Sarah is too young for sexual adventures with Aaron. But is she? Her twin brother, **Seb**, is now a junior star on a new series at Channel 3. **Charlotte,** their elder sister disappears. Does she return?

Lex Pettersen, Evans loving wife of over 20 years, is involved in a horrendous car accident that leaves her on life support and with her untimely demise, can the Star go on? How can he face the cameras and his fans after this devastation? He soon learns he has to do so as **Nigel** reeks his revenge for Phil's actions.

But can **Evan** continue to deliver his multi-awarded performance as the most fabulous Celeb Chef? And what will happen to "The Cooking Game....r u Game?"